THE HEEL OF ACHILLES

THE MEDICI SQUADRON

Jacquelyne Morison

Medici Publishing
Cheltenham

ISBN 978-0-9929973-6-6

Published by Medici Publishing in 2021

Revised and reprinted in 2022

Published by Medici Publishing in 2018 under the pseudonym of Berenice Caldecote

Cover design by GermanCreative

The author wishes to acknowledge with sincere thanks the assistance given by authors Sue Baker, Lyn Phillips and Michelle Wolfe-Emery who have meticulously read the typescript and given their invaluable comments.

CONTENTS

PART I
THE RIVER STYX

And he stood still, watching her as she panted up the way; for the moment an irradiated being, the epitome of a whole sex: by the beams of his own infatuation.

Thomas Hardy
The Well-Beloved

PROVOCATION

She judged that the time was now opportune. I'll strike now, she decided.

Accordingly, she slipped off her high heels and gently lifted his trouser-leg with her big toe. Then playfully she rubbed against his hairy flesh. She looked away but silently noted the inevitable reaction. Success!

James found himself promptly swallowing hard and his breath came in short spurts. The whole of his instinctive purpose in life burgeoned into play. His primary reason for being on planet Earth was awakened big time. His entire genetic history came to the fore as his unavoidable drive towards the act of procreation. He felt that nothing else in life had ever mattered or ever would – such was his total immersion in the prospect of earthy sex. He was bitten and hooked. His mouth went dry but he endeavoured to moisten his lips. Alas unsuccessfully. James wanted to take a gulp of the wine in his glass but his inner mind told him that he had more important tasks in hand. He replaced the wine glass shakily on the table. Poor sod!

He tried hard to look away from her but found his eyes glued to the silken folds of her skin. James observed with admiration the elegant aquiline slope of her jaw, the grey but sparkling eyes, the clear and creamy complexion, the slight curl of her brown hair and her slender shoulders – not to mention those alluring, breath-taking, ample, to-die-for breasts which undoubtedly had been sought after by many men before. And, indeed, they had. James looked forward to fondling them at length before soon and divesting her of that slinky black dress with pearl buttons, topped with a filigree oyster shawl.

James began to imagine what the rest of her might look like. Don't go there, chum. James wanted to study his surroundings in order to take his mind away from the temptress but, instead, his thoughts were absorbed and transfixed. He failed to notice the blue and silver lights at the bar, the waiters dodging each other expertly, the incessant inane chatter at nearby tables and the hum of the nondescript background music. How he wished he could concentrate on these external factors but it was not to be. Her presence was too strong a pull for him to resist.

A funky *"It Ain't Necessarily So"* jingled intrusively from her phone on the table. Fuck. I could smash that bloody thing. Poor, exasperated James.

She smiled mischievously, blended with an airy expression of apology, as she looked down nonchalantly in order to discover who the caller was.

"I am so sorry," she said coolly, "but I shall have to take this." She waived her delicate, slender fingers to illustrate the dilemma.

Calendula promptly left the table and made her way into the street outside the restaurant.

James spent the time in her absence productively. He imagined romping in the hayloft with her, having stripped her of a delicate, white embroidery Anglaise dress with a dainty blue ribbon pinned to the bosom and matching bows in her hair. He wondered what she would look like in the shower, when waking up first thing and whether she liked to be hugged during the night.

He envisioned sweeping the state-of-the-art crockery and the crystal wine glasses off the table on to the floor and breathlessly taking her in the restaurant there and then. He would care not about the reactions of others and, in fact, James relished the thought of the horror on their faces and wondered idly whether that obsequious waiter would come up to the table and protest that the other customers were dismayed by his wantonness. This idea was fun.

James would be the Adam to her Eve. He would be the Abelard to her Heloïse. He could even be Dracula to the not-so-innocent maiden. Or Blue Beard with his nubile, young wife, Judith.

Calendula Fortescue-Bligh, meantime, chuckled with glee as she answered the phone outside the restaurant in the crowded London street.

"Hello, my dearest darling, how are you, my poppet?"

"I am good. How are you getting on? Are you coming home tonight, poochie?"

"I'm doing wonderfully well. You would be proud of me. And, yes, I shall be in your arms just before midnight, lion cub."

"Well, I could come up to town and we could stay in the flat, if you like. That way I could see you sooner," he suggested.

"No, don't worry, I'll drive myself home."

"How's the gig going?"

"I've got as far as the toe-up-the-trouser-leg routine and I have him where I want him now, I think. Another couple of dates to tease him still further and then I will pick him off the tree. He hasn't talked shop yet but he will, I am sure. I have deliberately kept off the subject of politics or overseas dealings because I am, as we discussed, playing the innocent woman who just likes him for himself not for his political clout. And I don't want to give him any impression that I am fishing for scandal." Calendula took a breath.

"Well, I am glad you are coming home, in fact. I need you tonight, poochie panda. But maybe you had better get back to the mark. And you can use this call as an excuse to leave him in the lurch while, at the same time, leaving him wanting."

"Sure baby. Bye darling. Can't wait to see you. Love thee lots."

She returned to a bemused James Fetherington, drenched in his latest reverie, with a cheerful yet languid smirk.

"I do humbly apologise but I shall have to leave pretty soon. Business is business, you know."

James tried in vain to suppress his irritation and disappointment (he was so used to getting his own way, obviously) at the thought of not sleeping with her tonight as he had planned.

"What NOW, Verity? It's nearly 10 o'clock."

"My dear man, it's work." And James earnestly hoped he was her 'dear man'. "But, besides, if this client is willing to pay me the best part of £300K for one piece of my work, then he almost has a right to ring me whenever the mood takes him. Filthy rich men don't do office hours, you know. I also didn't know that I would be with you tonight, in any case, when I told Mr Purchaser that I would be free this evening. And I need the money."

James almost felt like offering her the £300K himself but decided that it was best for him to play it cool.

But before he could protest, she deflected his response. "What do you do, by the way?"

"I'm a Parliamentary Secretary "

"Oh, really, how interesting," she said, feigning but little interest. "Anyway, I must go soon now to discuss final terms with the buyer."

They left the Blue Lorikeet shortly afterwards, with James panting for more of her. She tantalisingly gave him a quick peck on the cheek, while simultaneously hailing a taxi, which she annoyingly for James refused to share. But he was slightly consoled by a promising, lingering look.

"It's been wonderful, James. I do hope we can do it again soon." She spoke soothingly and encouragingly and he was again captivated. Cupid's dart never misses its mark.

As the taxi departed, James Fetherington felt as if he had been stranded on a dessert island which was devoid of nourishment and sustenance, surrounded only by sea water which was undrinkable, the panic of hopelessness beginning to set in as he realised that he might never be rescued.

James returned reluctantly to the restaurant to pay the bill, giving the aforementioned obsequious waiter a generous tip in recompense for maligning him so during his earlier fantasies.

I didn't get much for my money this evening but, perhaps, I should view it as a long-term investment, really, James pondered.

This chapter was not yet over, he felt. James wondered what the waiter might be thinking about his semi-defeat but decided that he probably had seen everything in life and was, almost certainly, unconcerned by his predicament. That is, if he had ever even noticed it.

James decided to walk to his car, even though it was parked, at least, a mile away, if not more. He felt like a coiled spring. He needed to clear his head and assuage his disappointment at not spending the night in a luxurious hotel room with a beautiful woman. He even contemplated ringing up a former up-for-it girlfriend but decided that the hour was too late and that life would get too complicated if he did.

James thought long and hard about the woman who called herself Verity Baxter during his al fresco walk to the car. He wondered momentarily whether her phone call was an excuse to get away from him or simply to tantalise him but dismissed the thought as groundless. He believed her to be genuine and caring and not at all interested in his professional life which was a great relief.

He decided to ring Verity in a few days, play it chilly if he could, and suggest another dinner engagement with the proviso that she leave that bloody phone at home. In his own mind, therefore, James saw Verity as a potential sexual partner who might last more than a fortnight before he tired of her.

FABRICATION

James would like to have spent a languorous day (a 'do-fuck-all day' as his ex-wife used to call it) in his Mayfair flat just thinking about that irresistible troll who had put him under such a spell. But, instead, he had to make his way to the office in Whitehall where a pile of urgent matters awaited his attention. It was ever thus.

He arrived at a deserted office where the dregs of last week's problems had been swept away under lock and key for tight security reasons but the evils still chuntered along below the surface. There was the delicate matter of Tranty's double-dealing with the Elisian government, the financial cover-up over the latest budget figures and the trade secrets which had been sold to a low-life foreign journalist. James also suspected that Tranty might have syphoned off some funds from the petty cash before now.

Gregory Tranter's unscrupulous dealings with the Elisian government had meant that the British government were able to supplement their budget figures in time for the recent general election and this move had possibly swayed the fickle voters because a large majority had been gained nationwide. Tranty had received a backhander in return for the PM's commendation of the new Elisian Prime Minister, Johann Finkelbaum, at the last European parliament.

Why were politicians so corrupt? His former employer, in the Department for Environmental and Pastoral Matters (the Nosh and Not-So-Posh Brigade), had been the same and he was required to keep schtum that time too in spite of desperate odds. Fortunately, his new femme fatale was not interested in politics and she had, therefore, checked out in an exemplary fashion. James decided that it would be unwise to prolong any further reverie about that little minx until later in the day as more pressing matters were in hand.

James hoped that this little episode of Tranter's misdeeds had now died down but the press would still be left hungry for any whiff of impropriety. Political journalists had been hot on the trail during the election but James had managed to avert their gaze, he prayed, successfully. There had been a time when he had jumped every time the phone rang but, hopefully, the paparazzi were now becoming more interested in the gossip from the latest scandal about William Bredy in Scotland who had been found with his pants down with a little-known official for the Opposition. But, of course, his well-trained wife was sticking by him as he was simultaneously denying the charge.

Political journalists, on the whole, were a nasty breed, James mused. They studied politics, philosophy and economics (the tried-and-tested PPE mix) at Oxbridge and then put it to spurious use. What a waste.

James had personally made his way up through the ranks on leaving Oxford. After obtaining his PPE he also secured a master's degree in Business Administration in which he specialised in accounting practice. He then became a parliamentary private secretary on half-pay for a couple of years. As a PPS James had learned to keep his ear to the ground in order to track backbench opinion surreptitiously and he had served in a minor capacity on the Select Committee for International Trade Relations. His work on the Select Committee had led him to secure a lucrative trade link with a few Japanese automobile manufacturers and this deal secured him the admiration not only of Gregory Tranter but also of Ian Jepherson, the PM himself. As a PPS, therefore, James had cemented his skills for diplomacy, underhand dealings and playing the cards really close to his chest.

Finally, James became an MP by winning his marginal seat in Throxfield with a significant majority for the right wing. He then was appointed to his present post of Parliamentary Under-Secretary of State (Parliamentary Secretary, to you) for the Department for International Development with the blessing of both Tranter and the PM.

James perused some papers following an important meeting in Brussels but his skim-reading only revealed an accurate record of the proceedings and, therefore, he placed them in the filing tray dispassionately.

Beryl Wainwright, right on cue, came breezily into the office in order to discuss the day's work and to bid him a cheery Monday-morning greeting. She automatically swept up the filing papers from the tray and reminded him of a late-morning meeting with Simon Risborough from the Executive Sub-Committee for International Diplomatic Relations (ESIDR). He confirmed that he had the agenda and related documentation but lied about the fact that he had studied it over the weekend. Beryl was not deceived but her poker-face gave nothing away. James wondered whether she saw through his constant need for deception but naively concluded that he would never actually be found out.

At school and during his younger years James had always found it expedient to be economical with the truth in order to get the upper hand in his dealings with schoolmates, teachers and parents and, in particular, with his father who had ruled the household with a rod of iron. James had never lied to his mother because he knew that she suffered continually from his father's stern demeanour and his strict views on proper conduct. His current compulsive need for the deception of others, something of a self-deception even, and his desire to support the underhand machinations of others, stemmed from this period in his early life, although he failed to realise this salient fact.

A shrink would have concluded that his stormy relationship with his father had led him into a professional arena where corruption and duplicity were an accepted way of life. But Fetherington would never acknowledge such a truth even to himself. He simply believed that he had found it expedient to conceal the truth from others on many occasions as his way of being in control and not revealing his true motives to those who might possibly pose a threat. James wanted to be in command of any situation and to gain the upper hand and his propensity for lying was simply the easiest way of achieving this goal. James had concluded this tenet at an early age when vying for top-dog position at boarding school but, of course, he had then buried it as a forgotten memory. By the same token, he would have found it impossible to believe that others, like Verity, for instance, or Beryl Wainwright, were equally capable of truth-economy.

"You have had a call from Philippa. Would you like me to get her on the line?" the hyper-efficient, but boring, Beryl asked. She was eager to get on with the day's business, naturally. James had deliberately chosen to employ a sexual-turnoff secretary so as not to be at all distracted from his purpose.

"Yes, please," he responded abruptly but with a smile.

Philippa Gresham was the PR consultant for the Tories who handled press and public relations for the International Development Department and she managed generally to deflect any intrusion either at his home or at the House. Pippa was a strident woman whom he had no desire to seduce as he felt that she might dominate him in a way which he would have found uncomfortable. The odd flirtation would suffice but was not meaningful. Keeping her at arm's length, however, was a necessity. She would do her job better that way. It interested James that in a professional capacity he could, if necessity dictated, remain aloof but outside the office he was prey to any ravenous Jezebel who might casually come into his orbit.

The phone rang and, before he could get it to his ear, the forceful tones of Pippa announced that a press release was wanted urgently in order to deflect the nasty criticism of Tranty's implication that he might be becoming complacent about foreign trade figures. Apparently Tranty had been caught off guard at a dinner engagement when, in reply to a question from the floor following his post-dinner address, he had asserted that he was 'satisfied' (that is 'complacent') with the way things were going. How had this news broken? No-one could either recall or identify the questioner. Apparently, no-one seemed to have taken note but the error needed to be rectified pretty sharpish.

"I have drafted the press release which states that we are gratified but not sitting on our laurels yet. Shall I read it out? Jenny has faxed it over just now, I think, but you may not have received it yet," she enquired.

He asked for the gist of what she had said and she also read a few juicy phrases:

Gregory Tranter is reported to have stated that "he had no intention of misleading the public into believing that he was at all complacent about the foreign trade figures." Mr Tranter believes that he was

> *misquoted by a scandalmonger who is out to discredit his important work and that of his department.*

James decided to intervene here by making a few comments and to show who was in control. He felt that the word 'scandalmonger' should not be attributed to Tranty.

"Could we use the word 'scandalmonger' but not imply that it came from Mr Tranter's mouth?" he suggested.

Pippa acquiesced. "I'll change that to an 'opposition sympathiser' shall I?"

James assented.

Pippa then continued:

> *Sources close to the Cabinet Minister confirmed that the Department for International Development was optimistic but certainly not complacent since the publication of the overseas trade figures which showed promise and a definite improvement in recent months.*

At this point Beryl interrupted proceedings in order to deliver the said fax. James nodded his gratitude and she promptly left the office.

I do wish she would occasionally give more than a token knock before barging in. I could have been being immoral with myself.

"And change 'overseas trade figures' to 'international trade figures' too," he added.

Pippa agreed and a lull in the conversation indicated that she was scribbling on her copy of the fax.

"I have the fax in front of me now," James reported.

Pippa continued undaunted.

"Then go down to paragraph 6 in which I have said some stuff about last year's figures and the Department's general efforts to explore and boost trade links by sending a number of delegations to Japan and the

Middle East," said Pippa. "I have also mentioned, en passant, the success of the European Parliament in May," she concluded.

James decided it was time to end this conversation.

"OK, I will give it the once over and come back to you." He tried to make his tone sound authoritative and conclusive but Pippa persisted.

"Well, I shall have to get the thing out very soon in order to stem the tide on this one."

"I'll do it today, I promise," he asserted.

"This morning would be better," she countered.

"If I can but I must go now, sorry."

James instantly regretted having apologised to Pippa as he put the phone down. It was that compulsive need to lie again because James felt that Pippa was subtly manipulating him. He wanted to gain the upper hand naturally without having to play into her hands but now it was too late to rectify matters.

James read through the press release then and there and made some more small changes but neglected to hand it back to Beryl immediately. He would give it to her on his way to the meeting with Risborough that would delay things for the impatient Pippa.

James shuffled a few more papers most of which were again consigned to the filing tray, and some to the permanent out-tray for shredding, and he then dictated a sheaf of letters of a mundane nature. The mundanity of the correspondence meant that his thoughts had begun to wander back to last night and it took him some considerable effort to keep his mind on the job.

EXCITATION

The drive from London for Calendula was monotonous when ploughing through the town traffic but the scenery became increasingly delightful as she got nearer home. She was not only longing to see Barrington but she also desperately needed the comfort and slow pace of rural life which only their home in middle England could afford.

She longed for the sweet air, the pleasing red limestone architecture, the undulating terrain and, last but not least, their love-nest with its profusion of *Alchemilla Alpina* (alpine lady's mantle, to you), Japanese cherry blossom, delphinium and hypericum in the garden in summer. It was Barrington, however, who was the gardener but she took a keen interest in his hobby. She often wondered whether he had initially been attracted to her because of her name with its floral and herbal associations. He also grew most of their vegetables which made scrumptious fayre. What would I do without him?

The house itself was a modest four-bedroom detached – purposely not ostentatious so as not to arouse the suspicion of the affluent neighbours around who might, if the house was more in keeping with their true income, be inclined to be a tad too curious about the couple. Also the thought of endless dinner parties or coffee mornings revolted Calendula and so she purposefully avoided any long chats with neighbours in the district. Their London flat and the villa in southern France were more in keeping with their income bracket but these dwellings had been purchased from money secreted away into a numbered Swiss bank account long ago which was still looking reasonably healthy even after these home-purchases. And the pair were quite adept generally at fatiguing their bank accounts and flashing the plastic.

From the A40 she turned off on to the homeward road towards Grove Naxton Cross by the River Nax – that familiar final common path which the car knew so well. Before she had even switched off the engine, Barrington appeared to delight her eyes and to further lift her spirits.

"Poochie panda," he cried with outstretched arms.

"It's been a long day and too long away from my cuddly lion cub."

They instantly locked into each other's arms with triumph and expectation like two homing pigeons.

They hugged long and hard once inside the house too and they clung to each other while Barrington poured out the mulled wine. Making mulled wine with a good quality claret adding cloves, grated nutmeg, cinnamon sticks and blood-red Seville oranges was Barrington's speciality even in summer. They drank their warming drinks in the large L-shaped lounge with its sanded and stained floors, Persian chenille drapes and an Indian carpet which Calendula had picked up in a bazaar in Mumbai when she was out there gathering inspiration for her contemporary artwork and spying on a playboy banker whose fingers had been in the petty cash. The uplighter standard lamps glowed and created an atmosphere of intimacy in the room, devoid of central lighting, a touch perfected by Barrington for when Calendula returned home after a long jaunt.

"Now tell me all about Mr Fetherington, panda."

Calendula related the events which had led up to her dining with James that evening. She spoke of how they had met, accidentally on purpose, in an art gallery in London last week. She had explained to James that she was selling her paintings to wealthy purchasers and that her visit to the gallery was to check out the opposition and to make contact with prospective buyers and agents. That part of her story had been true to an extent at least. She had kept Barrington posted on progress with James, in principle, throughout as they had planned the coup together. But they still liked to gloat in detail on their success to date in reeling in the fish.

"I shall have to sleep with him, of course," she reminded Barrington and he gave her a warm hug by way of confirmation of his understanding.

In the smaller part of the L-shape of the lounge, a wrought-iron, spiral staircase connected the lower floor with the upper. After the mulled wine and some homemade cheese straws, they retired to the bedchamber up the spiral staircase in order to celebrate their reunion and their success with James so far. Both were actually confident and stimulated at the prospect of making a mint out of the Parliamentary Secretary.

After some impassioned bedroom activity, Calendula asked, "How are you getting on with Maisie," as they lay sleepily in each other's arms.

"What her of 'Hell's bloody tits' and 'God's bleeding knackers' fame?"

"Your accent is far too refined," was Calendula's cool rejoinder. "But you did remember to contact her, didn't you?"

"How could I forget Maisie Clifton?"

"I am relieved that your former conquests do not disappear from your mind the instant they are out of sight. I would worry for myself if they did. And did you give her all the documentation?"

"You are a very long way from being a former anything," he countered. "And, yes, she has all your beautifully forged documents, poochie."

"Has she anything to report?"

"She's going to be doing her thing at Harmony Holistics any time now, bless her."

"More details please?" she persisted.

Barrington grunted briefly before falling asleep.

She looked at him affectionately in his slumberous state. She observed his rugged skin, his dark hair, not yet showing any signs of early grey but, no doubt, it would have the potential once he had surmounted the big four zero. She felt his tall body around her and his broad shoulders and she believed him to be in the prime of his life. "And he's all mine," she pondered.

The couple awoke next morning to sense the light pouring in through the windows of their double-aspect bedroom. The pale morning sunlight prompted them to celebrate with further lusty exploits and a breakfast of naturally-cured smoked salmon and scrambled eggs, cooked to perfection by Barrington, suitably attired in his 'hard labour' apron, and served on a silver salver, complete with a garnish of home-grown parsley, lemon balm, lemon wedges, gherkins and soured cream with chives freshly picked that morning. These delicacies were all washed down with a couple of glasses of Veuve Clicquot which had been a gift from a grateful journalist for whom a very successful deal had been pulled off recently.

As they sat on their secluded patio, the summer's onset was evident in the morning air, still somewhat redolent of the dawn mist. A lone *Coenonympha Pamphilus* butterfly (small heath butterfly, to you), with its distinctive yellow-orange wings, had risen early to bask in the sunshine and was making a kit-inspection of the anemones and gypsophila.

Calendula admired the well-weeded garden and the newly-mown lawn, both evidence of Barrington's devotion to his task. The flowerbeds were kidney-shaped and hexagon-shaped which Barrington had toiled at long and hard for several years. A gravel path and some stone steps led to a gazebo-style summerhouse which they had often used for high jinks in the late summer evenings.

"Are those peonies and that lobelia new editions?" she enquired after a study of the familiar flowerbeds.

"Yes, I couldn't resist them back in the spring when planting was necessary. Especially the exotic Chilean Devil's tobacco lobelia. And I have also acquired some tree lilies and some more broad-leafed sage," Barrington replied while affectionately watering the patio pots.

"Any movement on the legal scam front?" she asked after a pause which heralded a change of subject.

"That one might come to fruition but I am still waiting to hear back from Bill."

Bill Frampton was a Post Room Operative (Post Room Boy, to you) who worked for Galbraith, Minchin and Claxton in London. Bill was a very reliable source of information on the machinations and misdeeds of the partners at GMC and, in this case, there was a more than usually unscrupulous partner in their Commercial Division whom they had had their eye on for some time.

"Apparently there is a possibility that Piers Wendell might be up to his usual tricks with the finances of one of his clients but, as yet, it does not constitute a goer. But the situation could change in our favour at any moment," Barrington reported.

Calendula smirked.

One the most important assets for a commercial lawyer was the need to have a profound understanding of the way in which a client's business ticked. This would mean that Wendell would have been party to privileged information about several multinational corporations and global enterprises which would open him up to corruption on a large scale. Wendell, for instance, would need to understand a client's inherent strengths and weaknesses, be thoroughly familiar with the organisation's financial standing and appreciate in-depth their forward-planning policies. Any whiff of scandal would, therefore, be a prime opportunity for Calendula and Barrington to ply their trade and the excitement was, consequently, mounting within both of them.

"But we must seal the Fetherington deal first, in any case," concluded Barrington.

Calendula decided that the first part of the day should be spent on finishing off one of her paintings, *Subterranean Ferocity*, as it was entitled, which she had promised to a discerning purchaser in Paris. This painting was worked in a heady mixture of oil pastels and gouache on plywood. The non-acidic oil pastels rendered a softness to the bold contours of the pointillist textures of the work which were achieved by vibrant, expressive strokes. A colour gradient in shades of bright red and wine, not dissimilar to their mulled wine of last night, had engendered the underlying menace of the work. The gouache, as a blend of acrylic and watercolour, included for its Parisian nuances, added an animated and luminous quality to the painting which Calendula hoped the buyer would appreciate. She often chose gouache for its opacity and heavier-than-a-delicate-watercolour texture as a contrast to the pastels and her contemporary work was noted for this hallmark.

Calendula was never, in fact, totally satisfied with her work but this one would do for the buyer. After about an hour and a half, with short breaks to drink some herbal teas (cranberry and orange, mint or camomile and lemon) which Barrington had lovingly fetched her occasionally, she was able to give the final fixative spray of gum arabic. On each occasion, when serving the tea, the waiter had given Calendula a peck on the cheek which made her murmur with gratitude. But Barrington knew better than to interrupt the craftswoman at her work for any slightly more amorous exploits.

"Would you like lunch in? Or shall we pop along to the Peacock's Feather?" asked Barrington once she had left her studio and cleaned up.

"Oh, the Peacock's Feather definitely. Let's splash out."

"You don't think we are hedging our bets by celebrating too soon?"

"Oh, ye of little faith. I shall land Fetherington like a non-slippery fish. Do you really doubt me?"

A table at the Peacock's Feather was duly booked.

DISSIMILATION

She donned a casual but respectable trouser-suit in faded organic lawn cotton and bamboo with a nondescript pattern in sub-fusc shades of sea green and lilac. She decided to adopt a television presenter's accent too for the occasion. Her training as an actress had provided her with a flexible wardrobe and a collection of impressive accents.

Her make-up similarly gave the impression of a sincere and dedicated professional using Dr Hauschka's organic skin care range. A quick spray with an Ecocert-labelled Vanille and Narcisse perfume by L'Occitane completed the picture. She also carried a discreet document case.

She stepped out of the taxi not too far from Harmony Holistics in order to make out that she had walked from South Kensington tube station.

At the reception desk she was greeted by a well-groomed girl in her early twenties.

"I have come to see Grace Norris. My name is Selina Mason." She did not want to give too much information to the receptionist.

"Oh, yes, Gracie is expecting you," the receptionist told her cheerfully. "But she is just finishing with a client, at present. She won't be long. Do take a seat, please."

Selina instantly liked the receptionist, unlike some of the stuck-up bitches she had met on other jobs. She took a seat by the window. Far enough away from the reception desk to be able to observe all unnoticed.

Harmony Holistics was a well-proportioned, elegant establishment, the epitome of respectability and high-class service. It would undoubtedly cater for well-to-do clients. The décor was understated but with a designer label. Sleek white lines and non-reflective surfaces were complemented by a blend of both Scandinavian and oriental furnishings of both rich and subtle shades in contrast. The lighting was also low-key which provided an inviting ambiance.

A female client, clad in a hot-off-the-press maxi dress, swept through the door straight out of an obviously chauffeur-driven car. The receptionist greeted her almost obsequiously but it was not overdone, the observer noted.

"Daisy will be with you shortly, Lady Vivienne," said the receptionist after putting down the phone which connected her to Daisy's room. "She's just coming down now."

"Thank you, Eleanor," said Lady Vivienne in reply. Lady Vivienne then took a seat by the reception desk and glanced somewhat distractedly at a copy of *Vogue* magazine.

Receptionist, Eleanor, noted the observer.

Lady Vivienne was shortly collected by the aforementioned Daisy, wearing low-heeled shoes and a white, clinical coat over navy cotton knee-length culottes.

After a few minutes Eleanor addressed the newcomer, offering her a glass of water from the water-cooler dispenser in the reception area. Eleanor seemed to appreciate that Selina had to wait longer than might be considered acceptable. Selina was sure that Lady Viv would not have wanted to be kept waiting but she was content to wait herself.

"Thank you," came the reply and a hard-plastic, see-though beaker with a *Lupinus Arboreus* (tree lupin, to you) decoration on it was promptly brought for the waiting guest.

In a trice, however, Gracie herself entered the reception area ushering out her client and inviting her to make another appointment with Eleanor's help for next week at the same time. Ex-client was then duly handed over to Eleanor as Gracie outstretched her hand to greet the newcomer after an inconspicuous prompt from the receptionist.

"Selina," exclaimed Gracie as if she had known her all her life. "Very nice to meet you. Sorry to have kept you waiting. Do come this way."

Selina downed her water promptly and the beaker was automatically taken by Gracie who had anticipated her search for a bin.

Gracie led the way upstairs, bidding her former client adieu as they left the reception foyer. They mounted a short flight of stairs and walked along a vaguely circular corridor, with windows on the left-hand side to the street, to a room marked "Private Office" in the corner of the building.

The private office, which overlooked the street, was reasonably spacious and functional yet inviting. A neutral-coloured, limed-oak desk had been placed centre stage and a low-level matching filing cabinet sat unobtrusively in a corner on which lingered some pot-plants of cacti and tradescantia (spiderwort, to you) with a small indoor watering-can beside them. Obviously, this part of the building was where the real business of the establishment took place.

Gracie invited her guest to sit down in a sort of visitor's area to the side of the desk where a small but comfy duck egg and cream check-patterned sofa and two matching armchairs surrounded a mosaic-inlaid coffee table.

Gracie opened the batting.

"We have twenty rooms. I will take you on a tour of the premises in a moment. But, of course, some are being used at present and so it won't be a detailed tour. The room I have in mind for you is Tuscany. It's just along the corridor. It will be free for a kit-inspection in a few minutes."

Gracie laughed at her own feeble joke while Selina merely smiled politely.

"It's quite roomy and well-equipped. We keep all the towels and massage oils readily available and there will also be a cabinet in which you can keep your personal belongings and any extras. All rooms have sinks and some have showers. Tuscany has a shower, of course."

Gracie drew breath. And so did Selina.

"There is also a nice view of the inner garden," she continued. "The building, as you probably realise, is sort of oval-shaped but with an open garden-space in the centre which can be seen from each floor and brings in a lot of light to the treatment rooms. Clients can also take light refreshments in the garden below on the ground floor where there is also a steam room, a sauna and a plunge pool. The main business goes on here on this floor and the upper floor where there are another eight rooms but the remainder of the rooms are on the ground floor. There are a couple of flats above but they have their own entrances. They are not part of us."

More breath was required by Gracie.

Selina began to feel that she was being bombarded with information but she appreciated that the description of the rooms and the layout of the premises was reasonably easy to follow and so she just hung on in there. She also realised that a lot of information needed to be imparted at this juncture.

Gracie recommenced, having replenished her lungs.

"Your slots will be Tuesday evening from 6.00 pm to 10.00 pm and Thursday afternoon from 2.00 pm to 6.00 pm, as we discussed."

"Yes," said Selina, feeling that she ought to contribute something to the discussion.

Gracie then went to her desk where she collected a sheaf of papers.

"Here are our Terms and Conditions for Room Rental and the Fee Structure. You will see that we ask for a monthly retainer fee up front and then the room charge for the sessions separately. You would be charged for two sessions, the Tuesday and the Thursday, and the rates are indicated here. The Terms and Conditions have a direct debit form attached."

Gracie also pointed out that invoices would be rendered monthly to Selina with the retainer fee being requested in advance and the room rental charges, plus any extras, such as massage oils, being asked for in arrears on each monthly invoice.

Selina murmured to herself as she studied the fees for the monthly retainer and the two separate room-hire charges. She was amazed at how high these charges were but she was really unconcerned because she would not actually be footing the bill herself.

"That all seems reasonable," said Selina.

"We set the fees for the clients and massage and aromatherapy are charged to the client according to this price list." Gracie handed Selina the said price list.

Again, Selina studied the fees to the client and hoped she did not give away her astonishment at the price of a massage in this part of the world. No wonder Lady Viv was a client. However, Selina noted with elation the fact that she would be making a tidy packet from this little job.

"You asked me to bring along my practising certificate and a copy of my professional insurance policy," said Selina taking these items out of her document case and replacing them with the documentation which Gracie had just given her.

"Yes, they are satisfactory," said the clinic proprietor after a cursory inspection. "Are they the originals? And may I take photocopies of these just for our records?"

"Of course," replied the other.

Gracie rose and opened a door, which Selina had not yet noticed, to the side of the desk. In this inner sanctum Gracie efficiently peeled off a couple of photocopies and returned the originals to Selina.

"What I would do is give the matter some thought and, if you are interested, then simply sign and return the Terms and Conditions, together with the direct debit form, as soon as you can. Now I can show you Tuscany, I think," said Gracie glancing at the wall-clock.

"That would be splendid, yes."

They left the room and Gracie took the lead down the corridor. Selina noticed that they passed Umbria, Piedmont, Auvergne and Limousin. Presumably the East End of London would not qualify here.

"This is Tuscany," announced Gracie who showed Selina into the bijou massage room. The décor was as elsewhere plus the addition of a massage couch, another water-dispenser and some storage space as previously indicated by the owner. The room was fairly small but perfectly suitable for the purpose and ample space was available for her to move around the couch when treating a client. The shower cubicle in the corner was pristine with tiled walls and an opaque, textured-patterned glass door. Selina wondered if such doors existed in Tuscany.

Selina was also introduced to Auvergne, Limousin and Andalusia very briefly before going downstairs. All had similar décor and looked about the same size, although Andalusia was used not for massage therapy but for talking cures or reflexology, Selina supposed, because of the absence of a massage table here and the presence of a recliner with matching footstool. Selina indicated her admiration on each occasion when the owner proudly displayed her wares.

"What other therapies do you do here, besides massage and beauty therapy?" Selina enquired.

"Oh, we do a full range of therapies from Acupuncture and McTimoney Chiropractic to Psychotherapy and Reiki Healing. I will give you our brochure when we get to reception." Gracie's actions fitted her words as she handed Selina a glossy brochure which detailed the impressive array of therapies which were on offer to moneyed clients in south west London and beyond no doubt.

"Do you just cater for local clients?" asked Selina.

Gracie self-importantly replied that their clients came from all over London and even from overseas as if she had been waiting all day to impart this impressive bit of knowledge.

"I see," said Selina looking suitably impressed.

"We often get tourists who come back here year after year." Gracie seemed inclined to want to elaborate for her guest.

Finally the meeting concluded with a warm handshake and an expectation on both sides that this would be a viable business venture.

Selina walked along the street and, once out of sight-line and earshot of Harmony Holistics, she pulled out her mobile.

"It's in the bag at Harmony Holistics," she sang when the phone was answered, reverting now to her normal cockney accent. "God's bleeding knackers, it's in the bag," she repeated.

"Maisie that is wonderful news. Well done, darling. Keep me posted," came the response.

Once back at her flat in the East End of London, Maisie threw off her posh clobber and donned her usual garb of jeans and a tee-shirt and then got down to a bit of form filling.

EXPECTATION

Beryl Wainwright was not so much plain as just rather frumpy. This was mainly because she was past her prime at an age when the begetting of offspring was not an urgent necessity, she had an uxorious spouse and she was dedicated to her work for the Tory party – a mission to which she had devoted the greater part of her professional working life.

She regarded James Fetherington as an upstart despite the fact that he was something of a rising star within the movement. She found his roving eye a tad worrying too and was interested to note (a little disappointed, perhaps?) that he never paid her any particular notice as a woman. Beryl was aware that Fetherington kept his philandering inclinations well under wraps but she herself was not deceived. She had noticed his gallant air in the presence of more than one attractive researcher or office administrator once too often in the past. And the way his eyes lingered avariciously just a fraction too long on the lips or the legs of some of the secretaries in the office was further evidence of his true nature.

Beryl also believed that he cut unnecessary corners in connection with his official duties. Most politicians took on a ridiculously backbreaking amount of work (and James was no exception) and then had to cut corners accordingly. James, however, shaved far too many hermetically-sealed angles and this tactic would backlash on him one day. She knew, for instance, that he had not studied the papers for the ESIDR meeting and she completely saw through his habitual lies. Was he trying to impress her or something?

She believed, in fact, that she was one of the few people who could detect his economy with the truth — perhaps because they had worked cheek by jowl for so long and, in such close quarters, the mask would slip eventually. She maliciously hoped that James would actually disgrace himself in one of the official meetings even though such exposure of Fetherington might not exactly be in the interests of the party.

Beryl's office was streamlined and efficient both in terms of design and functioning. She had organised and reorganised her precious filing system several times in the last year in order to ensure that papers in current demand could be instantly retrieved when necessary. She had insisted that the papers which were currently needed in hard copy be retained in her office and not sent to the central archive where they would be stored on microfiche or on the multi-storage computer.

This control-freak tendency on Beryl's part had attracted both criticism and favour from those about her. The secretaries under her jurisdiction, she knew, found her administrative system unnecessarily pedantic and a trifle unwieldy. But those in similar positions at her level of authority, such as Belinda Forbes and Jane Quentin, her opposite numbers in Innovative Enterprise and in the Global Affairs Ministry respectively, had often expressed their envy at her ability to keep track of things and to produce papers for ministers and officials instantaneously as if pulling rabbits out of a hat. Jane had often had to work very late in order to achieve such feats of conjuring. And Belinda had cursed the slowness of the computer system many times in finding and locating even recently-stored material.

The faithful amanuensis Beryl incorporated the amendments to James' press release and despatched it to Pippa Gresham post haste, answered the correspondence which he had dictated and replied to routine letters under her own name. Most of this work was completed by lunchtime. She also gave instructions to the office secretaries about the typing or amending of reports. Nancy and Zena were instructed to type up the latest reports on overseas policy, international trading figures and foreign delegations, while Claire was given the task of locating and transcribing the minutes of the think-tank Committee for International Trade Expansion and their accompanying papers.

When Belinda Forbes rang to suggest a quick lunch, Beryl agreed willingly but suggested that they go outside the Whitehall building to a small yet elegant bistro nearby. The pair went to Fisca's Bistro quite often because it had tables on the pavement which meant that they could not only enjoy the sunshine but were also afforded some privacy in the shade under the spreading parasols. The street noises also meant that what they said to each other could not normally be overheard by prying ears. They still, nonetheless, endeavoured to keep their conversations at low volume just in case anyone should overhear their gossip.

"I think Fetherington is on the prowl again," said Beryl.

"Oh, heavens," replied Belinda, "I do hope we are not going to have another political scandal from his neck of the woods all over again. Do we know who she is?"

"Not a clue but he came in this morning in a very distracted state which is indicative of when he is on to something big. He is not yet guilty of a dereliction of duties but it could be going that way and we would be powerless to stop it. He left on Friday with that familiar look of anticipation of sexual adventure."

"Can't you put an anti-aphrodisiac in his morning coffee?" quipped Belinda.

"I don't think it would work in his case," laughed Beryl. "But I don't think he is getting on very well with his conquest because he is now wearing a slightly worried look rather than one of elation."

Belinda had ordered a Nordic gravlax dish with a dill and mustard sauce, new potatoes and a spinach-and-pinenut salad. Beryl, less health conscious, had gone for a pasta dish of rigatoni stuffed with natural gorgonzola blue, courgette and red onion topped with a tomato, herb and chilli pepper sauce. Both shared a bottle of still mineral water. Alcohol was off-limits at lunchtime when a period of hard graft in the afternoon loomed.

A short silence descended over the table as Beryl and Belinda consumed their meal.

The young man at the next table was engrossed in his *Times* crossword while simultaneously tucking into the house speciality of the day, a French cassoulet of veal, smoked lardons, cannellini beans and root vegetables. He loved cassoulet because it reminded him of his mother's cooking which he only sampled occasionally now as she was so far away. He also reflected, however, that this cassoulet was prepared in the way that his mamma would like to have cooked it rather than how she actually served it. The youngster was also demolishing a large carafe of fruity Bordeaux claret.

"Do you think it might be someone connected with the party?" Belinda resumed when their meals began to diminish.

"I wouldn't think so because he has had most of the quality goods in the office. So I reckon it must be someone from outside. That is what worries me," emphasised Beryl.

"And you're worried that it might be someone who could cause a bit of damage?" replied her colleague.

"Yes."

Despite the fact that the young man next to them appeared to be fully occupied, and disinterested in his surroundings, his radar scanner was actually highly active and his instincts well attuned. He could just about hear the conversation at the next table despite the low voices. He recognised Beryl Wainwright who worked closely with James Fetherington at the Department of International Development and he knew that her colleague worked for Grant Proctor in the Department of Innovative Enterprise. He endeavoured to contain his excitement with a degree of sangfroid at this chance indication of scandal.

Beryl and Belinda decided that they would have an after-lunch coffee back at the office and so they settled the bill and left Fisca's Bistro with a promise to return soon.

The young man could now hardly contain his excitement at the prospect of reporting back to his superior. He imagined that this piece of information could possibly become a lead to something big which could be investigated. He hurried back to his workplace and made straight for the office of Ronald Turner.

MORTIFICATION

Stuart McGill took the steps up to his Kings Cross office two at a time such was his eagerness.

He lamented the fact that his boss, Ronald Turner, was not yet back from lunch and was, he knew from experience, unlikely to surface again in a condition which would be conducive to his approach. But Stuart left a message on Ronald's desk to the effect that he wanted an audience.

Graham Fifield, Stuart's immediate superior, was abroad chasing a lead in Elisia and so the Junior Reporter for Political Affairs at the Guardian Media Group plc, which incorporated both *The Guardian* and *The Observer*, had temporarily been required to report directly to Ronald. This Stuart viewed as a positive advantage despite Ronald's crusty temperament and unsociable drinking habits.

Stuart returned to his desk to sift through some urgent copy which required his attention and he, therefore, set himself the task of proofing, amending, approving and despatching the copy accordingly. He also undertook a bit of research on the Internet in order to verify some facts about the history of certain members of the House and checked *The Guardian's* own files against that in the public domain. Stuart was especially interested in the career of James Fetherington and his supposedly meteoric rise to fame. He wanted to check and update his knowledge before approaching Ronald with his juicy snippet and so, in retrospect, he valued the time in which he had to kick his heels before *The Guardian's* political editor-in-chief returned to the office.

Stuart McGill had had something of a stupendous rise up the greasy pole himself. He had studied PPE at Oxford. He had withstood the rigorous selection process at Oxford of being shortlisted and interviewed and was overjoyed to have been offered a place with a mini-scholarship at Exeter College after making an open application to the Oxford colleges. Exeter, one of the oldest colleges, had the advantage of being near to the Bodleian Library which Stuart appreciated because he was quite a keen student rather than being dedicated to party-going. His austere upbringing in Edinburgh had schooled him into this straight-laced frame of mind and had rendered him sober and serious-minded.

While at Oxford, Stuart's lifelong interest in journalism had been kindled further when he joined the Pembroke College Writer's Guild. He had also had some of his work published in *The Oxford Student* and *The Cherwell* rags which were published, he believed, because of his unique talent for investigative skills.

Stuart then supplemented his first degree from Oxford by going on to study for a Postgraduate Diploma in Journalism at the London School of Journalism. He also considered it expedient to take some additional masterclass-type courses at *The Guardian* in order to secure his present post which he coveted and prized as the precursor to a startling career and he was now doing all in his power to succeed exceptionally well in the profession.

He had found the London landscape to be a rude awakening after living in Edinburgh and Oxford where life was reasonably sedate even at the best of times. His initiation at the LSJ was, however, a mere taster of London dwelling when compared with life in the frenetically hectic newspaper office. But the LSJ had, at least, knocked the edges off him and had taken him down a peg or two in his own estimation.

Stuart's salary was also modest by any standards and he found that the cost of rented accommodation and living expenses in the capital left little change for niceties and entertainment and he was additionally saddled with his university funding loans which he would need to pay back now and in the future. Stuart, however, was cautiously optimistic about his future career – even more so if he could put his investigative skills to good use as he had done this lunchtime.

When he first joined *The Guardian* team, almost a year ago now, Stuart had been relieved to discover that his more senior colleagues were fairly congenial and on his own wavelength mostly. Ronald, Graham, Dennis Sexton and Manfred Hinds had all gained Oxbridge degrees. Ronald and Graham had done PPE at Oxford, Dennis had read History and Politics at Cambridge and Manfred had read Business Management Studies also at Cambridge. And so he did not suffer from being regarded as an upstart in the office as he had been warned could sometimes be the case in journalism where a college-boy was regarded askance by old-sweats who had learned the ropes the hard way over many years. But Stuart supposed proudly that this was because he was working with a quality journal.

Later in the day the phone on Stuart's desk rang insistently to inform him that Ronald Turner was back in the saddle and that he was accordingly summoned before the chief.

Stuart straightened his tie as he stepped out of the elevator on the third floor and made his way to Ronald's plush upper-storey office. The third floor was like a temple to the gods with many pilgrims coming to worship at its shrine.

"You wanted so see me, young 'un?" came the stern greeting from Ronald as soon as the office door was opened but Stuart detected a grimace which tended to dampen down the brusqueness of these words.

Ronald stood looking out of the office window thus revealing only his back to the newcomer into the room. The view from the window, which overlooked the canal-boats on Regent's Canal, was often worth looking at and offered Ronald a distraction from the cares of having to see a junior hack after his return from lunch when he simply wanted to snatch a bit of shut-eye for ten minutes.

The Regent's Canal, which perambulates around Central London, runs from the Grand Union Canal at Paddington in north London to Limehouse in Docklands in the east, meandering over a fourteen-kilometre stretch. It was a much favoured haunt for tired newspapermen who wandered along its towpath on bright days when they wanted to temporarily escape from the sturm und drang of office-life. The towpath of the Regent's Canal was where a tired office-worker could behold life in perspective by sniggering at the American tourists, watching the dog-walking locals, peeping into the lives of the canal-boat owners and observing the wildlife some of which came from nearby offices.

Ronald's office was lush by newspaper standards with its steel and glass desk, its pale blue walls and its low-level filing cabinets. A rank of phones sat on the right-hand desk-extension and an Apple Mac computer on the left-hand arm of the desk which formed a U-shaped desking arrangement. The front part of the desk itself was strewn with papers, mostly reports, articles and back-numbers of *The Guardian* and *The Observer* as well as copies of rival papers, such as *The Times* and *The Telegraph*, in typical pressman style. An adjacent office with a connecting door both from Ronald's office and from the corridor outside was reserved for VIP visitors and important meetings.

Stuart wondered to what extent the big man would be sober, if at all. He, however, observed that Ronald was not that bad for 4.00 pm. But then, he reflected, it was still only Monday. The situation would rapidly deteriorate towards the end of the week, of course.

Stuart took a breath as much to clarify his thoughts as to give himself courage. He found himself shuffling somewhat from one foot to another on the quality Vinyl, mock-wood-effect designer flooring.

"I think I have picked up a lead in Fisca's Bistro this lunchtime, sir, from James Fetherington's PA from the Department of International Development," Stuart began.

The use of the word 'sir' frequently annoyed Turner immensely but he decided to let it go for now.

"I know who James Fetherington is, thank you!" Ronald's irritation filled the room.

"I know, sir, but apparently he may be putting it about a bit."

"Well?" Ronald demanded with his intolerance of delay mounting rapidly.

Stuart began tentatively but soon picked up momentum and told Ronald as succinctly as possible about the way in which he had earwigged Beryl Wainwright and Belinda Forbes discussing the possible doings and misdoings of James Fetherington. As he spoke, he regretted not having more specific details to report to his supervisor and so his confidence began to wane towards the end of his narrative. Stuart, however, trying to recapture his kudos, stressed the worry which the two chatterboxes had conveyed in their lunchtime conversation.

Ronald grunted. He was tired. It was the end of the day nearly. And his lunch had been more than adequate. He was, however, rather impressed with this young man, although he was at pains not to show it. He allowed an embarrassed silence to ensue for the sake of discomforting the junior reporter.

"But you could not speculate about who this new conquest might be?"

"No idea, sir."

"There is no need to keep calling me 'sir'. You are not at Oxford now, sonny."

"No," replied a deflated Stuart, biting off his automatic response of "No, sir." Stuart also neglected to mention that the use of the words 'sonny' and 'young 'un' were similarly patronising to him.

"Well, I knew that there was something in the offing but what I need to know is WHO Stuart! WHO?" added Ronald.

"You knew?" Stuart attempted not to sound too spluttering but, in truth, he was astonished and devastated.

"That's what I said, didn't I?" returned the other.

"Yes, sir ... I mean, yes," Stuart stammered.

Stuart wanted to leave the office now as quickly as possible in order to lick his wounds. The ground was obviously not going to swallow him up and so a hasty retreat would be a consolation prize. He felt as if someone had taken his last gumdrops from his precious stash during the night. He felt like a kerb-crawler who had been deprived of satisfaction because some workmen were digging up the road. It was as if the young man had desperately wanted to lose his virginity but an alien abduction had rid the planet of the females of the species.

"Just keep nosing around, lad, and we will unearth the rat yet," said Ronald but this only partially mollified the disappointed young journalist. "Have you yet got anything on the Elisian affair from this end, then?" continued Ronald.

Stuart admitted that, as yet, he had heard nothing and wanted to quit the office even more promptly than a moment ago. Finally his dismissal from the presence came like manna from heaven.

Once Stuart McGill had left the room and Ronald had heard the almost-silent lift descending, he swiftly picked up his mobile and rang through to his informant.

"Beryl Wainwright has got wind of Cal's seduction ploy," said Ronald when the phone was answered.

"That just means the whole plot is working," replied Barrington Flint coolly from the other end. "So, given time, we should have some result for you within the next few weeks, Ron."

"Brill. Keep at it."

"O, she will," replied Barrington with a chuckle. "I'll report back as soon as we know something. Take care and give my regards to Dotty."

Ronald stated that he would do as Barrington had requested and the conversation came to an end. Ronald then looked at his watch and decided that it was now time for his afternoon nap.

Stuart, however, was still reeling when he returned to his desk with his hopes of promotion and recognition dashed against the rocks and shattered forever.

TREPIDATION

While not exactly having one foot in the grave Simon Risborough had many years ago relinquished any hope of becoming a Tory party superstar. He had a safe seat in East Bressex which he had retained for many years and he had served in various capacities which suited his temperament, appeased his vanity and catered for his aging self.

He knew that retirement would be inevitable in the not-too-distant future but, in meantime, having jobs, such as chairing the Executive Sub-Committee for International Diplomatic Relations which reported directly to the PM, was more than sufficient to interest him and to occupy his time. He thus regarded himself as one of the denizens of the London parliamentary scene because of holding the coveted position of chair of the ESIDR.

Another day is yet another opportunity to get it right or to give up. Simon's office was not prestigious enough to hold today's sub-committee meeting and so, at just before 11.00 am, he made his way along the corridor to an appropriately-sized conference room where his ESIDR colleagues were due to assemble. The lunchtime sandwiches had already arrived and he inspected them with anticipation. Hot beverages and mineral water were, however, more appropriate for this hour of the late morning and so he availed himself of a cup of black coffee with a dash.

The first delegate to arrive was Vernon Lee from the Finance Division, a faithful party-worker who knew more about manipulating figures than a Soho tart did about non-stop titillation. Vernon was followed shortly by the efficient Vanessa Hargreaves who was the Minute Secretary. Vanessa had learned her craft in politics over many years but she still exuded a degree of freshness and enthusiasm.

The next to arrive was Fetherington himself accompanied by Ruth Angell, the Senior Researcher for International Affairs. Fetherington had, in fact, bided his time so that he could arrive at the same time as the delectable Ruth.

Trust James to arrive with a female – the randy bugger, thought Simon.

Idle chatter was the order of the day until the final dregs of the sub-committee had arrived. The team each helped themselves to tea or coffee with the exception of Ruth who judiciously opted for the mineral water in order to avoid over-stimulation by the dreaded caffeine. And it helped to neutralise the mouth-drying effects of the alcohol which she had consumed in copious quantities the previous evening.

The latecomers were Daniel Faulkes and Edward Cummings. Daniel Faulkes represented the Department of Innovative Enterprise as Parliamentary Private Secretary and Edward Cummings was the Chief Administrative Executive at the Global Affairs Ministry. Edward bustled in very late and was full of apology, as was his usual practice, which most other members found slightly irritating. Daniel, however, did not seem to be perturbed at all that others had been waiting for him.

Arrogant bastard, mused Simon.

Vanessa, over and above the call of duty, obliged by getting hot beverages for the late arrivals.

"Shall we commence, gentlemen ... and ladies, of course?" enquired Risborough.

The females in the room were by now used to the fact that Simon Risborough was of the old school where women were only meant to remain in the kitchen and, on demand, to supply sexual relief and babies when summoned. But he was adjusting gradually, poor sod. Ruth Angell tolerated him as a necessary evil but would not weep at all when retirement came for Simon.

Everyone grabbed a chair in their usual places with Simon at the head of the table as was the tacit agreement for the chair of a meeting.

"You all have copies of the Agenda?" asked Vanessa whose question was greeted either by silence or by mumblings from the room. "Leonard has sent apologies for absence because he has been delayed by a crisis in his constituency," she added.

We'll manage without that bloody little upstart, thought James.

"Are you all happy that I sign the minutes of the last meeting?" urged Simon who was eager to press on.

"I think we should amend item 3.4.2 (ii) which states that the Danish Diplomatic contingent was sent out last March because, in fact, they went out in both March and April of last year," corrected Daniel.

A bit of paper-shuffling ensued for those who were interested in the precise wording of the minutes but James remained aloof.

"And the figures in Appendix III for Travelling Expenditure for the recent excursion to North Africa should include Tips and Gratuities at £15,947 as a separate item and I think it has been overlooked," chimed in the pedantic Vernon Lee.

"I thought those figures were included under the general travelling expenses item, Travel Sundries, if I am not mistaken," argued Simon. He didn't really care about the details but he liked winding Vernon up.

God! This is going to be one of those really fucking boring meetings, thought Fetherington. Perhaps I have been cursed by the Incas of Peru for misdeeds in a former incarnation for having to attend these dreadful meetings. James could have been right given his track-record in this life.

Simon Risborough, anxious to get on with the actual business of the day, agreed readily to the amendment to the minutes for the Danish contingent and signalled to Vanessa to make the necessary change for his signature. She was also requested to double check the North African travel figures in order to pacify Vernon.

"I will liaise with you later Vernon before I sign them," said Simon. "Let's now move to item 1," he urged.

The first and most pressing item on the Agenda of the ESIDR was the report on the Elisia government delegation.

At this juncture James began to show unmanly grief. He had in the back of his mind Tranty's double-dealing with the Elisian government but he was fairly certain that it was not common knowledge among any of the members of this working party. He vacillated between remaining silent as much as possible or, alternatively, deflecting attention away from any possible chit-chat. It was a diplomatic committee after all. As a compromise, James decided to take the bull by the horns and submit only a brief report.

"All seems to be going well," James began. "The Elisian delegation are making much headway. The draft report and accounts have already been circulated and a finalised version will be submitted to Gregory Tranter shortly and, of course, copies will be made available to this committee."

James hoped that this short announcement would suffice and surveyed the room in order to take a straw-poll of the smiles and the frowns. On the whole, he believed that his submission was quite adequate. But he was mistaken.

"Do you not have an interim verbal report which we could minute?" asked Simon. Daniel and Ruth also enquired about the reasons why there had been a protracted delay in finalising the report.

James mentioned that a lengthy series of meetings with Elisian political, industrial and commercial leaders had taken place as well as a full trade convention which would need time to commit to print following the work of the translators. His interrogators were reluctantly assuaged and he began to breathe once more. It appeared that James had surmounted that particular sticky hurdle. But he was wrong again.

"I have been looking at the accounts which you submitted. I gather we have received some spurious funding from Elisia. Is that quite in order?" demanded the implacable Ruth Angell just as James was beginning to relax into a false sense of security.

James was only slightly disconcerted by her cutting remark. How do I scotch this one? Shall I flatly deny it or shall I feign ignorance?

"We have received a backdated subsidy, I believe, on some imports but that's all the information I have," James lied arrogantly in reply.

"That's all the information you wish to reveal you mean. That's not what I heard," came the acerbic rejoinder from the embittered Ruth. Angell by name but not angel by nature, obviously.

"You're mixing in bad company, Ruth. It's not good for you, you know." James could not resist a jibe at her, voluptuous though she was.

Simon interjected swiftly in order to defuse the situation. "Hearsay is not the remit of this committee, Ruth," he stated firmly. "If you have facts then please present them here but only facts, not tittle-tattle," he added emphatically.

Ruth sighed, somewhat deflated. She'd get that bugger Fetherington one of these days, she resolved.

James thought that this hiatus would now neutralise. However, his mind turned to more interesting fantasies. I'll tame that bucking bronco (fucking bonko, more like) yet, if it's the last thing I do. Although James really hated Ruth, she also held a very strange sexual fascination for him, as if by ravishing her he could subdue her entirely. James did not even understand the phenomenon himself. The oxytocin drew him to her and began to reach the parts which other hormones could not access.

"Can we move on then, please?" said Simon, much to James' relief and to Ruth's annoyance.

Ruth could not reveal her unconventional sources as the information was unconfirmed but she was sure that what she had heard via the bush-telegraph was correct. She had, in fact, heard the potentially explosive news via a press-hack who had traded this tasty morsel of secrets about her departmental chief, Gregory Tranter, in exchange for news about the impending resignation of a top-flight cabinet minister.

"Item 2 is Middle East relations," Vanessa reminded Simon who had temporary mislaid his agenda beneath the minutes and other documentation.

"Yes, can we have your report on the Middle East question please Edward?" requested Simon.

Edward Cummings reported on his trip to a little known dominion which was rich in rare and precious mineral deposits and energy fuels. But getting Sultan Vacca Bakripp to divulge the extent and nature of his country's discoveries was like extracting enthusiasm from a mule. The UK government suspected that Derrehan had an abundance of zinc, copper and gold, which were desperately needed by the manufacturing industries in the north of England, but the Sultan was playing the cards deliberately close to his chest. Edward had not managed to penetrate the social barriers in Derrehan but reported that he was received hospitably and that no fundamental disagreement had been in evidence during his talks with the political leader.

Edward's written report, to back up his verbal summary to the sub-committee, was handed to Vanessa.

The ESIDR then turned to discussing trade relations with Japan which gave Daniel Faulkes his chance to report glowingly of his success when visiting Tokyo recently to meet with the captains of commerce and industry. No comments ensued from Daniel's account of his trip and this provided a much-needed respite from the gloom of the morning and a lead-in to lunch.

When Simon suggested that the sub-committee members break briefly for lunch, this suggestion was greeted with much acclaim from those present.

James ensured that he helped himself generously to the prawn, lettuce and mayonnaise on granary because, he knew, that this sandwich combination was favoured by Ruth. She thus had to content herself with crab, lettuce and spring onion instead. James inwardly simpered with delight. He, however, made a point of chatting to her briefly over lunch by way of showing no hard feelings for their earlier contretemps, endeavouring to instil in her mind the prospect, at least, of a bit of rumpy-pumpy on offer and to advertise the fact that he had got to the prawn sandwiches first.

After their repast the conference table was repopulated by the sub-committee members, although Vernon mentioned that he had another meeting at 3.00 pm as his way of urging matters forward and laying the foundations for an excuse to leave early.

The next item for discussion was the draft annual report for the PM on the work of the ESIDR. At this juncture James had to wing it. This was the paper which he had lied to Beryl about reading. Accordingly, he stole a quick perusal of the abstract and introduction of the report but elected to remain as silent as possible during the subsequent discussion.

The report, however, only summarised the work of the sub-committee and, therefore, no detailed discussion at this stage was necessary. Simon, in fact, suggested that they wait until the report from the Elisian delegation had been finalised and submitted before discussing the final draft submission of the ESIDR report for the PM in detail. All present agreed to this stratagem.

Phew! thought James. I think I have managed to get away with that one. I'll read it later, he promised himself, although his promises had often been broken in the past. Self-deception is overtly cheating others but often covertly cheating oneself.

Vanessa then reminded all delegates of the date of the next meeting and stated that she would circulate the final draft of the report for the PM well before that date.

The meeting adjourned and James hurried off in order to avoid any further enquiries into his activities or his opinions.

ELEVATION

Mariella Wendell sat in the garden of her substantial six-bedroom abode, Willows Cottage in Market Drayton, with its extensive acreage and breath-taking views of the rolling hills and valleys, sipping a dry sherry. She surveyed all that she and Piers owned outright and felt safe surrounded by such wealth. Willows Cottage, which could hardly have been described as a cottager's dwelling, had been financed partly by a small inheritance from her late father but mostly by Piers' ability to make money fast and in huge quantities. But, somehow, she did not feel happy.

Mariella was concerned about Piers' tendency to secrecy and the fact that large injections of cash seemed to appear from nowhere into their joint bank account. She also believed that Piers may have much more stashed away about which she knew nothing. And this suspicion was even more worrying.

She had gone into his home-office, which Piers ostentatiously called his library, once or twice when he was at work to see if she could discover anything. But she did not really understand how to look stuff up on the computer. She never really had got to grips with this new technology. She could just about work out how to send an email but that was where the story ended. And she certainly did not know how to open his securely locked desk. Mariella suspected that he kept his desk tamper-proof deliberately and he never let the key out of his sight. Piers obviously did not trust her. And she certainly did not trust him.

Mariella was by now, after twenty-four years of tedious married life, bored to death with Piers and his workaholic ways. He often worked at weekends and once or twice they had to cancel a holiday at short notice because of the pressure of his work.

This enraged her beyond anything. On one particular occasion, when he had elected to cancel their vacation to the Bahamas at the eleventh hour, she had gone away herself in a monumental huff. She had spent a week by herself in Norfolk where her sister lived and she was seriously tempted never to return. Piers made a half-hearted attempt to find her but, she noted, he did not try very hard.

Mariella wished that she had possessed the courage to leave Piers now that the children had left home for good. But, somehow, she did not relish the thought of the upheaval and the hardship which a marriage-breakup would entail. And, in any case, she would have to sell her home and perhaps live in less salubrious surroundings. Mariella had not worked for years and certainly her skills as a library assistant would now be well out of date. And she was more or less computer illiterate.

Mariella was, therefore, at a crossroads of indecision. And it was unlikely that she could jump over the cattle-grid. She would like to have left him but she was scared of residing on her own, she did not want to drop her standard of living and she did not wish to look flea-bitten because she could not afford the things to which she was accustomed. Hence Mariella's quandary.

Her dilemma, of course, was brought about by her lack of courage and impetus. If Mariella had been a fiery get-up-and-go individual, she would have had no problem. But she was instead a mopey-type, a procrastinator and an escapist who took to having her hair done or ringing up a friend if and when she got down in the mouth. But her friends were beginning to dwindle or were often too busy to listen and certainly disinterested. And often she did not have the energy to pick up the phone anyway.

Mariella decided, however, that she should make an effort to stop herself brooding and so she elected to go for a toddle round the shops and perhaps buy herself a new outfit. This seemed to cheer her up enough to propel her slowly from off the garden hammock and into the car.

The main town of Henchmead, some seven kilometres from Market Drayton, was a thriving market town packed with boutiques, trendy restaurants and an off-beat shopping arcade.

Mariella's first port of call was Café Antique in the Skylight Loggia arcade, so-called because it was a wide portico-type affair covered by glass at the top in order to prevent the poor-rich shoppers from being deterred from spending money by getting wet if it rained.

Mariella treated herself to morning coffee and a raspberry tartlet. She surveyed the establishment for anyone she might know but found herself friendless sitting at a table for two only. The café was quite busy and buzzing but a woman at the next table also sat alone and seemed to reflect Mariella's vein of despondency.

"I thought I'd treat myself to a raspberry tartlet. They are so delicious here," she ventured by way of making a casual remark to the stranger and hoping that she would take the bait. The woman smiled and nodded but she looked as if she were not going to respond. Mariella sank back into her thoughts and lugubriousness. She wondered what else she could buy for herself. A new dress? A long, slinky cardie? Some shoes, perhaps? Another handbag?

"I am thinking of ordering one too," said the woman. "It can't do that much harm to the waistline."

Mariella was awakened with surprise by this response.

"Go on. Treat yourself. Just one won't harm," Mariella replied.

The woman called the waitress over and a raspberry tartlet was duly ordered. Mariella waited patiently for hers to arrive.

Both women giggled when their delicacies arrived and the ice had been broken. They began chatting about the weather, then their reasons for visiting the town, then their domestic arrangements and, finally, where they could have lunch after a heavy shopping expedition.

"Would you like to join me," enquired Mariella who had invited her new best friend, Dorinda, to sit at her table. The waitress was certainly very relieved because Café Antique was beginning to get crowded and tables were becoming scarce. The waitress hastily cleared Dorinda's vacated table and prepared it for the next consignment of customers for morning coffee and raspberry tartlets whom she soon ushered in with enthusiasm.

Dorinda apparently lived locally and she too was a bored housewife who had been deserted by an over-conscientious spouse and university-bound children. Her husband also apparently was married to his work as an industrialist. Both women shared the same complaint. They were bored and vexed but did not have the courage to up sticks and leave. Mariella's new-found friend was obviously a soul-mate.

The two jaded women moaned continually about their lot in life and, once the tartlets had gone down the right way, they, therefore, decided to engage in a shopping spree together. Accordingly they visited every dress shop in town and, of course, bought the most expensive creations on the market in the latest fashion whatever it was. Below the surface, however, nothing changed other than the satisfaction of spending some of the money earned by their neglectful husbands.

They, of course, had lunch in the best restaurant and ordered a sumptuous two-course lunch of avocado with prawns followed by John Dory with creamy mash and courgette spears for Mariella and roast lamb cutlets in red wine sauce preceded by brandy-infused chicken liver pâté for Dorinda. Both shared a bottle of the best Beaujolais that the waiter could recommend. They decided, however, to skip the dessert course in view of the number of raspberry tartlets which had been consumed earlier that morning. Coffee and liqueurs, however, went down a treat with the pair.

"Do you fancy going to a tea-dance tomorrow afternoon?" enquired Dorinda. "I am going with my cousin and his friend."

Mariella was excited by the idea but highly embarrassed at the thought of having to dance – and with a stranger.

"I can't really dance. I have not done so for years," she protested.

"Oh, it's all very casual and there's no pressure. My cousin and his friend are not any good on their pins either. Go on. It will be a real laugh."

Mariella was sorely tempted but still hesitated.

Dorinda continued to egg her on, stressing the it-will-be-a-laugh angle and emphasising that it could do no harm and Mariela could leave if it was not her cup of tea (pun intended). And when she mentioned the prospect of more raspberry tartlets together with strawberry scones and cherry cheesecake at the posh Meadow Bridge Grand Hotel, Mariella was powerless to refuse.

Mariella thus found her excuse for buying yet another new dress with matching jacket and some new shoes to complement the outfit, with the help of Dorinda, especially for the occasion.

The two new friends exchanged contact details, made the final arrangements to meet at the Grand tomorrow and kissed affectionately on parting.

Mariella felt that her life had taken a new and refreshing turn. She looked forward tremendously to her outing the next day but deliberately forgot to tell Piers, who would not have been the slightest bit interested in any case, about her new companion.

The next morning Mariella was up with the birds, having gone to bed with the fairies, and could not wait to begin the process of preparation for the event which began at 2.30 pm. She sat in her own in-house sauna for half an hour first thing, she took a long leisurely bath laced with floral-scented stress-buster bath oils and finally had her hair done mid-morning. Mariella then donned her elegant new dress and jacket ensemble in navy and rust shot silk together with her new shiny navy shoes and sparkly clutch-purse which she often used for evening wear.

She arrived at the Meadow Bridge Grand in good time to greet her new friend Dorinda and Dorinda's cousin Anthony. Mariella was also introduced to the dashing Nicholas Benson who instantly took her hand and kissed it like a knight in shining armour. Mariella was rendered breathless and coquettish at this greeting.

Nicholas was attentive, gallant and one of those dancers who managed to make a woman feel as if she did not need to do anything but merely exist. He glided her expertly across the dance-floor and Mariella did not need to even think about her steps. It was so easy-peasy. Mariella's troubles and despondency disappeared instantly.

The lapsang souchong with lemon and lime slices and the cream cheese and cucumber sandwiches garnished with mint followed by raspberry, strawberry and apricot tartlets, strawberry-filled scones, cherry cheesecake and mille-feuille also went down a treat although Mariella pretended to be abstemious in terms of her intake of carbohydrate in the presence of Nicholas.

Dorinda and Anthony smiled knowingly.

INSINUATION

Simon Risborough returned to his office in a mood of intense contemplation.

He had strived not to show his astonishment at the remark made by Ruth Angell at the ESIDR meeting to the effect that some financial skulduggery had occurred with the Elisian government. But Simon was a little more than curious to know more of this possible misdemeanour. His instincts told him that something potentially serious was afoot and he wanted to be in on the ground floor when the news broke. Intuition is knowing something without being told it. Instinct drives the human organism, of which Simon was a typical specimen, without thinking too much about it.

Simon considered taking Ruth out to lunch, getting her tight and pumping her gently for further information but he then deemed it inappropriate to ask her directly himself. Ruth would soon get wind of the fact that he was fishing and this might prove very embarrassing for him to be openly seen to be prying into the departmental affairs of another politician.

Simon asked himself many questions but answers were not always readily forthcoming. Who else could I recruit to do some ferreting around? It would have to be someone I could trust which significantly narrowed the field. No politician could ever be trusted. A politician is a creature who promotes himself under the darkened umbrella of promoting the welfare of others. A politician is like a man who marries a woman and obtains a stepdaughter just in order to be able to get a glimpse of the said stepchild, under his guardianship, in her underwear.

Simon also wondered about getting a complete outsider to do a bit of idle nosing around but he then concluded that this tactic would be fraught with danger and, if it ever got out that he had employed a mole, then he would certainly be in for the chop.

He also paraded the secretarial and administrative staff before his mind's eye in order to decide whether any of them would be a suitable snooping candidate but again he rejected his conjecture.

Simon then wondered about the absentee from today's meeting – Leonard Fletcher. His mind landed on Fletcher as a young recruit who was always anxious to please any of his more senior colleagues. But could he be trusted as an aspiring politician? Perhaps the young man had not yet learned that underhandedness is the life-blood of the political scene? But Simon believed that he could actually deny it if the lad were ever too loose with his tongue.

But I just must take the risk. And if I can present a tasty tiddler of information to the PM then my stock would inevitably rise. And the remaining days left in this sphere of operations would be a lot more pleasant and tolerable.

Temptation is an irresistible bedfellow. She is an enchantress who will brook no opposition. Simon further pondered what other jobs he might usefully be assigned to if he had the PM's ear. The prospect of becoming the blue-eyed boy with brighter days ahead spurred him onwards. The siren Temptation was growing in stature and allure.

He rang through to his secretary, Susie Melrose.

"Susie, when will Leonard Fletcher be back in the office, do you know?"

"I don't know precisely but I can find out," replied Susie obligingly.

"Do that will you please and let me know. I want a word with him as soon as possible."

Susie picked up the urgency in his voice although Simon had endeavoured to restrain it.

Susie, another who was always delighted to please, rang several of her colleagues and then went to Leonard's desk in the Central Administration Office in the hope of finding a note in a diary or a written message which would indicate the scheduled time of his return. But nothing obvious transpired.

She learned, however, from an administrative assistant, who worked in the same part of the open-plan office as Leonard, that he would be working late that evening in his constituency because a press-leak about a possible defection involving a party-worker had erupted. The elected minister for Westbury North, Helena Dartfield, did not want any taint of complicity on her hands and so Leonard Fletcher had been deputised to quieten the press interest and to defray any hint of truth about absconding on the part of the said party-worker.

Susie decided to try to make contact with Leonard directly and so she began by ringing the party headquarters at Westbury North.

When the phone was answered a helpful drudge informed Susie that Mr Fletcher was out of the office at an informal press conference but that she did have a mobile contact number. Susie herself was not normally given access to personal mobile numbers of minor officials but, on this occasion, she felt that it would be in order to reach him by this route. She was also dumfounded that his mobile number could be obtained so readily on a lame pretext by a mere phone call. After all she could have been anyone masquerading as a bona fide personal assistant from the London office.

"Leonard Fletcher," came the response when the mobile phone was answered.

Susie gave her name and stated the nature of her call. A summons from Simon Risborough with an asap price-tag attached gave her licence to interrupt whatever young Leonard might be doing.

"I am just about to attend a press conference," said a slightly harassed Leonard Fletcher, "but I should be back later tonight, if all goes well which it should."

"OK, but can you ring Simon on his office number as soon as you are free, please? He said it was fairly urgent."

Leonard consented knowing that the office switchboard would be manned until 10.00 pm that evening. Leonard interpreted 'fairly urgent' as 'ultra-urgent' in his mind.

"If I am not free before 10.00 pm, say, should I ring Simon on his mobile, if it's that urgent?" enquired the young man.

"I'll find out and let you know whether it can wait until tomorrow at least," replied Susie. She believed that it would not be politic to give out Simon's personal mobile number because he was a bit old-fashioned in that respect. She was amazed, in fact, that Simon even possessed a mobile phone, but he had only recently acquired one. Why mobile phones could not be standard Conservative Party issue, Susie failed ever to understand.

Leonard proceeded to his press conference with a new spring in his step. That he had been summoned by Simon Risborough he considered to be a great honour and an opportunity not to be missed.

Susie rang through to Simon to inform him of the lie of the territory and the whereabouts of Leonard. Simon felt it would be prudent not to urge such a degree of urgency even though he coveted it.

"It's not that vital," said Simon casually, "but just as soon as he can. What time will he, in fact, he back in the office this evening?"

Susie flushed. She had stupidly forgotten to ask. She must be losing her touch.

"Before closing time if at all possible or, if not, tomorrow first thing," she lied.

"OK, well, just tell him to contact me as soon as he can, then."

"Of course."

Susie then left a message on Leonard's mobile and told him to contact Simon on the land line when he could and left it at that.

Leonard's press conference was very much a perfunctory, one-way affair as he merely read out an official statement from the MP for Westbury North to the effect that the defection of one Sandra Mullingar was a malicious rumour. Unfortunately Mrs Mullingar was not available for comment.

Fletcher then answered a few challenging questions from the floor with evasive answers of the no-comment variety and hurriedly concluded the address to the, as yet, local reporters. He speedily wound up the proceedings by assuring all present that a further update would be issued if any additional information came to light. The gathering reluctantly dispersed.

Leonard knew that if the scandal worsened and the national press became interested, then he would not be the one to have to rescue the day. Fletcher appreciated that he was only sent down to Westbury North simply because he was, in fact, a junior backbencher, a tactic which had been designed to play down the seriousness of the occurrence.

Leonard walked back to party headquarters as it was on his way to the train station. In one of the smaller offices there he rang Simon Risborough. The phone in Simon's office rang at about 9.45 pm and he hesitated before answering it. Could it be Leonard or would it be someone who intended to keep me even later than usual at the office?

It was the insatiably keen Leonard Fletcher.

They spoke briefly about the press conference and then Simon asked when his junior colleague would actually be back in the London office. On learning that Leonard would be back on the morrow, Simon arranged a meeting with him scheduled for 12.00 noon on the following day rather than first thing.

Simon felt that he had some time between now and then to decide whether Leonard could actually be trusted with a snooping-around task while Leonard glowed with satisfaction at being called before one of the big white chiefs for a pre-lunchtime get-together or, possibly a lunchtime meeting, if he was lucky.

Leonard wended his way homeward with an air of anticipation and curiosity.

Simon closed and locked the office for the day and made his way home laboriously because he was jaded after a tiring day.

Sandra Mullingar was already at home and in bed but not asleep. Her husband slumbered peacefully beside her. She wondered how she had ended up in a situation whereby her loyalties to a party which she had served all her life were being seduced in the opposite direction. Was she to become an insomniac?

DELIBERATION

It was a short but pleasant drive to the Peacock's Feather along some winding lanes and across the undulating countryside until they reached the restaurant by the river's edge. The roadside verges were decorated with red campion, *Anthriscus* (raven's wing, to you), and the lilac-coloured *Scabiosa Columbaria*, a relative of honey-suckle, which were much admired by the travellers.

Barrington commented that the *Scabiosa* and the *Anthriscus* must have self-seeded from a nearby garden as it did not normally grow wild although *Anthriscus'* more common relative, cow parsley, was usually in profusion everywhere as a wild flower.

As regular customers, the restaurant manager heartily greeted them both by name and with a warm handshake. Good tippers were invariably remembered.

"A table in the garden beside the river, Mr Flint? Miss Fortescue-Bligh?" enquired the solicitous manager.

"Thank you, Pedro," came the reply from Barrington.

"I wonder how we have managed to secure a garden table here, buttercup," whispered Barrington.

"Pedro always sees us right, poppy."

They were given a spacious circular table with wooden chairs in matching Swedish redwood covered with plenty of soft, mock-velvet cushions. A white damask tablecloth was unobtrusively pinned in four places at the corners of the table in order to counteract the slight breeze. Sheffield silver cutlery and Waterford crystal glasses graced the table and, of course, all this luxury was reflected in the price.

"Some cocktails to start, Mr Flint?" said Pedro sporting a drinks menu, "Miss Fortescue-Bligh?" Cocktails were a speciality of the house.

"Thank you, Pedro," said Barrington. Calendula proffered her winning smile.

They scrutinised the cocktail menu for a few silent moments. Barrington quickly plumped for his usual Whiskey Sour with bourbon, lemon and honey. Calendula selected a Mojito, a traditional Cuban highball made from white rum, lime, mint, icing sugar and sparkling mineral water but, in typical female fashion, speedily changed her mind and opted instead for a Bellini consisting of Prosecco and nectarine purée. They placed their orders which were soon brought with a smile by Amanda.

"Could we also have some olives, please Amanda?" requested Barrington and Amanda consented and shortly obliged.

The lunchtime menus were the next to arrive.

Calendula decided on the sea bass with an apricot and almond stuffing, minted new potatoes, braised celery and a green side-salad for the main course and a roasted tomato and basil soup to start. Barrington decided on a smoked salmon and broad bean tart for a starter but then, in typical male fashion, vacillated between a rack of lamb with dauphinoise potatoes, lemon-glazed carrots and a root ginger and kale compote, on the one hand, or a breast of duck with a cranberry and wholegrain mustard sauce, sauté potatoes and buttered spinach with almonds, on the other. He still couldn't decide even when Pedro returned quite a little while later to take their orders. Calendula told him to have the duck and be done with it.

Barrington also ordered a large bottle of mineral water and a bottle of Chilean Pinot Noir for them to share.

When the starters arrived, they both found that they were quite hungry and consuming the food occupied their attention for a while until the silence was broken by Barrington.

"There may be a lead we can follow-up on from *The Guardian*," announced Barrington. Calendula murmured her curiosity. "I learned from Ronald Turner that they are planning to send a local reporter down to Westbury North to a press conference there tomorrow. Apparently one of the senior party-workers may be defecting and it has caused something of a stir. I will hear more tomorrow night."

Calendula's creative mind started to churn. "If there is a defection, or even a rumour of a defection, from the party it may be someone we could pump for information," she pondered. "How much would a local party-worker know about what goes on in London, would you say?"

"Apparently it is someone who works either in or fairly close to Fetherington's mob and so she could know more than would be expected of a local operative."

"It might be worth following up, in any case. Got anyone in mind for the job?" asked Calendula.

"Poochie panda, of course I have."

"Who?"

"Maurice."

"Maurice? Isn't he normally a bit young for a senior party official in the provinces?"

"Precisely," replied Barrington with significance.

"I see. Ingenious. A nice little toy-boy in the offing. Clever old lion cub."

"I know. I can't help it."

Calendula pushed him on the arm playfully and he gave a deep-throated, masculine-type giggle in return.

They got up and walked to the river's edge hand in hand while the starter plates were being cleared and they were waiting for their main courses. Barrington plucked a magnolia blossom from one of the trees in the garden and presented it to Calendula.

"For my true lady-love," he announced gallantly, on one knee.

"Why, thank you, kind sir." She gave him a mini mock-curtsey.

"Don't mention it."

He placed the blossom in her hair but it promptly fell out and they both laughed almost hysterically. They walked back to their table just as the main courses were arriving.

Pedro made a point of repositioning them at the table by holding out their chairs and flourishing their napkins as they sat down.

"This duck is delicious," announced Barrington as he tucked into his meal with relish. "What a good job I chose the duck," he teased. "How's your sea bass?"

"Heavenly! Shall we go for a walk along the river afterwards, lion cub?"

"Of course, poochie."

They declined any dessert but Calendula imbibed a pot of camomile tea made from fresh camomile leaves – no teabags in this posh establishment naturally. Barrington indulged in some mature Stilton, both the blue and the white varieties, and some creamy Wensleydale with celery, radishes, cherries and dates. Of course, Calendula afforded herself a nibble or two of the cheeses from her lover's platter now and then.

Calendula and Barrington had visited Stilton for the annual cheese-rolling on May Day a few years back and had actually met the landlord of the Bell in Huntingdonshire, who had invented this famous English cheese. They also planned to visit the Yorkshire Dales, the home of Wensleydale, when pressure of work permitted, for similar reasons.

While on their meandering riverside walk, they talked about Barrington's son, Charles, and Calendula's daughters, Chantal and Juliet, briefly as the meal wound down.

Charles was an accountant based in Scotland who had married a local lass and raised two lovely children. The paternal grandparents had been invited for a weekend later in August and so the pair anticipated some relief from the hot summer weather down south.

Juliet, the younger of Calendula's two offspring, was in her final year of a degree in education, that is Education, Psychology and Learning, at Cambridge. Once her degree was in the bag Juliet had plans for further study in order to do a PGCE and, perhaps, then go on to a master's degree in Education. Calendula and Barrington had recently visited Juliet at Cambridge but, because of her impending finals, they supposed, she seemed unwilling to devote any time to them and so the pair explored Cambridge a little instead before returning home.

Chantal lived in Paris and worked hard as a freelance fashion designer for an international fashion house out there. She had yet to secure the breakthrough which all fashion designers aspired to but she did own a small and upcoming company set up about five years ago with more than a little financial help from Calendula.

They sat down in the shade on the river bank. The river was in full spate just now and shimmered in the summer sunshine. Its reedy banks were lush green at this time of the year. Mallard ducks, dippers and grey wagtails provided a sight which delighted the observers. The male mallards, with their green heads, grey wings and undercarriage, strongly contrasted with the brown-speckled plumage of the females. The fast-flying dippers, with their startling white bibs, emitted a high-pitched squeak at the top of the birdsong harmonic range. The insect-eating grey-wagtails, famous for their distinctive yellow breasts, were recognised by the couple because of their rapid tail-wagging antics.

"Shall we take a quick weekend trip to Paris sometime soon if pressures of work are not too onerous?" suggested Calendula. "Then we can look in on Chantal if she's not too busy."

"Brilliant idea," came the instant response. "What about the weekend after next? We could probably get a last minute booking on the net."

"Let's do it. But maybe wait a few days while I put some further effort into Fetherington."

"Agreed."

"And how is your old school-chum doing in the researchers' office?" enquired Barrington.

"Oh, Faye?"

"Yes."

"Haven't heard from her lately. I might chase her up, although I am sure she will report back immediately if anything transpires," replied Calendula.

They contemplated finding somewhere quiet in order to make love but decided that the whole river footpath was too densely populated even on a weekday. A return home was indicated, therefore.

When they arrived home Barrington elected to do some piano practice on the Steinway grand. He regarded practising as a tedious chore (he was not really a muso) but he usually found time to do it at some point during the day when they were in Naxton.

Calendula went upstairs to practice her yoga and then prepared a cold supper of chicken salad for when they became hungry later in the evening.

After her yoga practice, Calendula went into the office where the accounts for her art and design business were sitting patiently waiting for her approval with an unsigned Accounts Approval Form due to be returned to the accountant. She read as much of the accounts documentation as she could understand and signed the said form. Barrington had already given her accounts the once-over and his subsequent seal of approval.

Calendula's business accounts were reasonably straightforward and so were simple for the Inland Revenue to follow. As far as the taxman and their lame-brained local accountant were aware her income was derived partly from her freelance earnings from the sale of her high-priced paintings but chiefly from the investments which she had made with the money she had inherited from her titled father, Sir William Fortescue-Bligh. Barrington was put down as a sleeping partner in the business, Two City Designs, but he himself also derived a small income from his late father's estate in Shropshire. And certainly no-one knew about their cash-only dealings from the work of the Medici Squadron.

Both the Inland Revenue and their accountant, Sidney Bingham Clarke, were, of course, unaware of their numbered bank accounts in Switzerland and the existence of their properties in the south of France and central London. Calendula considered it prudent to give the production of her accounts for Two City Designs to an outsider in order to rubber-stamp her business in the eyes of the Inland Revenue. By this means she could appear open and above board. Barrington, of course, could have completed her accounts easily himself but he had, in fact, suggested the merits of out-sourcing them for the sake of credibility in the eyes of the Inland Revenue.

AMALGAMATION

Piers Wendell sat in his office very late one Wednesday night considering his financial position. And it needed to be reviewed too because it was so complex.

Piers surveyed his numerous bank accounts in various names across the globe into which he had secreted monies from ill-gotten gains. He also inspected his investments and his semi-liquid assets which were distributed in offshore accounts. Piers then checked his anticipated remittances and in-payments and all seemed to be in order, fortunately.

Wendell idly wondered what he would do with all this money but he decided that such a problem could occupy his time on another occasion. It was as if he needed to make the money and then ruminate at a later date on how to spend it. He was also in two minds about whether to spend it or not. He wanted to live the high life but he also wanted to retain something of a nest-egg in order to ensure that he would have enough money to live on in luxury for the rest of his life. He certainly did not want to defenestrate his earnings in a frivolous manner and then be chewed up as a result of his losses.

Wendell had mixed motives when it came to money. He had hailed from a family who had lived on the bread-line and this start in life had coloured his view of finances. His mother had worked long hours in order to make ends meet but his father had put most of their income down his throat in the semblance of drink and tobacco. Poor sod!

Piers was constantly a home-alone kid which may have accounted for the fact that he preferred his own company in preference to socialising. Piers only got married, in fact, because he felt it was expected of him. He had not had many girlfriends before his marriage and he had never been able to feel close to his wife or even his own children. He regarded Mariella merely as someone who organised his home affairs rather as his secretary, Leanne, ensured the smooth-running of his life in the office. Not for one moment did he ever believe these women in his life to be an embodiment of humanity but then he was hardly alive himself.

Wendell had been a bright boy and he had managed to excel in his study and fascination for the law and its practice as adulthood came upon him. After his assiduous training in commercial law, he had joined a firm of corporate lawyers who had quickly recognised his talents and had speeded him up the greasy pole at a vast rate of knots. Piers then changed jobs a few times in order to gain the requisite experience for dominating the field of commercial law. Currently he held the position of senior partner in the firm of Galbraith, Minchin and Claxton (GMC), a city-based concern in London. Wendell often gloated on his success which delighted him continually because he felt that it was his only true achievement in this world.

Some of his earnings had gone into buying his house in Market Drayton, a holiday pied-à-terre with moorings and a sailing craft in Turkey and a couple of flashy cars. Piers, however, was not the playboy-type and so he never indulged in the kind of activities, such as gambling and womanising, which his colleagues habitually enjoyed while their wives turned a convenient blind eye or did likewise. And as Piers certainly never would have won first prize in any beautiful bouncing baby competition, he was not sought after by any of the female population.

Piers was, moreover, contemplating making a few property-purchases abroad as a means of disguising his assets from various government departments worldwide. The lawyer, by this means, could fiddle the books by undertaking his own negotiations and conveyancing without declaring his assets to the British government or any other superpower for that matter. Not that he believed the UK government to be anything more than a noisy and blustering, yet utterly ineffectual, ruling party. The hype was just that – flimflam and propaganda.

Piers reflected on his recent dealings for one of his multinational clients, Wyatt Enterprises Incorporated, which traded in oil from the Middle East but had interests across the globe with regard to investments. Wendell had handled Wyatt's legal affairs for some years and he had built up an enviable reputation with the outfit. He had expertly negotiated takeover bids and mergers with other corporations until Wyatt's had become a really big fish with little in the way of competition and much in the manner of interest from the

Monopolies Commission who themselves had a monopoly on being a regulator of organisations who were playing monopoly with their assets and business practices.

Wendell had also negotiated one or two cunning moves for Wyatt's when dealing with oil barons who were not at all averse to selling a few drugs here and there or doing a bit of money-laundering on the side. Like the wives of his colleagues Piers elected to turn a blind eye when necessary and so he had received a handsome payback when the fruits of these operations had proved their worth in terms of time-investment and human effort.

Wendell, moreover, had also negotiated some deals of his own through the contacts which he had made with the oil-producing magnates via his work with GMC. Arms, for instance, had been shipped across frontiers and exported to those who were desperately in need of them. Remittances from far and wide had, consequently, scudded across the planet like a fast flasher's exhibits when he believed Robert Peel's brigade to have been hot on his trail.

Having put his finances in order, Wendell's attention then swooped on his latest under-the-table transactions for Wyatt's and for the advertising agency Braithwaite and Kelleridge plc.

For Wyatt's he was negotiating another takeover bid with a transportation business, On the Road Distribution, who specialised in shipping goods to countries in Africa. This transaction would enable Piers to get a rake-off when a deal was struck with On the Road because he had secured the agreement of Wyatt's chief executive, Jason Cunningham, to this effect. Wendell's fellow partners at GMC, of course, knew nothing of these transactions.

Piers was helping Braithwaite and Kelleridge to decide on their forward-planning policy in terms of financial investments and asset-acquisition. For this organisation, Wendell's rake-off would transpire because he was in cahoots with their finance director, George Allingham, who had promised to line his palm with gold if he, George, was recommended for promotion by Piers in the course of his reporting to the Board.

His mobile warbled and Piers wondered who the hell was ringing him at this time of night unless it was from abroad. He looked at his watch. At nearly 10.00 pm it could be from somewhere west of where Piers sat.

Wendell did not recognise the voice at the other end of the line but he could identify the accent.

The caller announced herself as Kadienne Patrell.

Wendell's mind went into overdrive. What a stupid name. Who the hell was she? And how the blazes did she get my number? What's she selling? He waited for an explanation before terminating the call.

Kadienne explained that she was ringing from New York as the personal assistant to the chief executive of Wyatt's. Ah. Now he was interested. Good job he hadn't put the phone down with a parting expletive. His dealings with Wyatt's personnel were exclusively in Europe to date but he wanted keenly to expand his field of operation for this client.

Would he be able to come over to the big apple (well, she didn't actually use those words) to discuss a deal? More information? It was in connection with a vertical integration scheme which the US division of Wyatt's was hoping to pull off with a pharmaceutical company who bought and processed the by-products of oil. Wendell continued to listen attentively. A trip to the States would not go amiss. And maybe he could check out the tourist properties for investment there at the same time?

Kadienne mentioned that a Skype meeting could take place at a suitable time for both sides of the pond in order to discuss the preliminaries. Well, that would be OK, certainly. And she also inferred that his work was highly valued by Wyatt's and that, therefore, he had the stamp of official approval which the US operation valued. What a nice woman, thought Wendell. A Skype meeting was accordingly arranged for the following day for late afternoon for him and early afternoon for them.

Wendell pondered on the prospect of widening his net across the Wyatt's conglomerate and of getting the chance to look into the affairs of the organisation worldwide rather than concentrating his efforts merely in Europe. He then decided to jack it in for the day after the call and to wend his way homeward with thoughts of greater adventures in the future.

Mariella was, of course, asleep in her room when Piers arrived home. Piers made himself a hot chocolate and retired for the night. Mariella was not, in fact, asleep but she neglected to acknowledge his return.

As usual Piers left early the next morning in order to return to his beloved office before Mariella had ventured forth. They say that on a man's deathbed he often regrets spending so much time in the office. In Piers' case this adage did not apply.

Mariella, of course, designed her life around avoiding her husband so that, even though she was awake that morning, she elected to read quietly in her room just so that they could avoid each other. These days she even ignored his farewell greeting. That way she could pretend she was not married to Piers except when she was spending his money.

MAGNIFICATION

Back at the factory James discovered that life was chuntering along as usual once the ESIDR meeting was over.

Beryl Wainwright looked up expectantly on his return and, as was her custom, more or less pounced on him with a barrage of messages, requests for phone calls which he needed to make, his post for signature and a number of the typed reports for his perusal.

James lingered by her desk before returning to his own office so that he could get an eyeful of the other younger office members, namely, Claire and Zena. He would have loved to spend the night with either of them or, better still, both at the same time but, in fact, he confined himself to merely ogling them because he felt that they were just a weenie bit too close to home.

Zena smiled as James nodded his head in her direction and he noticed the inviting cut of her blouse. The summer was an interesting time for James because it revealed more of the average woman's body. In the case of Beryl and Nancy, however, he cursed the summer because what they could display, he did not want to see.

Claire also attracted his attention because she wore a figure-flattering dress in an attractive cotton print. Perhaps he could make an exception in her case, despite the fact that she was close to his doorstep, provided that she showed some interest in him which, so far, his prowling radar-scanner had failed to detect.

Nancy, despite being a snappy dresser and rather fashion conscious, he could definitely leave out of the equation. Nancy had a face like chip-shop vinegar after it had developed a highly offensive mould. Nancy's saving grace was that she was monstrously efficient – more so than the officious Beryl with her world-famous filing system and her ability to rule the office with a rod of iron.

James became aware of Beryl's summing up of his thoughts and, therefore, he beat a hasty retreat into his office.

Let's try Claire out for size one day and see if she might be willing to take the bait? I might find an excuse for getting her in my office alone for a protracted period of time perhaps when watchdog Beryl takes her prying eyes on holiday, James contemplated. However, to business.

James skim-read a number of the outstanding reports, returned the lighter reading to his filing-tray and put the weightier ones in his briefcase with the usual consignment of promises. He signed his letters, indicated some corrections to one and looked down the list of those who sought his attention on the phone.

The afternoon was reaching that time when his blood-sugar was at its lowest ebb and so he decided to indulge in some speculation and fantasy under the guise of studying various bits of documentation in case anyone crashed in unannounced.

With a weighty document in hand, he indulged himself with thoughts about Verity Baxter. When would it be politic to ring her again? Perhaps towards the end of the week? Don't want to appear too keen or desperate. But he was beginning to feel desperate about her. The oxytocin and testosterone combined were up to their old tricks again. The former to draw him towards her like a magnet and the latter to raise the stakes and enable him to step up to the plate.

Fetherington fantasised about caressing her thighs and stripping her naked on a hot summer's day in a shady, deeply-wooded glade surrounded by fragrant wood anemones, bergenia and campanula while listening to the plaintive birdsong of the chiffchaff and the nightingale. Birds might make vicarious observers but they would never be able to tell any tales.

James next vividly imagined ravishing her in a luxurious four-posted, somewhere in France's Gorge du Tarn, encased in lavender-scented sheets.

James thoughts then turned to the fourteenth century *Sultan Ahmet Camii* (The Blue Mosque, to you) in Istanbul where he might lounge around in a Turkish steam bath with Verity, as if as a spiritual homage to the God of Voluptuous Gratification, and watch the sweat running down between her firm and upturned breasts as she sat on his lap. This image recalled a time when James had dabbled with a Scandinavian girl (Linnea? Lovisa? Lalla? Something like that) in a Swedish sauna in a hotel in Amsterdam.

The phone on his desk interrupted his reverie. Bugger! What was it about phones that had the habit of interrupting the serious business of life? He was reminded of another phone that had rung at an inopportune moment last evening. What, was is only yesterday?

Philippa Gresham was back again to report that the press release on the foreign trade figures matter had already scotched most of the rumours but that they also needed to have a meeting about the promotional material for the Russian trip planned for next year. They co-ordinated diaries for possible dates for a meeting with Tristanica Rezze, the creative design agency, in order to discuss the artwork.

No sooner had this conversation terminated than Beryl rang through to enquire whether she should also get some of the more urgent calls for him now. James agreed to her obtaining about half of those who had requested a telephone audience. He had to keep Beryl on her toes by not acceding to all her demands which encroached on his fantasy-time.

James spoke to the chief official at the Westbury North constituency, Harrison Smythe, who reported that Leonard Fletcher had given a good account of himself at the informal press conference held there and that Sandra Mullingar had been suspended from duty pending an enquiry. Tranter had asked that James be kept abreast of any developments on this issue even though it was really Helena Dartfield's patch. James believed that Sandra's suspension was the reason why the press boys had become interested but, nevertheless, he still thought it was a wise move even though she may have been entirely blameless. A mole in the camp, because she had become disenchanted by policy decisions or because she was generally disgruntled with her lot in some way, was a potential time-bomb for the party. James bid Harrison good-bye and promised to have lunch with him when they next met either in London or Westbury.

Fetherington had retired to his private washroom when the next call came through but he felt disinclined to offer an explanation to Beryl for his delay in answering.

It was God himself, well semi-god, and he had kept him waiting. Gregory Tranter wanted to know what had occurred at the ESIDR meeting that morning. Because the sub-committee consisted of members from various walks of life, it was a potential hot-house for gossip, rumours and useful information.

James was able to report on Ruth's knowledge about the Elisian business and the fact that the Danish report had been delayed. James delighted in telling Tranty tales about Ruth's ungovernable tongue. Both ministers spoke in veiled terms when referring to these matters, even over a secure line, just in case the eavesdropping piranhas became over-aggressive. They also generally discussed the various trade missions and the fact that the Russian foray was being planned and organised well in advance. James was also able to mention to Gregory the news which he had just received from Westbury North.

James offered to confirm their discussions in writing by way of an interim report but Gregory declined to want anything in writing at this stage.

Simon Risborough also called just to make sure that there was really no funny business with the Elisian government, the topic which he had adroitly suppressed at the ESIDR meeting. Simon felt he could risk contacting James using the excuse that he just wanted to make certain that Ruth's assertion was simply a rumour. Risborough adopted the tone that he was acting out of the best of all possible motives.

James was interested to note that Simon had been curious while still feigning indifference and appearing to quell any scandalmongering at the meeting. He also wondered what use Simon would make of any information which was imparted to him. Fetherington speculated about whether a similar phone call had been put through to the shit-stirring Ruth. The Parliamentary Secretary, therefore, became very guarded in his replies to Simon as his antennae perceived a possible trap which would have disastrous repercussions for him.

"The situation is just as I said at the meeting, Simon. There was a backdated payment from Elisia, that is all. I am not at all sure what all the fuss and fizz is about? And where did Ruth get her unfounded information from, I wonder?" complained James. The last throwaway remark was actually his means of fishing for facts.

"Ruth seems to think that her interpretation of the figures is correct. But I am not sure why," came the response from Simon. He was careful not to give anything away.

"In other words, it is purely hearsay and speculation," replied the other. "Ruth Angell should learn not to be such a meddling woman. She is only a researcher after all."

James would like to have called Ruth a meddling, muck-spreading blabbermouth but he chose to doctor his language appropriately for Simon's benefit. He also, of course, wanted to make life difficult for the irrepressible Ruth if he could.

"I think Ruth, as a researcher, is acting above her remit by passing on or even questioning anything at all, under any circumstances, that she might have been exposed to whether good or ill," James continued. He sought to appeal to Simon's entrenched old-school, women-should-never-have-got-the-vote attitude. He felt that this stance and his response would propitiate Simon's nosey-parker proclivities.

Simon noted the emphasis in James' voice and this, strangely enough, made him even more suspicious. Could he be hiding something or was he telling the unadulterated truth? Did he simply just hate Ruth and was he trying to make life difficult for her? Was he covering up for Gregory Tranter? Was the suspect information likely to leak out? Did the PM know? That was the question.

When the call had finished James wondered whether Simon did not have his own agenda when making his seemingly casual enquiries. Was he genuinely concerned about the accuracy of the accounting? Did he believe the replies he had been given? Was he on a mission to curry favour with the PM by feeding him some juicy snippets which would discredit Tranty's sphere of operations and then destabilise the whole department? Interesting considerations. Interesting times.

James thumped the desk petulantly. Fucking Ruth Angell! Yes, I wouldn't mind. And, if it would keep her mouth shut, that would be a big bonus.

CERTIFICATION

Leanne Ingram sat at her desk filing her nails in between bouts of filing papers in the filing cabinet. She could afford to be lax because she had an office to herself – a privilege often afforded to a senior partner's personal assistant as she liked to style herself. The only other occupant of her office was Silvia Reed, a junior secretary in the Corporate Client Department, but she was on holiday at present.

A tap on the door interrupted her nail-filing routine and she hastily threw her emery board into her desk drawer before answering the door.

Bill Frampton stood before her beside a stranger whom he introduced as a bloke who had come to mend the computer network cabling in Mr Wendell's office.

Leanne was unaware that the network system was down but she agreed to admit the two into Piers' office as he was away visiting a client that morning. Leanne, therefore, indicated that the two could go into Piers' office as long as they were not too long.

"Shouldn't take a moment," declared the stranger who seemed to answer to the name of Norman when Bill addressed him.

Leanne returned to her desk and only then noticed that the internal intranet system was out of action and so she was forced to complete the filing for the week. Most of the stuff was held on the computer but occasionally documents had to be printed out for reference and eventual archiving when a matter was completed. And so Leanne was saddled with the filing which had built up, particularly because Silvia was away.

Bill then emerged from Piers' office and announced that the cabling problem had, at last, been rectified and that Norman was now rebooting the system at Piers' terminal.

"Will it now be up and running?" enquired Leanne.

Bill consulted Norman who informed him that the system would also need to be rebooted centrally but that this would take place shortly.

Leanne wanted to get out her latest spy novel in order to finish the next chapter which she was reading but she refrained from doing so until the two men had left the office suite. After all she couldn't do any work because the computer was down.

The two men left the office with thanks from Bill and a smile from Norman the techie.

Leanne instantly grabbed her novel, opened it at the place which she had bookmarked and continued to read it with her desk drawer wide open just in case Piers should return unexpectedly. He would have to pass through her office in order to get to his own because the office suite was arranged in that manner in order to deflect any casual callers who tended to interrupt Wendell's thought processes. Leanne regarded him really as nothing but a boring git. But it was a job, at least, and so she played the game.

Bill and Norman then made their way back to the main information technology centre in order to inform the IT staff that a reboot of the hub should reinstate their computer network after which all should be well. And it proved to be the case so that the work of Galbraith, Minchin and Claxton could continue as normal.

Bill then bid farewell to Norman who made his way down in the lift to the ground-floor exit.

Piers Wendell returned to his office later that afternoon in time for his Skype meeting with New York. He gave some instructions to Leanne but then bid her adieu because she would not be needed by him for the rest of the working day. Leanne was entirely happy with this arrangement.

The Skype conference call came through from Kadienne Patrell and Adelina Murphy, the CEO of Wyatt's and her side-kick in New York, on time and without hitch.

Neither Adelina nor Kadienne were the pusillanimous type and so the meeting kicked off to a prompt start.

"We wondered if you would be willing to come over to the States to handle the legalities for our takeover of Grant Houghton Pharmaceuticals. Jason Cunningham speaks very highly of you, sir. And I gather you handled the deal with On the Road really well. And we want your type over here," began Adelina.

"Right," thought a slightly bemused but typically English Piers.

Adelina didn't wait for a reply and continued to ply him with the details of the vertical integration scheme which she had planned and wanted executed forthwith. This would entail his going to the USA and negotiating with the lawyers for the other party, Liarbridge Law Practice. Wendell had certainly heard of this outfit and was flattered somewhat to be asked to deal with such a giant in the industry. He rubbed his hands with relish beneath the desk and grabbed his diary in order to make a date for his trip to New York.

Adelina also stated that she would send much of the paperwork in advance so that he could digest the background on the matter before his arrival. Wendell was delighted to have another excuse for staying late at the office.

They flagged up a few details and points for further discussion during the online meeting but essentially the conference call had served its purpose.

Wendell was going over in his mind the way in which he could organise things at the London end. He would assign most of his outstanding matters to two of his legal staff, Nigel and Emily, who could be trusted to delegate work as required, but he would take with him Kate and Ainsley. Kate Falmouth would go down well with the women out there but Ainsley Chrythorn was brilliant at negotiating with the enemy as if he were a Rottweiler on steroids.

Wendell had told Adelina that he would be delighted to bring his team over as soon as conveniently possible and the New York team agreed to set a date in the not too distant future.

The Skype session concluded with much in the way of 'have a nice day' wishes.

Wendell now planned the trip (a good chance to get away from Mariella for a week or two) and decided when he would travel. The details were soon finalised and Leanne was given instructions to plan his itinerary and to make the necessary bookings on the following day.

The documentation came through on time and was duly digested and Wendell's team was assembled with a degree of enthusiasm which satisfied all parties.

Kate Falmouth said adieu to her flat-mate who helped her to pay the mortgage and Ainsley Chrythorn bid his wife and new-born baby a fond farewell and all three made their way to Heathrow with optimism and exuberance.

Wendell began to envisage with great pleasure the lucrative rake-off he might personally obtain from such a deal.

Bill Frampton, meanwhile, became a very satisfied employee of the Medici Squad once he had received a tidy sum for his ability to warn Barrington of Wendell's forthcoming US trip and its purpose. Bill was also instrumental in enabling another associate of Calendula and Barrington to gain access to Wendell's office. Jules Axminster had managed to record Wendell's online conference and had also put a bug in his desktop computer and his laptop which would keep a tally on the lawyer's activities both here and across the pond.

PERTURBATION

Faye Windsor-Harris sat at her computer in the open-plan administrative offices of the Research Division, known colloquially as Research Central, acting for the International Development Department and the Department of Innovative Enterprise based in Whitehall.

Faye was employed by Gregory Tranter as a Junior Researcher who reported directly to Senior Researcher and Section Head, Ruth Angell, with whom she shared an office. The office also housed a number of other researchers, supported by some secretarial and administrative staff.

Ruth sat at a desk adjacent to Faye's but Ruth sat with her back to the window while Faye sat sideways on, with the window on her immediate right, in the corner of the room. The two desks thus formed a disjointed L-shape, with a gap of a couple of metres between them. Faye, if she cared to, had a full-on view of Ruth in profile. Very convenient.

To the left side of Faye's desk abutted a number of other desks where some more junior researchers, also reporting to head honcho Ruth, beavered away. A partition then separated the bank of researchers from the administrative and secretarial staff.

The part of the office which the researchers occupied was, on the whole, normally quiet and the workers remained fairly static at their desks while the administrative staff were more prone to chatter and movement.

Faye was analysing voters' preferences and polling trends following the recent provincial elections. A survey had been conducted which asked voters to state whether they were in favour of retaining the regular surgery which their local MP usually conducted on a weekly basis, whether they felt that the presence of the MP in their constituency was adequate and what local issues they would like to see addressed.

Her training as a statistician enabled her to collect data, organise it, analyse it and deliver an interpretation quite speedily. Faye's degree in statistics from Imperial College London, in which she had specialised in predictive analytics, had paved the way for her getting a job with the government because she could extract data and then predict future trends which was what her employer required.

Faye was also studying for a part-time, mainly home-study, MSc in statistical and corporate research at the London School of Economics as a means of furthering her career. She felt that her government job was a good grounding for a future move into the corporate sector. She saw no long-term prospects in this neck of the woods but she intended to cast her net wider in the not too distant future because she had held her present post for nearly four years and it would shortly be time to move on. Faye's master's degree would be completed later in the year and then she could begin to search for jobs elsewhere.

Faye was in the final stages of preparing her report, entitled *Voting Trends and Preferences: A Predictive Analysis for Forward Planning*, which set out her suggestions for action in order to meet the demands of the electorate in Gregory Tranter's constituency at Morganbury Bridge, a large and safe seat in Cambridgeshire. This report had been commissioned by backbencher James Fetherington who was responsible for assisting Tranter as the Cabinet Minister for the department. Faye regarded the upstart Fetherington as a predator from whom she elected to keep her distance before his wandering eyes and hands could target her. She purposely intended to retain him as a backbencher in her life as well as in the House.

As the day was drawing to a close Faye glanced periodically at the clock at the top of her screen in order to see when she might be free to leave the premises and dust away her thoughts with a glass of wine. She wanted to get the report today to the stage whereby she could simply give it a final read-through tomorrow, make any last-minute corrections and generally put the finishing touches to it, before printing it out in draft for Ruth to finally appraise. They would then discuss her findings and conclusions before its despatch.

Because of the flexitime regime in operation at the office, most of the administrative and secretarial staff and many of the researchers had already hit the homeward road. In her section only Carol Wilkes, a newly-recruited junior researcher, remained.

The equilibrium of the office, for those still at work, however, was abruptly disturbed by the return of the fiery Ruth Angell who entered the room in a flurry of temper and obvious frustration.

She threw some papers down on her already untidy desk which threatened to cause a cascade of other documentation on to the floor. This situation, by chance, was narrowly averted, however, on this occasion. Faye was, by now, accustomed to Ruth's temper tantrums and, on a number of occasions, she had managed either to prevent papers from falling on to the floor or had retrieved those which had actually made it.

"Bloody Fetherington," Ruth exclaimed sotto voce but loud enough for Faye to catch it, although she brought down the iron mask in order to give the impression that she had not heard anything at all. Faye did not, in fact, even look up until Ruth was well and truly seated and then only glanced at her to the extent that social mores dictated. Faye knew that by ignoring Ruth she would cajole her into starting up a conversation in order to secure an outlet for her discomposure.

Faye bided her time. She was aware with her peripheral vision that Carol Wilkes was quite taken aback by Ruth's disposition and so she studiously avoided any exchange of eye-brow raising with her.

Ruth got up and began to pace the room. Faye remained impassive and apparently concentrating hard on what she was doing with her head pointing well down towards the desktop. In despair at not securing an audience, Ruth flounced out of the room.

Faye focused hard on her computer screen in order to pretend not to have noticed Ruth's exit and so as to avoid any eye-contact with Carol too. She certainly did not want to engage in any prattle or banter about the situation with this relative newcomer.

Faye wondered why Ruth had left and where she might be going. Was she going to confide in another, perhaps? Was she going to the loo for a decent rant or a good ball? Was she going to have a blazing row with Fetherington? Surely not? She was not that stupid. How long would she be absent from the office? She did not normally leave at this time of the day.

Faye began to speculate further. Had Ruth managed to seek solace elsewhere? And had she found a sympathetic shoulder to cry on with another? No, perhaps not. Most people were sick to the back teeth with Ruth's volatile outbursts and her petty tiffs with James Fetherington.

Faye could not understand why the two of them could not just get together and relief their respective sexual frustrations and put an end to the dramatic tension between them. It was obvious to her that the two of them had a love-hate relationship in which passion, in its various incarnations, would surface come what may. Beatrice and Benedick were no match for those two. So why didn't they do something about it? James, after all, would shag anything with a pulse and so why not the passion-stricken Ruth?

Twenty minutes or so elapsed and Faye was beginning to pack up her things and to lock her desk when the irascible Ruth returned to the office. By this time no-one else, apart from a few secretaries and Carol, was about. Ruth sat listlessly at her desk and then addressed the air around her generally.

"Anyone fancy a glass of wine at Hatty's?" she said vaguely. When no obvious response was forthcoming, Ruth resorted to a more direct approach. "Faye? Carol?"

This was Faye's chance. Seize it, gal.

"Yes, that would be nice, Ruth. And Carol will come too," said Faye almost commandingly. She knew that Carol was too timid to refuse.

But here would be an opportunity for Ruth to unload and, if anything interesting did transpire from their conversation, she, Faye, would both have a witness and someone else to blame if there was a leak. Perfect.

The three researchers made their way to Hatty's Wine Bar on Horse Guard's Road opposite St James's Park. Hatty's was an art deco establishment which overlooked St James's Park and which was presided over by Joe, the waiter. It was happy hour but they soon found a corner table near the window and ordered their drinks. Ruth ordered a full bottle of Spanish house red, Carol discreetly chose a glass of Rosé while Faye, wanting to keep utterly sober, simply asked for a mineral water with fresh lime.

Ruth wasted little time in bearing her soul. "That damned Fetherington got my goat at the meeting today," she began.

"Oh, how did the meeting go?" enquired Faye casually, wanting to know about any major developments of the work of the ESIDR sub-committee just as much as about the war between Ruth and James.

"The usual thing. No real decisions or progress. No change there."

Faye nodded her acknowledgement of this derogatory fact.

"But Fetherington got my back up," said Ruth wanting to get her point across. "When I questioned him about the financial irregularities in the trade figures to accompany his report on the Elisian project, which I have already had sight of, he simply said it was an import subsidy back-payment. Back-payment, my arse! The man is covering up something big, I am sure. And then that misogynist Risborough blew the whistle on any discussion. Typical."

Carol drew breath but said nothing. Shock had registered but she was too bashful to voice her thoughts in front of these two minor luminaries.

"Financial irregularities? What made you suspicious of the figures? I thought they had been checked and double checked, even in the draft," queried Faye. She endeavoured to make this a casual throwaway question. It was, in fact, the first time she had got any inkling of something being afoot and she hoped that Ruth would get increasingly inebriated in order to loosen her tongue still further.

Ruth threw caution to the wind. "I heard about it on the grapevine. I can't reveal my sources except to say that it came from outside. But I wanted to rattle Fetherington with the knowledge."

Faye believed that Ruth's ill-considered move would have threatened her position as Section Head considerably but it would certainly have rattled the lascivious backbencher. How can an intelligent woman be so reckless? She speculated still further. Could it have been a newshound or an ex-employee? I wonder?

However, Faye said aloud, "Is it a reliable source? It's quite an accusation to make if the claim is based on a shaky foundation?"

Ruth considered a while and then said, "Well, as far as I know it's genuine."

There's possibly a mole in the camp concluded Faye silently to herself. Often some insider information can leak out to the press and then the hacks will endeavour to make trouble by selling their information back to those in the government departments who are likely to stir up the most trouble within the ranks on the divide-and-conquer basis, she thought.

Carol had drained her glass and looked as if she wanted to leave. She eventually plucked up the courage to say, "Well I must be off. My husband will be getting concerned."

Ruth made a vain attempt to get her to stay but Faye took pity on her and fought her corner. Carol left in a bit of a fluster of embarrassment. She hurried down the road with relief and confusion.

Faye wondered what other information she might now get out of Ruth if she put her mind to it.

Ruth's narrative continued. "He even flirted with me at lunchtime. The bastard. And he pinched the prawn sandwiches!" Ruth's voice was getting louder. She needed to be quietened down and so Faye put a restraining hand on her arm. The confidante had arrived.

Faye concluded that it would be advantageous to let Ruth talk without interruption, despite the fact that she would have to sit through hearing about her pugilistic relationship with Fetherington.

Ruth obliged by rambling on and ordering another bottle of house red. She admitted to fancying him a lot but she had made a policy decision not to get involved with such an infamous Don Juan. This obviously caused her a lot of inner turmoil and, perhaps, some sleepless nights. Faye just made sympathetic comments in the most appropriate places and continued to play the role of Ruth's kindly confidante.

After about an hour of Ruth's outpourings, Faye thought she had obtained as much information from Ruth as was necessary and she was beginning to tire of the drunken sot. She made her excuses and left while Ruth continued to consume the house red and become more morbid and vulnerable as the evening drew on.

Faye, meanwhile, picked up a posh Thai takeaway and made for her flat in Pimlico. She augmented the Thai cuisine takeaway with a bag of green salad dressed with lemon juice and olive oil.

Once home Faye had a quick look at her overdue course work for the MSc. She despaired now of ever getting this assignment in on time and so she sent a begging email to her tutor for an extension of the deadline to which he normally obligingly consented.

As the meal was being digested, refuelling her and giving her a pleasant sense of satisfaction, she poured herself another glass of wine and then picked up the phone to call a friend.

EXHILARATION

Barrington Flint had originally trained to be a corporate lawyer. He had a degree in law and a career-oriented postgraduate diploma in business management.

He had formerly worked for a short while as an in-house lawyer for a multi-national conglomerate which manufactured and sold the hugely popular perfume range, Brevity Bliss. This schooling in corporate law at management level had given him the grounding which he needed in order to understand managerial tactics, human resource management, forward planning, tax accounting and marketing.

After his stint with Brevity, Barrington worked for a number of years as a freelance business management consultant, a period in his life when he had acquired large amounts of money and invaluable experience but his life lacked lustre. This episode in Barrington's life felt aimless and purposeless and it proved to him that money was not its own reward. His constant need to travel was also a burden which he could have done without. It actually increased his feeling of restlessness.

It was not until he had met the lovely Calendula in Paris that his business and personal life changed irrevocably and he never now looked back. The two of them plotted together to form what they affectionately referred to as the Medici Squadron. This clandestine enterprise had gone from strength to strength and had become successful beyond their wildest dreams.

Barrington was one of those rare men who made a distinction between making love and having sex. Some men only make love and, therefore, lead a curtailed existence with but one woman all their sexually-active life. Sex thus is not meant solely for procreation but merely as a way of wasting time until it is time to get up and get on with the chores of the day. Category number two are men who only have sex and so bed-hopping almost becomes a chore and differs only by the day of the week or the bedroom décor of the latest conquest whose name cannot usually be recalled the next morning. Sex, for this latter type of Casanova, is getting it up until it is time to get up.

With Calendula he made love with true affection and heightened pleasure. Barrington loved her sincerely and intended to spend the rest of his life with her. He could not, in fact, have existed without her and Barrington could not even contemplate the notion. She satisfied him in every respect. As a child Barrington had felt completely detached from both of his stuffy parents, now deceased, but he had, in later life, found the love which he had formerly craved in Calendula as the embodiment of all that was missing from his past.

The only useful function which the death of his mother and father had served for Barrington was that he had obtained a small inherence from which a modest income could be derived.

For occupational necessities, Barrington Flint could manage to have sex with a series of females but emotive involvement was not on the agenda in any respect. It was as if he had a belt-and-braces lifejacket which prevented him from ever becoming attached to anyone but his adorable Calendula.

While Barrington was the hard-headed business brain of the outfit, Calendula was the artist of the pair and she provided the creative input which drove the bus.

Calendula had trained in contemporary fine art in prestigious art colleges in London and Paris. When Calendula had left art school, she made Paris her home for a while. During this period of her life she had been everything from a pavement artist to a fashion designer. She had been anywhere, in fact, where she could make money. Times had been hard to begin with but she soon found a way of surviving. Selling some of her more serious works to Parisian aristocrats had been the start of her own freelance business, Two City Designs. It was, indeed, a tale of two cities as Calendula had maintained an art studio in both London and Paris within five years of launching herself on the open market.

It has to be said also that Calendula was highly gifted and so it was no wonder that her works, which sold for ridiculous prices, were much sought after. She became known by all the London and Parisian art dealers as well as others across the globe. Calendula had sold her work as far and wide as Japan, Australasia and the US as well as to the more local European markets. Although Calendula was now making a mint of money out of selling her oeuvre. She also had the safety-net of her inheritance from the Fortescue-Bligh estate.

During the early days of her Parisian domicile, Calendula had also acquired another talent for seducing those French aristocrats and ditching them once she had gained a sizeable chunk of coinage from each and every one. Like Barrington, she too had learned how easy it was to detach herself from whoever occupied her bed with her mind only on the prize left not always on the mantelpiece but slipped to her in various discreet and unobtrusive face-saving and tax-avoiding ways.

It was not until she met Barrington that she gave up the practice of hooking unsuspecting candidates in favour of starting the new undercover operation with him. Having made their first million or three within a couple of years, the proprietors of the Squadron had intended to retire. But idleness they found tedious as their adrenal glands had become acclimatised to the buzz of it all as if it were a drug and they were two hopeless addicts.

While lying side by side the morning after their excursion to the Peacock's Feather, Calendula and Barrington decided to take a long, lingering shower together. Calendula turned on the jet-stream and sprayed Rose Garden Mist around their en suite wet-room. As the soft water began to engulf them, and their bodies intertwined, they could hear the phone chiming *"It Ain't Necessarily So"* in the bedroom.

"Will you get that or shall we leave it to the butler?" enquired Calendula cheekily.

"Let them leave a message. We have more important things to do right now," her partner in love and crime declared.

"It could be something important."

"Who cares," he said insistently caressing her. Calendula, at this juncture, was inclined to agree with him.

The telephone number in liquid crystal was displayed on Calendula's mobile phone screen when they emerged from the shower. She recognised the caller and rang back instantly as they lay panting and drained on the bed.

"Faye Windsor-Harris' office," announced a secretary.

"Is she there, please?" replied Calendula.

"Yes. Who shall I say is calling?" came the voice at the other end.

"It's Isabel Franklin."

Calendula could hear an exchange of words at the other end of the line and then a curious but guarded Faye came on the line.

"Ah, I see, it's you," said Faye who had recognised Calendula's voice instantly.

"I'll do the talking, if it helps. I got your call. Do you want a quick lunch or would you prefer to make a date to call back?" asked Calendula.

"Yes, Miss Franklin, there are a number of issues I would like to discuss with you sooner rather than later," said Faye who was getting used to having conversations with her ex-schoolmate draped in indecipherable code.

A date was duly made for lunch on Thursday, two days hence, at noon.

"That was Faye with some news," said Calendula when the telephone conversation had concluded. "She will have some info for me on Thursday."

"Yippee! I hope it's good," replied Barrington. "I must also get on to Maurice to set the ball rolling in that direction too."

After a breakfast of scrambled eggs, raw prosciutto crudo di Parma imported directly from Italy, sun-dried tomatoes, marinated asparagus spears and black olives, the love-birds went their separate ways until lunchtime. Calendula went for some yoga practice and then set to work on getting *Subterranean Ferocity* shipped via courier to her buyer.

Barrington made for his office to call Maurice Moreau.

"Bonjour, Monsieur Moreau. C'est Barrington Flint ici."

Maurice instantly recognised Barrington's English accent and the remainder of the conversation was conducted in Flint's mother tongue because Maurice had a superb command of the English language. Barrington was, of course, relieved because his French was adequate enough to order a drink or to chat up a waitress but, apart from that, he spoke French comme une vache espagnole.

"I have a little job for you," said Barrington.

"How wonderful," replied the Frenchman.

Barrington briefly outlined his proposition to Maurice who agreed that it would be a pleasure as well as a tantalising challenge. Maurice also liked the kind of money which he would be paid for such a job. The future looked rosy and inviting in every respect.

"I will fill you in on the finer details in due course," said Barrington.

"I await your call," replied Maurice.

As he put down the telephone Barrington thought that he might have another go at the Beethoven sonatina which he was endeavouring to master on the grand piano. He knew that his lesson was looming and, therefore, he wanted to get to grips with some of the difficult bars and the links between phrases. But he also knew that his teacher was encouraging, knowledgeable, efficient and non-judgemental – the perfect combination of skills for one who found little time for practice yet wanted to progress and had the tenacity to stay the course for many years.

Because it was another beautiful day, Barrington also decided to do a stint in the garden. He had earmarked one or two beds which could do with some more weeding, trimming or pruning and he needed to visit the vegetable garden in order to get some lettuces, new potatoes, carrots and fresh herbs for lunch.

Barrington was also planning a number of surprises up his sleeve for Calendula in the garden. He had an idea to build a pond and he wanted to make sure of the ideal spot before he began the digging.

Barrington also wished to build a swing for which he had already ordered the materials from a nearby builder's merchant and wanted to test out the stability of the ground to see whether he needed to organise for a hard-standing area to be erected or whether it could just be sited anywhere he chose. He finally decided that a grass-standing would be best and he discovered that he could rig up a swing under one of the trees. So romantic.

Barrington knew that these surprises would give Calendula pleasure so he did his inspection of the garden with barely concealed pride and eagerness. But it was an all hush-hush operation until the deed had been carried out in her absence.

EXPLORATION

She sauntered into the Garden Lawn Hotel on Bond Street. She looked around enquiringly as if searching for something in particular.

The receptionist on the desk glanced at the stranger as she made her casual entrance. The receptionist secretly admired the visitor's stunning good looks and her alluring aura. She noticed the silk puce chiffon of the halter-neck maxi dress with side-splits topped with a contrasting bolero-style jacket in black velvet. And a soft black leather shoulder bag. Probably Jaeger. Or Gucci. Something posh anyhow.

"Can I help you, Madame?" questioned the receptionist.

"I am looking for the Lawn Border Restaurant ... ah, but I think I have found it," replied Calendula who had noticed the sign pointing towards a corridor on the left.

"That's right. It's just down the corridor at the end. You can't miss it, Madame," responded the girl at the desk.

Calendula was ushered to the table by the window which had been pre-booked. The restaurant was fairly empty. Just a few guests and one or two non-residents sat at tables a goodly distance away from Calendula's position. Calendula thoroughly approved of the location of the table. She ordered a bottle of still mineral water with lime and lemon but no ice.

Calendula wandered out on to the patio which led to the garden itself. She toyed with the idea of requesting a change to an outdoor table but then felt that the noise of the traffic and the heat of the day would have been too oppressive and intrusive.

The hotel was the epitome of elegance with high ceilings, filigree drapes and monochrome décor. The only colour was afforded by the olive green and pale pink checked tablecloths and the upholstered chairs also in olive green. Chandelier lighting complemented the scene. She and Barrington had stayed at the Garden Lawn once or twice some while ago themselves before they had purchased their riverside apartment on the South Bank near Vauxhall.

The waiter showed Calendula's dinner-date to the booked table and then indicated that her host was enjoying the garden outside. Faye came over to Calendula with an appreciation that she may have kept her friend waiting. Calendula brushed her momentary lateness aside as being of no consequence when the two friends hugged warmly.

"Darling, I am so pleased to see you," emphasised Calendula as they walked back into the restaurant arm-in-arm and headed towards their table. The waiter was soon in attendance, handing them menus for both the table d'hôte and the à la carte fayre.

They opted for the two-course table d'hôte offering which made things simpler and quicker all round. From the choices available Calendula ordered a halibut steak with broccoli and sweet-potato mash with a grapefruit and almond cocktail to start. Faye ordered an avocado parfait as a starter followed by a rack of lamb with sautéed spring vegetables. Faye agreed to share the still mineral water, which Calendula had ordered previously, as an accompaniment their lunch – alcohol was not conducive to a productive working lunch. A waitress arrived intuitively, after a discreet signal from the waiter, with another glass laced with lime and lemon slices ready to receive the mineral water.

Calendula began by asking Faye about how her degree was coming along but her compatriot merely groaned and wanted to change the subject. Faye could not wait for the course to be completed and for her to have submitted the final dissertation. Her study was beginning to drag and, as it had been undertaken for career-advancement purposes only, her heart was not truly in academia for its own sake.

Calendula, in her turn, spoke briefly of her idyllic life in the country with Barrington and the success of her work with Two City Designs.

"What news?" began Calendula eager to commence business once the lunches had been ordered.

"Well, first of all," said Faye, "there is the Sandra Mullingar question. She's a long-standing party official who works partly in London but also mainly in Westbury North for the constituency there."

"Who holds the seat there? Remind me," enquired Calendula.

"Helena Dartfield."

"I see."

Calendula discreetly extracted a small notebook and a propelling pencil from her shoulder bag and made a note of the names provided. Calendula was very glad to be filling in the background on this one.

"Well," Faye went on, "she has been seen hobnobbing with the left-wingers and generally taking an interest in their activities in an unhealthy manner."

"And this has caused a stir, I suppose."

"Very much so," continued Faye, "she has been suspended pending an enquiry. And a press conference was held for the local press with Leonard Fletcher, low-level backbencher, but one who has applied to stand for a powerful constituency at the next round of local elections. Because Fletcher is still quite a low-key figure, he was asked to conduct the press conference so that Dartfield would not get her hands dirty and her absence would play down the significance of the event."

"What's Fletcher's background," asked Calendula.

The starters arrived and they consumed them while the business carried on. Calendula made more notes while this hiatus ensued.

"Fletcher started with a degree in political science and a public speaking course – the usual highway for a budding politician. He stood and won a seat as an independent candidate somewhere in the north and was elected some while back. However, Fletcher joined the Tory party recently and organised some very, very successful fund-raising campaigns for them before applying to stand for election. He is undergoing the selection process now while remaining an independent. He is as keen as mustard and endeavours to curry favour with everyone and anyone. He has even got himself on to the ESIDR."

"The what?"

"The Executive Sub-Committee for International Diplomatic Relations, which is headed by Simon Risborough, and reports directly to Jepherson."

Calendula made another note but she still needed to clarify some of the facts.

"Who's Simon Risborough the MP for? Somewhere down south?"

"East Bressex," confirmed Faye. She also explained that he was heading for retirement but still pandered to the PM.

Calendula was beginning to find this lunchtime meeting very exciting and the scope for meddling intervention was fermenting in her mind. This information was certainly worth the price of the lunch and the rake-off which Faye would in due course receive.

The narrative was suspended while a waitress cleared the plates and the waiter refilled their glasses with mineral water.

"Tell me about Sandra Mullingar?" continued Calendula after the interruption. Even though the Medici Squadron were already on to this one, Calendula still wanted to know more. Calendula felt she wanted to know more about the protagonists themselves in this drama because many of the background facts she could almost certainly research on the Internet.

Faye went on to explain that Sandra Mullingar had been a faithful party-worker for many years, that she was married and that she led a reasonably plain and staid life living at Lymingworth near Westbury North. Calendula's enthusiasm was blossoming still further.

The main courses arrived and looked delicious. Silence ensued until the serving staff were well out of earshot. Again they ate and talked simultaneously as Faye was, of course, tight for time and Calendula wanted to know the full story.

"But there's a lot more about the internal politics in the House," said the apparently unstoppable Faye. She wanted to earn her keep and was saving the juiciest bits for the last. She noted Calendula's obvious elation but was saving her trump card for now.

"Well, even more interesting is the fact that my boss, Ruth Angell, has discovered a discrepancy in the figures for funds received from the Elisian government. I took a sneaky look at these figures myself and I think she might be right. It stacks up. Apparently Fetherington is maintaining that the Elisians recently paid a very large, backdated import subsidy but Ruth believes that it was a backhander paid to Gregory Tranter which arrived in time for the general election."

Calendula was now concentrating like mad on Faye's words. Faye noted this reaction with intense pleasure. It was nice to be appreciated.

Faye recommenced her narrative. She also explained that Jepherson had openly lent his support to Johann Finkelbaum, the Elisian premier, which added spice to the facts on paper when considering the back-scratching and palm-crossing tactics of politicians. She also wanted to elaborate on the relationship between Ruth and James.

"Ruth and James Fetherington have an explosive relationship. Ruth revealed her knowledge about the dodgy figures at the ESIDR meeting and it threatened to spark a big row but it was suppressed by Simon Risborough."

Faye then went on to describe the relationship between Ruth and James and the way in which Ruth had poured out her inner feelings to her at Hatty's Wine Bar.

Calendula was on the point of yelling with joy. She asked more about the personality of Ruth. Obviously, she knew quite a bit about Fetherington but wanted to keep this information out of Faye's knowledge-domain.

Calendula learned that Ruth was a volatile but passionate female who could have done with a good dose of counselling and a good lover. Just the kind of disposition which Calendula could exploit. The price of this posh lunch would be repaid a million times over, she decided.

Faye stated that she needed to get back to the sweatshop and Calendula picked up the tab for the lunch. She could swing this one on expenses as entertaining a prospective art buyer.

The lunch-date concluded with more hugs, a handsome cash payment for Faye, a fond farewell and a promise to do it again. The two friends parted and went their separate ways both with a warm and cuddly feeling.

INITIATION

After her meeting with Faye in Bond Street, Calendula took advantage of an opportunity to check out some of the West End clothes shops. She loved aimlessly idling around the shops and deciding what next might be a useful addition to her wardrobe. Here she managed to pick up a few items which she could use as seduction fodder.

Calendula acquired a petrol blue maxi dress with oyster-shell buttons stitched on haphazardly for purely decorative purposes from the Haute Griff collection. She also purchased some more summer sandals and one or two diaphanous scarves to add to her collection.

Calendula then took a taxi to Regent Street to the Liberty store where she bought an almost-matching skirt and jacket with a white frilly blouse which gave her a slightly businesswoman demeanour as if she were working in an office. Calendula could easily have walked to Regent Street but she used her shopping purchases as an excuse to arrive at Liberty in style via taxi-cab.

This shopping spree meant also that Calendula needed to take yet another taxi back to her riverside flat in Vauxhall because of her several purchases. The twenty-minute journey, of course, took double that amount of time because of the traffic build-up. But Calendula spent the time usefully in reviewing her purchases and planning the next move or two which the Medici Squadron would take.

The block of apartments in which the couple lived had five storeys including a penthouse which formed the entire fifth floor where they lived. The penthouse overlooked the Thames on three sides of the building. The flat was built only three years ago but its purchase price had doubled in the time in which they had owned it and so it didn't owe them a penny. But it was a sound property investment which they could realise at any time. The convenience of this London base, however, made the location ideal for the times when Calendula and Barrington needed to be in the capital usually for work.

Calendula ascended in the smoky-mirrored lift and inspected her hair and complexion as she moved heavenward. The lift opened to reveal a small hallway and a door almost opposite which was the entrance into their penthouse apartment.

Calendula was greeted by the uxorious Barrington who had driven down to London with her that Thursday morning. Because Barrington had heard her fumbling with the key at their door, he was able to save her the trouble by opening it himself. He wanted to take her in his arms but instead he was forced to relieve her of her many packages first. Once she had been divested of her purchases, they could then get down to catch-up business on the physical contact front.

Calendula and Barrington spent much time in admiring the new editions to her wardrobe and Barrington hung them up lovingly in the hallway closet with the rest of her gear.

The hallway had a number of rooms off it – their bedroom with en suite bath and shower room, a hall cupboard and their wardrobe off to the right and the main bathroom and the guest bedroom off to the left. Both bedrooms overlooked the river and both sported a Juliette balcony. The hallway led into the lounge-cum-kitchen at the far end which was an open-plan area with floor-to-ceiling windows on two sides. The kitchen-diner was tucked away to the right of the lounge area. From the lounge the couple could walk out on to their balcony which overlooked the river and housed a number of pot-plants and a table and chairs.

In typical London riverside-apartment style, the dwelling was of an ultra-modern design which Calendula and Barrington had complemented by minimalist furniture. A small upright digital piano in white, moreover, in keeping with the décor, ensured that Barrington did at least some piano practice while in London. The floors were of solid oak throughout and the walls painted in a very pale cream, enhanced by oak furniture from Denmark. The kitchen units were in a similar oak-effect with built-in oven and appliances.

They stood locked in an embrace while looking out on to the Thames from the lounge area, a constantly changing view which never failed to fascinate the keen observer.

"Shall we have a swim, poochie?" asked Barrington when they were drinking a glass of an Italian sparkling white wine of the spumante variety together. Calendula squealed with delight at the prospect and they gathered their swimming gear excitedly.

The small Lagunita Spa Leisure Complex was situated only a few minutes' walk away from their flat and was shared as a privately-owned facility which only the residents within a short radius were permitted to use. They sauntered across a quadrangle and descended a short flight of steps which led to the locked door which Barrington opened with a pass-code.

The reception area of the Lagunita Spa was little more than a waiting area with seating on two sides with some more steps leading down into the leisure centre itself. On this lower-ground floor there was a small but well-equipped gym and doors to the male and female changing rooms. A vending machine, which was frequently out of order, also sat in the passageway together with a water-dispenser.

Calendula and Barrington parted to change into their sporting gear. Barrington did a short stint in the gym using the treadmill and some muscle-strengthening devices while Calendula took a turn on the exercise bicycle. Neither Calendula nor Barrington would qualify as fitness-freaks. A gym instructor and poolside attendant was on the premises in order to assist patrons and to deal with any emergencies which might arise. The pair acknowledged his presence with a nod and a wave but they did not have any need of his services as either fitness-trainer or swimming instructor.

Next the couple took a plunge in the pool where they both felt more at home. The pool was a small twenty-five metre affair with a decorative Roman-bath style pattern painted at the bottom surrounded by complementary Roman-style tiled flooring with numerous sun-loungers designed for relaxing by the poolside and recovering from any strenuous bouts of activity.

Barrington was a fast, strong swimmer while Calendula was more equipped for long-distance swimming which she only curtailed because there was not enough fat on her body to keep her warm in the water for any length of time. Calendula, therefore, decanted to the large Jacuzzi long before Barrington began to tire. He joined her, and a few others whom they knew by sight but had never before spoken to, some while later.

Finally the sauna was the target for their relaxation time and fortunately they had the place to themselves. Dozing rather than chatting, however, was the order of the day and both Calendula and Barrington partook of this activity pleasurably.

Another round of swimming and then a shell-out in the steam room was the next on the agenda for the pair before they decided it was time for a walk in Vauxhall Park before dinner.

They strolled around the entire circuit of the park taking in the view of the lavender garden, the rose arbour, the model village, the children's play-area, the dog-walking area, the disused water fountain, the football pitch and the tennis courts. Barrington had considered buying a bench which he would donate to the park but he then decided that he was not charity-minded enough and did not want to leave this life with a legacy. Calendula, however, had donated some money for replanting in the rose arbour but she chose to remain anonymous when doing so.

"Where shall we dine?" asked Barrington. "Do you fancy that Italian on Nine Elms Lane down by the river?"

"I didn't know an Italian lived there," she replied, "What does he look like? Is he my type?"

They both laughed but agreed that an Italian riverside restaurant would be ideal for an early evening meal.

Luigi greeted them warmly as old friends and led them to their usual window table.

"Or would you prefer to sit outside," Luigi enquired solicitously.

"No, the usual will be fine," replied Calendula.

At the Trattoria Della Siciliani they enjoyed a delicious seafood risotto with red mullet, scallops, mussels, crevettes and black olives washed down with a bottle of chianti followed by Sicilian ice cream. The Trattoria Della Siciliani was a homely restaurant rather than an upmarket establishment but it held the charm which the lovers much appreciated when they were away from their rural domicile.

They did, however, decide to take their coffee and herbal tea outside on the pavement after the meal and so retired to a table there in due course.

"So how did lunch go?" asked Barrington.

The subject of business had been avoided for the best part of the afternoon and evening but now Barrington's thoughts turned to work. And Calendula responded accordingly.

"Well, I have some more information which will get Maurice on the simmer."

"Great!"

Calendula then proceeded to fill Barrington in on the details of her lunch-date with Faye. She also outlined ways in which Faye could be further exploited. She could find out more about James for her, for instance. She might even be able to shed some more light on the antics of Ruth Angell and the financial discrepancies which had arisen. She might also get a line on Simon Risborough and Leonard Fletcher. The custard was beginning to thicken. The strategy was fermenting further in Calendula's mind. She was, in fact, maturing her felonious little plans big time.

Barrington clapped his hands with expectancy.

"I'll ring him tonight. He is already biting at the leash in typical Maurice style."

"And, and, and," she paused dramatically for effect, "and ... I have a little job for you."

Calendula's remark had the desired effect.

> *'Curiouser and curiouser!' cried Alice (she was so much surprised, that for the moment she quite forgot how to speak good English).*

Lewis Carroll
Alice's Adventures in Wonderland

PART 2
THE TROJAN WAR

Not a sound, on the way, had passed between us, and I had wondered – oh, how I had wondered! – if he were groping about in his little mind for something plausible and not too grotesque. It would tax his invention, certainly, and I felt, this time, over his real embarrassment, a curious thrill of triumph. It was a sharp trap for the inscrutable!

Henry James
The Turn of the Screw

INVESTIGATION

It was Tuesday morning and Simon Risborough was feeling jaded for no particular reason, except that he was concerned about his forthcoming meeting. He was reading a number of reports which had been prepared in connection with his constituency matters but even this essential, albeit boring, reading did nothing to distract him much.

Time passed and the morning inevitably grew older just as a young lamb will one day stop skipping about because spring has turned into summer and then autumn. Or a fish will eventually give up the ghost if it spends too much time out of water.

Simon sighed heavily.

The phone on Simon's desk rang and he picked it up after deliberately allowing it to ring several times before he answered it. But it was something of a welcomed interruption.

"Mr Fletcher to see you, Simon," announced Susie Melrose.

"Oh, is it that time already? Can you ask him to wait a moment? I just need to make an urgent call before our meeting starts," lied Simon. He knew the hour perfectly well, of course.

"Certainly, shall I get the call for you?"

"No, just give me an outside line, if you would."

"Certainly."

"Thank you," said Simon as he waited to hear the dialling tone on his line.

In truth, of course, Risborough did not have any urgent anything to do. But he did make a call to a restaurant in order to alter the time of his arrival this evening. He often ate in this restaurant in order to save having to cook for himself. That would satisfy Susie in case she might be listening in on the call, although he knew that such practice was not really in her box of tricks. He was fortunate in that respect. There were some very underhand employees in the department but not, fortunately, in his office.

Simon visited his en suite cloakroom in order to waste a bit more time and to deliberately keep Fletcher waiting. Once back in his chair, he leisurely rang through to Susie and asked her to wheel in the young man.

A very tentative knock on his door indicated that Leonard was in his usual subservient mood.

"Hello, Leonard. How are you?" said Simon, extending his hand for a handshake greeting.

"Fine," came the response, as Fletcher shook hands with Risborough.

"Do take a seat. Take the weight off your feet."

They exchanged a few more pleasantries of an inconsequential nature.

Leonard made himself comfortable in the chair opposite Simon who remained at his desk in order to ensure a safe distance between them and not to appear over-friendly. Simon felt it politic to keep Fletcher at arm's length as a junior.

"I gather you have been down to Westbury North?" began Simon. But not waiting for a reply, he continued, "How did you get on at the press conference, then?"

"It seemed to go quite well. I read out the statement on behalf of Helena Dartfield and I managed to field a number of the questions effectively," Leonard replied enthusiastically in the hope of impressing his superior.

"No hitches, then?" enquired Simon.

"None to speak of," said Fletcher, "but I am not sure whether the conference has managed totally to allay any more press interest."

"Let's hope it will, at least. But what of Sandra Mullingar would you say? What is the position there?"

"Well, there will be an internal enquiry made by the local officials but I am not sure what, if anything, they can discover. She has been suspended, of course."

"Is that merely a political move or is there any foundation for the claim about her defection? I ask because the PM's office might be questioning me." This assertion on Simon's part was not particularly true but he wanted to provide himself with an excuse for asking Fletcher about the situation in Westbury North.

"I am not sure, at present," admitted Leonard rather sheepishly. He felt that he should have been better informed about the current situation but he had chosen purposefully to distance himself from the fracas now that he was back in the London office. Leonard felt that he had fulfilled his mission at the local press conference and that the ball was now firmly in Helena's, or someone else's, court.

"Well, keep me posted if you hear anything, will you then, Leonard?" Simon suggested.

Risborough believed that the fact that he had mentioned the interest of the PM would be sufficient to stir the aspiring Fletcher into action. And any information which Fletcher could acquire and pass on to Simon would only serve to enhance the elder's standing if anyone should enquire about what he knew. Risborough also knew that Tranter, via Fetherington, had been asked to be kept informed of developments and so he, Risborough, wanted to be sure to get there first when it came to briefing the PM.

Because Simon felt that this subject was now, more or less, exhausted, he then turned to the real object of his meeting with the young man.

"Nothing much happened at the ESIDR meeting on Monday but the minutes will be circulated in due course," said Simon.

Fletcher nodded his understanding.

Simon then braced himself for what he intended. He explained the position with regard to the PM's report and the fact that it could not yet be completed until the report from James Fetherington about the Elisian delegation had been finalised.

Leonard thought this was all very interesting but he did not quite see how this idle conversation could in any way be classified as urgent in view of the fact that Simon had requested to see him sharpish. Then came the crunch.

"There was a query about the figures for the Elisian report. Apparently, there could be some suggestion of," and he chose his words most meticulously, "a slight anomaly, shall we say."

If Leonard had not been awake previously during this exchange, he certainly was now. So that's why the old boy called me in. He wants me to do a bit of digging. And I'd be up for that all right. Fletcher then thought it expedient to wait and hope that Simon would continue his narrative.

Simon obliged, right on cue.

"I haven't actually seen the final figures myself, but James Fetherington maintains that the discrepancy is a backdated import subsidy while Ruth Angell believes there is something amiss. We shall have to look into it, of course."

Leonard was working out how to react to this bombshell. Should he volunteer to become a super-sleuth or should he wait to be asked?

While trying to make up his mind, Simon broke in with the solution to Leonard's dilemma.

"Have you heard anything about this yourself? You have seen the figures, surely?" continued Risborough.

"Yes, I have but I have not studied them in any detail."

Fletcher thought things were looking up. But he still elected to bide his time and let Simon show the initiative. After all, if Simon failed to actually ask for his assistance, he could still make his own discreet enquiries and, if he came up with something succulent, he could then legitimately score a brownie point by feeding it back to Simon without actually being asked.

Simon's eagerness, however, got the better of him and he, once again, resolved Leonard's quandary.

"Well, if you do hear anything, perhaps you could let me know as chair of the ESIDR, please?" said Simon as if to bring the interview to a close. "In confidence, of course," reassured the elder statesman.

"Of course, Simon. If I hear anything, I will let you know," said Fletcher, proud of the fact that he had become the chosen one. Leonard realised that this mission was obviously the real purpose of the meeting but he assumed a nonchalant air of indifference in Simon's presence.

The meeting concluded with more social niceties and a cautiously jubilant Leonard left the inner sanctum. He believed that if he could shed some light on the 'anomaly' or the 'discrepancy' then his stock would increase all round. What an opportunity. Perhaps Ruth Angell could be invited out for a drink one evening? Fetherington he dared not approach and Leonard did not, in any case, have an excuse for an audience.

Simon began to worry slightly that Fletcher had tumbled to his game. But there was nothing he could do about it now. The die was cast. The worry persisted, however.

VACILLATION

Sandra felt anxious, wearied with lack of sleep and utterly confused by her own indecision. To take her mind off disturbing matters, she went into Briarford's to pick up a few urgent things, to have a spot of lunch and a cup of coffee.

At the entrance to the supermarket Sandra collected a shopping basket rather than a trolley. Just a few bits and bobs would suffice. She had done a big weekly shop at Briarford's a few days ago.

She bought a few lemons and peaches which were reduced in price because they were nearing their sell-buy date. Sandra Mullingar thought that she herself was fast approaching her own sell-by date and she wondered if she would soon become half-price or, worse still, left on the shelf and then tossed on to the compost heap.

She wandered down the toiletries aisle and looked to see if there was something there which might cheer her up – something to put in the bath or an essence to spray in her hair. But this was fruitless speculation. Nothing would cheer her up. Nothing would shake Sandra out of the doldrums. She bought a bath oil, however, because it had a picture of a girl on it with a happy face. But not even this move made any difference.

At the fish-counter, she deliberated about buying some prawns or mussels, say, to enhance tonight's dismal supper. But indecision prevented Sandra from taking any positive action. Instead she opted for some samphire and some Japanese sea vegetables from a nearby shelf. Something different, although Ted, no doubt, would turn his nose up at them. She felt a bit defiant when she dropped them into the basket, nevertheless. I will shove them down his throat if he objects and he will.

Sandra next sauntered along the diary-produce aisle and shivered with the cold which emanated from the freezer cabinets. She felt cold and lonely herself. Her husband did not seem to understand her predicament or to offer her any support at all. Ted never had shown any interest in her ever since they had been married which is why she had buried herself in her work. He regarded her troubles as a tedious impediment to the smooth-running routine of his life. Ted just wanted her to keep herself occupied until it was time for her to cook his supper. Sex was not on the agenda in their relationship either, which she regretted not a bit because she didn't find Ted at all attractive any longer, although she did feel unappreciated by his physical neglect.

At the laundry section she piled her shopping basket high with the latest rinse aids and fabric softeners. Then, almost absentmindedly, she tripped over a pack of toilet rolls which had fallen off a nearby shelf and, in her confusion, she careered into a man with a trolley. The contents of her basket spilled on to the floor. Sandra felt ashamed of some of her purchases, such as the bath oil and the four bottles of rinse aid. The samphire fell to the floor and the container in which they were housed split open. The Japanese sea vegetables were also crushed underfoot by the man's trolley.

"A thousand apologies, Madame. A thousand apologies, Madame. I am desolated. 'ow can I ever repay you," said the man with a strong French accent.

"Oh, I wasn't looking where I was going," she protested.

"No, I am to blame. I am the king of stupid men. I am an imbecile. I am the, how you say, the dunce in the corner?"

Sandra was slightly lost for words and dumbstruck by this effusive man.

"I must replace the purchases I 'ave ruined for you. Ruined, Madame! I must make it up to you."

"No, it's quite all right," she found herself saying and, simultaneously, getting rather embarrassed by the small crowd staring at her. Some people tried to pick up the various items which were strewn about the floor. But the man halted them in their attempt and ushered them away while, at the same time, outpouring apology after apology into her ears. He then hurried to the fish counter and replenished the samphire and seized an even bigger packet of Japanese sea vegetables from the shelf. He then put everything back in her basket.

"I will buy these things for you, Madame," he declared and, before she could stop his wave of enthusiasm, he seized her basket from her hand and took it to the counter, picking up a high-priced bottle of wine on the way.

Sandra was still flustered and reeling from shock when he returned and presented these items to her in a 'Bag for Life'. She was overwhelmed with embarrassment but a little flattered at the attention which she was receiving from this gallant and dashing Frenchman.

"And now you must allow me to escort you to your car. I inseest."

"Well, I was just going to have a spot of lunch here," she replied. The instant she had imparted this news, she regretted it because it left the door open for more insistence on recompense from the man.

"I will buy you your lunch, Madame. It will be a pleasure. It is the least thing I can do. I inseest!"

And, indeed, he was so insistent that she felt disinclined to refuse or to protest any further. It was just too much effort for her weary self. And why not? What's the harm in it? I need to be cheered up especially by an attentive and good-looking young man.

"Well, if you are sure."

"I most certainly am, Madame," he retorted and, to her outer horror but inner delight, he took hold of her hand and bent over it and kissed it French-style.

It works every time. Maurice sported a mischievous chuckle.

At the supermarket café she ordered a Parma ham sandwich and a cup of latte while he requested a baguette filled with tuna and salad for himself, all bought and paid for by the flamboyant Frenchman.

Maurice could see that she was vulnerable. An ideal set-up.

"I am called Rousel and may I 'ave the pleasure of knowing your name, gracious lady?"

"Sandra," she said simply but she was beginning to become fascinated by this solicitous stranger.

"And what are you doing 'ere today in the town? You are on holidays like me?"

"No, I live not far from here. But I have some time off work just now."

"You work in the town then?"

Sandra just nodded absentmindedly.

"Madame Sandra looks sad. Sandra has some unhappiness," he proffered. Maurice always exaggerated his French accent and deliberately omitted to get his grammar right.

Sandra was rather taken aback by this remark. She was certainly not used to anyone noticing how she felt or showing concern for her feelings.

Sandra Mullingar felt the urge to spill out all her troubles, such was her state of mind at present, so she took this heaven-sent opportunity to do so. She enumerated her troubles in brief, of course. The doubts which she had about her work for the Conservative party campaign in Westbury North. The way in which her work and the late hours she kept were continually unappreciated by her immediate superior, Harrison Smythe, the chief official at the party headquarters in Westbury. Not to mention that Helena bloody Dartfield. She was a right cow!

Sandra wanted also to tell of how she had had talks with the opposition parties, Labour and the Green party in particular, in order to consider whether their cause and their working conditions were more conducive to her beliefs in citizens' rights and freedom of speech. Sandra was beginning to believe that the Tories were getting a bit above themselves and becoming police-state minded. Were they merely pandering to the wishes of the electorate and then, once in power, did they do their own thing far too frequently? She had lost faith because she felt that she was not supporting a good cause any longer. But she kept this information to herself.

She wanted to explain about the fact that her husband was unsympathetic and uncaring. Ted was only really interested in his own work as a Computer Database Manager for a local engineering firm.

He had little time to devote to her, to show her affection or even to talk as they used to do. But she kept very schtum on this matter too.

All this amounted to a mounting state of hopeless despair and deep depression. Sandra wanted to break free from the Tory party, from all political parties, from working long hours, from a heartless spouse, from the drudgery of running a home and worrying about the kids who had left home yet threatened to be making a mess of their lives in unhappy relationships or dead-end jobs. She was fed up with it all.

Maurice observed her distress with an inner knowing. This would be easy money.

When the meal was coming to an end, Maurice offered Sandra another latte but she refused. This time because she genuinely did not want one.

"I shall make your life happy again. We shall go for a walk in the park. I am on holidays. You are not at work. We can take a journey in a boat on the river," he suggested.

"Oh, no, I couldn't possibly. It would be a great imposition on your time," she replied nervously. "My husband would worry," she added, although, in truth, he probably would neither know nor care if she was a bit late back from the shops unless, of course, his evening meal was not prepared on time.

Maurice suddenly took her hand in his and kissed it again. This time caressing her hand with a tenderness which she had never before been shown. Sandra froze and tingled all over – even in places which she had forgotten had existed.

"No, no, I couldn't, Rousel," she protested again but, this time, more lamely.

Maurice brushed her excuses aside and led her from the shop in a daze. He carried her shopping to her car as if it were Dresden china.

"We must take a boat by the river. I inseest," he declared. That word again, laughed Sandra inwardly. "It is not far to walk from 'ere."

Sandra considered the proposition. Maurice was very good at insisting. Perhaps 'inseest' was one of the first words he had learned in her language and he had never forgotten it?

Sandra hesitated. He was handsome, attentive, caring, considerate and available. What would be the harm in it? It would only be a short boat-trip? Nothing improper could happen on the river, surely? She was perfectly in charge of herself and would not permit any impropriety, obviously. And Rousel was a gentleman, of course. She would tell Ted when she got home that she had met a friend. But why would she need to lie? She gulped. The thoughts swirled interminably in her mind like a whirlwind. Hurricane Gustav had not yet whipped up a tropical cyclone in the Atlantic.

Maurice noticed Sandra's fluster of indecision and rejoiced.

He took her hand and drew it up to his lips again. This one would be a push over. And she was not that unattractive for an older woman. Her hair needed to be loosened somewhat and a new wardrobe might not go amiss but, basically, she was a not-too-bad looker.

The hand-clasp did the trick, as usual.

"Well, if we aren't too long," she said tentatively.

Gotcha! Maurice smiled inscrutably.

Maurice loaded her car with the shopping, retained the bottle of wine which he had bought earlier and walked towards the river with Sandra. He took her hand again but held on to it this time. She was definitely beginning to respond to the treatment.

CONTEMPLATION

Wendell and his team arrived in New York rather jaded after their eight-hour flight from Heathrow to John Fitzgerald Kennedy Airport in New York and, consequently, they welcomed a hearty meal at their hotel on arrival at about 2.00 pm.

They were greeted at the hotel later in the evening by Kadienne Patrell who was bright and perky in contrast to the way in which the team felt. Wendell felt very flattered by this overture from Wyatt's as they sipped their drinks, commented on their transatlantic journey and made arrangements for a meeting on the following day.

The triumvirate then retired for an early night in order to further compensate for the build-up of jetlag. Sleep deprivation was becoming the order of the day. It had been a long day for all parties from GMC.

The next day heralded a preliminary lunchtime meeting at the offices of Wyatt Enterprises Incorporated with Kadienne Patrell and Adelina Murphy as a precursor to a meeting on the following day with the lawyers, Harvey Grimshaw and Jack Siskins Jnr from Liarbridge Law Practice, who represented the other party of Grant Houghton Pharmaceuticals.

Kate Falmouth found the experience of meeting some high-level women in the professional world very stimulating and she endeavoured to curry favour with Kadienne and Adelina as congenial companions as well as clients. The men were slightly envious of her instant acceptance by the bigwigs in Wyatt's but Wendell was also secretly pleased that he had made the right choice in bringing her with him.

Ainsley Chrythorn was also eager to make a favourable impression on the female executives but he was unable to decide how best this could be achieved. Flirting looked as if it would be off the agenda totally but he believed that he would excel and outstrip the others at the negotiating table.

When the lawyers from both sides of the equation, plus Kadienne in attendance, got together the next day the main import of the conference was set to discuss the terms of the draft agreement which had been drawn up after negotiations by both sides. And, in fact, the unvoiced dispute focused on money. Well, of course. Wyatt's wanted to pay less and Grant Houghton wanted to receive more. Obviously.

Reading between the lines Piers got the impression from the Liarbridge lawyers that Grant Houghton would be quite amenable to a takeover bid but that they wanted their pound of flesh out of the deal. Grimshaw did intimate that GHP were also in talks with another corporation about a takeover deal but both Piers and Kadienne suspected that this was just posturing on their part in order to up the antes.

Back at their hotel the three musketeers from GMC went their separate ways when the working day was over. Wendell decided to re-read some of the legal documentation in order to ensure that he was really up to speed during further negotiations. Ainsley phoned his wife for a bit of billing and cooing. Kate went off on a self-indulgent shopping spree with Kadienne.

Piers got the impression that GHP would be up for the deal provided that they got a bit more cash out of Wyatt's. While these thoughts were running through Wendell's head a knock came on the door of his hotel room and he rose to answer the call.

Sally Plumley announced without ceremony that she was the right-hand woman to Felix Taynton, the CEO of Grant Houghton Pharmaceuticals. Sally was a cool slick chick who was sure of herself in no uncertain terms. Wendell felt it was quite irregular for him to have any direct talks with anyone from Grant Houghton because of the conflict of interest but, simultaneously, he was insatiably curious to know why this female had called on him personally.

"If GHP got more money out of Wyatt's then the deal would definitely go ahead," announced the intruder. Wendell began to get the impression then that women actually ran the show in the USA.

Piers spluttered. "I really am not in a position to discuss this matter with any representative of Grant Houghton Pharmaceuticals because of the conflict of interest which means that we are ostensibly in contention. I must, therefore, insist that you go through the proper channels in your negotiations on their behalf, Miss Plumley," he countered with some pomposity and venom injected into his reaction.

Wendell confidently believed that his degree of assertiveness would settle the matter and avoid any embarrassment on either side. But he was wrong.

"We understand that you have, shall we say, been co-operative in the past when such deals are going ahead," Sally replied nonchalantly.

Time stood still for Piers Wendell. How the hell did she know that? Where did she get her information from? What can I do now? Shall I deny it? Well, I had just better deny it. But could I turn the situation to advantage, perhaps?

"You are misinformed," Piers asserted stiffy as if he would brook no argument.

Sally then calmly quoted two occasions, giving names and precise details, when he had received a lucrative backhander from a company in negotiations over takeovers or mergers.

Wendell wanted to die. His mind went into overdrive. But he remained silent as the grave.

"You don't have to make a decision right now, of course," said Sally in an attempt to allow Piers to recover his composure. Well, what was left of it anyway.

"What assurance would I get from you?" Wendell had decided to take the bull by the horns.

"You don't," countered a triumphant Miss Plumley. "But it will certainly be very worth your while, I can assure you."

Piers found that his gaze was dropping from her face in favour on the floor. He was still undecided about what to do but was naturally very interested in this proposal.

"I will make contact again tomorrow evening," concluded Sally as she airily left the room with a knowing grimace.

Wendell grabbed a whiskey from the mini-bar and gulped it down in one. God! Is this a trap? Is this a heaven-sent opportunity? Or is this merely a test of my stamina? And have I given myself away in any event? Well, I suppose I have really. Had anyone observed this woman coming into my room? Have my colleagues witnessed something which they could hold against me? The turmoil in Wendell's mind raged like an out-of-control furnace. Piers decided that he would have to face his colleagues and then maybe he would get a chance to gauge whether they had observed the ingress of Miss Plumley.

Dinner was an interesting occasion for the two men from GMC. Piers and Ainsley went out to eat together at a nearby restaurant while Kate continued to have fun with Kadienne.

The conversation at the restaurant for Wendell and Chrythorn was stilted. Both men seemed lost in their thoughts – Wendell contemplating his next move with Sally and Ainsley worrying about his wife and child and planning the way in which he would move negotiations forward successfully for the client on the morrow. Both men, of course, hated the fact that their female colleague was out having a good time with the client.

The next evening a call came through from Sally who offered Wendell a sum which he could not understand in exchange for upping the money paid over to Grant Houghton from Wyatt's. Wendell, still indecisive, however, could not resist the sum on offer and, therefore, he agreed to see what he could do but without making any promises.

Sally suggested that if the offer on the table could run in excess of £75 million then he would be handsomely compensated for his efforts. Currently the sum on offer was much less than that amount but Wendell could possibly see a way of raising the stakes if the negotiations failed or even looked like failing.

Another round of talks between Liarbridge and GMC took place the following morning at which Chrythorn's negotiating skills were exhibited like a ship in full sail. But he was still unsuccessful in bringing matters to a satisfactory completion.

Wendell could now see that his position was beginning to clarify and, perhaps, he could get some price leverage now particularly as negotiations were threatening to become a protracted affair. And even deadlock was looming on the horizon.

At a meeting in the afternoon with Adelina and Kadienne, Wendell put his cards on the table. He believed that if the takeover bid stakes were not raised, then deadlock or even failure would occur. It amounted to the fact that if Wyatt's wanted this deal to go ahead, and it seemed, from his reading of the situation, that the organisation definitely did, then they would have to decide to pay considerably more than that which was currently on offer. And someone else might, of course, pip them to the post.

Wendell could see that Adelina was wavering and, therefore, GB pounds sterling began to shimmer before his eyes.

The next morning saw a final decision made on the part of Wyatt's and the remainder of the day was spent in ironing out the finer details of the agreement. The takeover bid then went ahead at the speed of light.

Another call from Sally the next day sewed up the deal which she and Wendell had struck under the table. A new bank account had been opened in New York for Piers in his own name by Sally. Wendell noted with pride the substantial sum which had hit his newly-opened bank account in the USA.

A final day in New York saw champagne flowing and a sumptuous meal for the GMC team and the Wyatt's people.

The next day a reluctant Kate but an eager Ainsley returned to London.

Piers decided to spend a couple more days in the US capital in order to tie up a deal on the purchase of some holiday properties in Florida for rental to money-laden tourists. This gave Piers a chance to stay away from Mariella for another couple of days before the return voyage to London. He had checked regularly in order to ensure that things were running smoothly in the London office and so he felt quite justified in spending a few extra days away from the stresses and strains of life in Britain. Piers, however, had not bothered to check whether his wife was OK.

MAXIMISATION

Friday mornings bring a new optimism among all workers in that the end of the week is nigh. The weather, however, was inclement and the rain muddied the pavements as Thor wielded his hammer and thunder clouds broke again and again.

James sat at his desk looking over the preliminary sections of the report from the Elisian delegation. The members of the delegation had asked for his initial comments on the first three sections of their semi-finalised report and James was expecting to receive the final two sections, which included the now-famous figures for the Elisian excursion, later that day. James made one or two marginal notes with post-it stickers as he read so that he could remind himself of what to say to the delegation members when the telephone-conference meeting, as yet to be arranged, took place.

Fetherington had seen the accounting section in draft previously but he was now anxious to receive and study this part of the report again in a completed form in order to make sure that it was clear that no malpractice had taken place, even though he knew that it had.

James wanted the accounts to reveal what he wanted them to disclose and nothing more. He also hoped that the sum which had been queried by Ruth would actually make clear that the amount in question was a legitimate backdated payment and not a backhander. He was confident, however, that the bean-counters working on the figures would massage them convincingly enough but would they deceive Ruth Angell and Simon Risborough?

While lost in his hopes and daydreams, his mobile phone vibrated. It was usually his ex-wife or his lawyer or a personal friend when he was disturbed in the office. All other callers usually rang on the land line and Beryl, or one of the other minions, in the antechamber would put the call through via the official channel.

James hastily picked up the phone and hardly glanced at the name of the incoming caller whose number he did not instantly recognise.

"Hello, honey. How are you?"

The velvety voice at the other end of the line stopped him dead in his tracks. He recognised the sensuous voice instantly as if it had been ringing in his ears since time immemorial. He drew breath, loosened his tie and moved uneasily in his chair as his loins stirred into action at the sound of her dulcet tones. He had forgotten that he had given Verity his private number.

"I'm fine. Busy as always but fine. How did you get on with your art-buyer?" he enquired, as if casually.

"Painting sold, paid for and despatched," Calendula replied. "But I was wondering what, if anything, you were doing for lunch?"

James would obviously have liked their next engagement to have been an evening one with obvious after-dinner consequences which would satisfy his sexual appetite. But maybe lunch would be a start.

"You see, I have to be up in Scotland tomorrow, taking a late evening flight, for a couple of days and I didn't want to go without seeing you again," she continued.

James was decidedly excited by this news. The stars must obviously be aligned in my favour. And, he supposed, that lunch would be another sound investment towards getting her clothes off and thrown on to the floor. He sat on the edge of his seat with a hand resting defensively in his lap and made a promise to himself to have a glass of iced water brought in as soon as the telephone conversation was over.

"It would have to be a late lunch," James began, "because I shall be tied up in a team-meeting until late morning," he declared.

"You name the time and place and I will be there," she replied.

James thought a bit and then suggested the Chai Chillia in Knightsbridge, a fashionable and favourite haunt for well-to-do London office workers. He knew that she lived out of town but was not sure where and so decided on a smart London venue for the lunchtime bite.

"Shall we say 1.30 pm at the Chai Chillia in Knightsbridge?"

"That will do fine. Not sure where it is," she lied, "but the taxi will easily find it, I am sure."

Calendula had sometimes taken a prospective client to the Thai restaurant for lunch but she did not think anyone would recognise her. It would be worth the risk, anyway. She ended the conversation and then snuggled back into Barrington's arms with a satisfied smile on her face.

"Well done, poochie, you're reeling the fish in splendidly," he said.

The rain continued to teem down and showed no sign of abating before lunch. James watched the rain from the corner of his eye while in his team-meeting.

James took his umbrella and a taxi to the Chai Chillia and arrived shortly after 1.20 pm. He had taken the precaution of booking a table but he sat in the bar to await his guest. Calendula arrived about 1.40 pm, purposefully late, but she greeted him with another warm peck on the cheek by way of compensation. James approved of this start to the lunch meeting. But he hoped that a perfunctory peck on the cheek was not going to be his ration forever.

"It is so good to see you again." She had opened the batting.

James reciprocated the sentiment while admiring her two-piece outfit. It looked new. Had she bought it specially to meet him?

"Will you have a drink before lunch, Verity?" he enquired.

"No, thank you," she responded casually looking towards the restaurant.

He got the message.

"Shall be go through to the dining area then?"

She murmured in reply which he took to be an affirmative response. And they linked arms on Calendula's initiative. Calendula looked round and glanced towards the windows. James, picking up the clue, asked the waiter for a window table but he was disappointed because the restaurant was crowded and he had not specified a window table when he had originally booked. But she didn't appear to be disappointed. They were seated at a table but not in the centre of the restaurant and, therefore, not in the full limelight.

"How's work? Busy?" asked the delectable female in front of James' eyes.

"Oh, the usual worries connected with the job," he replied nonchalantly.

"Worry? Oh, my poor dear, what worries do you have?" she asked solicitously.

"Office politics, you know."

"Office politics?" She tried to pretend innocence as if an artist knew nothing about the world of backstabbing, double-dealing and power-games.

"Such troubles, my dearest. I am so sorry for you," she said touching his hand.

James reacted in a manner which was typical of the sex-hungry male who was locked in lust with the female of the species. He stirred uncomfortably in the seat and wondered if there was anyone in the restaurant who might recognise him and, worst still, note his reaction.

James would have liked to elaborate in detail about his dilemma with Ruth as a means of unloading his baggage but thought it better to play it in a low key. And, in any case, he wanted to talk of more interesting things in Verity's presence.

"Oh, it's just that there are a number of difficulties at work with someone," he hesitated to mention her gender, "who seems out to get me," he said dismissively.

She looked affectionately concerned and brushed his hand. He approved of her responsiveness.

"Anyway, shall we order? I cannot stay too long, unfortunately. Affairs of state are pressing."

Calendula smiled sympathetically and let go of his hand in order to pick up the menu.

The waiter bustled over to their table and drew their attention to the day's specials which were up on a board on the wall.

Calendula, after inspecting the list of specials, ordered a green Thai chicken curry with jasmine rice and a steamed pumpkin salad to start. James, grateful that this lunch was not going to cost him an absolute packet, chose a tom yum soup with lemongrass, lime leaves, chilli peppers and prawns followed by the kai jeow moo sab (pork omelette, to you) from the specials fayre. James also ordered a bottle of Monsoon Valley white wine to accompany their meal.

They chatted idly about her artwork business and her imminent Scottish trip and she spoke enthusiastically about the new projects she was working on. James did not really follow some of the technical terms his companion used but smiled encouragingly. His knowledge and interest in art was only judged by what he saw and his reaction to the finished product.

She then mentioned a forthcoming trip to Paris to see a number of potential buyers. And she seemed to be inviting him over to join her. James then listened more attentively. But Calendula promptly changed the subject to London life.

The starters arrived as an interruption to more interesting negotiations. These were soon consumed as they were both hungry at this late hour.

They discussed some of the latest films and stage-shows in London and it was clear that Calendula was not at all au fait with what went on in the big city. She did, however, know what was on at all the art galleries and the two opera houses.

Highbrow tastes, obviously. James concluded that he could make use of this information.

"Would you like to do the opera with me one night ... perhaps when you are next in London?" James was trailing his coat.

She responded in the affirmative but was non-committal about when she might next be in the capital. Perhaps she is doing her slippery-eel act on me again? James began to worry slightly.

Calendula asked James about whether he had seen *Der Rosenkavalier* at the Garden or *Die Zauberflöte* (The Magic Flute, to you) at the Coliseum. He confessed to having seen neither but he would certainly be interested to go with her, if she wanted. He tried not to make his response too tentative, for her sake, even though he would much rather have gone to a musical.

The main courses and the chilled wine arrived shortly after the starter plates had been cleared by the waiter. Calendula complimented the waiter on the pumpkin salad starter and he, in turn, trusted that the curry would please her likewise.

The conversation slowed as they tucked into their main courses but the eye-contact intermittently remained.

James was encouraged by the way things were going for him and Calendula rejoiced in her success so far. Nothing had been decided but the field-markers were in place for both of them. An evening date, following by a hotel room for the night, was merely a phone call away they both thought.

Soon after they had finished their meal, James felt that he must tear himself away as another meeting loomed back at the ranch. He apologised profusely (well, not too profusely) for cutting short their meeting and this prompted Calendula to promise to contact him again when business life for her had clarified, particularly with regard to the Paris trip, once she had returned from the highlands.

The rain continued to pour as they left the restaurant and so they decided to hail a taxi. As they were heading in opposite directions, it was not possible for them to share a taxi but, because James had thoughtfully brought his umbrella, he was able to chaperone her to one which was waiting conveniently nearby.

James was delighted that she linked her arm into his and squeezed it tightly while under the umbrella but he regretted the fact that they did not have to wait long for a taxi. He was even more delighted when she gave him a long, lingering kiss on the check on her departure and a promise to be in touch soon.

"Oxford Street," said Calendula as she stepped into the taxi.

James took the next available taxi back to the office and he felt that the memory of this lunchtime encounter would see him through the rest of a bloody boring afternoon.

He was also looking forward to his Friday night massage which had been booked with Jean Paul at Harmony Holistics for 9.00 pm. He wanted to use this opportunity to dream about her unless the massage and his thoughts had embarrassing consequences for him.

In her taxi, Calendula instructed the driver to ignore her previous instruction, once she was out of vision-range from James, and the taxi-driver did a U-turn and obediently took her back to Vauxhall.

EXASPERATION

Leonard Fletcher felt that he had been handed an opportunity to make his mark on a silver platter.

Fletcher had come out of Simon Risborough's office on Tuesday in a state of elation because of the challenge which he believed he could easily meet to spy for Risborough and, thereby, secure an ally for life. Leonard saw himself as being on a special mission which only he could accomplish. He had become the chosen one. He even visualised the PM patting him on the back and filing his name in the back of his mind for future reference.

Leonard soon came up with a plan. If Ruth Angell was the key to the mystery then he could easily find a way of chatting her up and extracting the truth after a bottle or three of wine. After all she had a reputation as a fire-cracker and she liked to drown her sorrows in the nectar of Bacchus. James Fetherington, however, would be a harder nut to crack but he could worry about scaling that particular mountain once he had got all he wanted out of Ruth. He knew that Ruth, like himself, would be put upon by those in authority and this would make them kindred spirits.

Fletcher began by noting her typical movements and habits. He discovered, for instance, that she often skipped lunch, or brought a sandwich in to work, but she then made up for lost time at the end of the day in Hatty's Wine Bar particularly on days when frustration became the embodiment of her job. She seldom patronised the staff restaurant, except to buy a packet of crisps or nuts when her blood-glucose levels were at a low ebb in mid-afternoon. Perhaps he could bump into her accidentally on purpose one day?

Leonard's office, in Admin headquarters, where he occupied the only suitable desk which could be found for him in the building, had a glass panel through which anyone could see who passed by in the corridor. Leonard knew that if Ruth was intent on visiting the staff restaurant then she would have to pass by his office. He could then follow her and start up a conversation at a time, in the late afternoon, when she might be in need of someone to talk to or a shoulder to cry on.

He waited and when, on Friday afternoon, a rather jaded Ruth made her way along the corridor with a face like thunder, Leonard decided that now was the time to bestir himself. Sure enough Ruth was making for the restaurant and she looked fraught in the extreme. The end of the week was certainly a good time to make an approach when everyone had endured enough of long hours, electrifying office-politics and excessive harassment from senior staff. Leonard followed her along the corridor and down the stairs into the restaurant.

Fletcher approached the counter shortly after Ruth who was, as predicted, buying a couple of packets of crisps.

As he sidled up to his target, he opened the batting.

"Well, what a week of frustration and aggro this has been."

Ruth turned towards him and agreed with his sentiment. She had spent the best part of the day trying unsuccessfully to convince Guy Chaffinch, some upstart of an MP in the Department of Innovative Enterprise, that her report on *Opportunities in the Far East* was based on a sound statistical analysis when, in fact, what he had actually wanted was for her to doctor the figures in his favour. Ruth's frustration had, consequently, been mounting for most of the afternoon and the bomb was just primed to explode.

"God, I can't wait to get out of this hell-hole and start the weekend," continued Fletcher, believing that he had captivated his audience.

"I feel the same way," she responded, "the people round here sometimes make me sick."

This time it was Leonard's turn to agree.

"I wish I could just go out and get drunk after a day or two in this place, let alone a week."

"I often do just that most days of the week," replied Ruth.

"Oh, where do you go? Is there a quiet spot where one can just let the troubles of the day go without having to walk too far or take a taxi?"

"I know the very place," said Ruth.

"Where is that, then? Anywhere I know?"

Leonard bought a bar of chocolate from the counter but made sure of keeping Ruth within earshot as he did so.

"Hatty's Wine Bar. Just round the corner."

"Do they do a decent glass of bubbly, do you know?"

"They certainly do and I, for one, am heading there straight after work."

Fletcher thought he would risk it.

"I am not sure where it is. Do you mind if I join you? Just for a glass or two."

Ruth felt that she had found a friend and a possible drinking buddy.

"OK, pick me up from Research Central at about 6.00 pm. I should be through by then ... in every sense of the word."

Fletcher was as happy as a pig in piss.

At about 6.00 pm, as instructed, Leonard strolled casually into Research Central and approached Ruth's desk.

"Well, here I am," he announced.

Ruth switched off the PC, cleared her papers and locked her desk. She felt better already. Someone to moan to who might possibly not look bored when she began one of her rants. A fellow sufferer.

"Just got to pop to the loo and then we can be off."

Fletcher patiently waited in the corridor for her return. And then they departed for a short walk around the corner.

Hatty's Wine Bar was crowded. It was Friday night after all. But Ruth always managed to get a table, possibly because one was automatically reserved for her on a Friday evening.

Leonard ordered a bottle of red burgundy and two glasses. Nothing like sharing the poison as well as the gossip. He forgot about the bubbly.

"So who is causing you all this grief?" asked Fletcher, expecting that this ploy would open up the desired can of worms.

Ruth spoke about her encounter with Guy Chaffinch. Leonard listened dutifully in the hope that the conversation could be swung round to more interesting matters. She spoke at length about the fact that Chaffinch was an out-and-out self-seeker who had only commissioned his report so that he could promote his own corner. Ruth had tried to point out the fact that the statistical analysis could not be altered to suit the occasion but Chaffinch had argued against this reasoning and an impasse had ensued in which both parties had become increasingly irate. Had Ruth been a man, Guy might have hit her. Whether or not Guy was a man or a mouse, Ruth was certainly on the point of hitting him when a secretary interrupted with an urgent message from his constituency headquarters. No bodily harm was, therefore, sustained by either party but Ruth had left Guy's office foaming at the mouth.

In view of Ruth's reaction, Leonard wondered whether he should put an asbestos sheet beneath her in case Hatty's Bar caught on fire. She certainly was a very fiery lady. And she looked as if she needed a damn good shag too. But he was not about to volunteer for the post. No way, José!

Leonard spoke briefly about his troubles of being pulled from pillar to post, being at the beck and call of his superiors and how Helena Dartfield often wanted to use him as the fall-guy in order to keep her own powder dry.

"How did the meeting go on Tuesday? I had to be in the constituency at a press conference," said Leonard, wanting to change the subject and to keep the conversation away from himself.

She, in turn, admitted to the contretemps with Fetherington and stated that she disagreed with the Elisian figures. This was a start.

"But I thought those figures had been checked and doubled-checked by Vernon Lee?"

"Yes, but I am sure Fetherington is hiding something or covering up some shady deal somehow."

Leonard ordered another bottle of wine without asking Ruth. When it arrived, he poured her another generous glass, again without asking. But she didn't seem to notice, much less object. Blimey, she could put it away. The rumours of her capacity to consume the stuff were not exaggerated obviously.

"I am so glad to have a compatriot to talk to," remarked Ruth. "I often don't want to talk to the other researchers, like Faye and Carol, but an outsider-insider who understands is much better. We must do this more often."

Fletcher swelled with pride and anticipation. He'd keep that 'more often' card in reserve. He couldn't, however, stand too much of Ruth. But he wanted her to elaborate about Fetherington's misdeeds for his unofficial report to Simon Risborough.

"What makes you think that the figures are deliberately wrong and that Fetherington is on a whitewashing campaign?"

"Well, I heard, that's all."

"Oh." Leonard paused, hoping that she might elaborate. He stared at her long and hard. Should he try the seduction angle? No, too dangerous. And too distasteful.

"Well, I've heard nothing," Leonard said instead.

"I gleaned it from an outside source, that's all." There was an ominous conspiratorial tone to Ruth's voice which Fletcher felt was encouraging.

Fletcher murmured and raised an eyebrow but he decided to stay mute in the hope that she could not keep the secret to herself. He poured her another glass of wine. It must have been a spy of some kind, a reporter possibly or an aggrieved employee? He began to ponder and speculate seriously.

Ruth did not continue as she had started and so Leonard prompted her with, "A reliable source?"

"I think so."

She was still playing the cards close to her chest. How could he resolve this gridlock?

"Well you would have to be very certain before you made any further accusations," he warned.

The dam burst.

"Well I heard it from a political journalist," she admitted, "who infiltrated the Elisian government offices somehow and he believes that they paid out a sum to Tranter, just before the election, in exchange for Jepherson's public support for Finkelbaum. Tranter then persuaded the PM to support Finkelbaum."

Fletcher decided that it was time that he absented himself from her view and headed for the gents in order to mull over his thoughts. This news was a bombshell. He could certainly make capital out of this little lot. Phew!

He toyed with the idea of pumping her for more information but decided that this could be done at their next meeting, if necessary. He brought his interrogation to a close by telling her that he had to leave. They parted really good friends.

Ruth stayed to finish the bottle of wine and Leonard danced along the street in a homeward direction.

PERAMBULATION

Gemma Gallagher realised with regret that it was high time to get up. She, therefore, slithered out of bed so as not to disturb her much dishevelled and sleepy lover. Lying in bed with a man is like lying on a grassy bank – except that it breathes.

She put a pot of coffee on to brew while she showered and then donned her most masculine trouser suit in pinstriped navy with a flouncy blouse. Comfortable shoes were also the order of the day for Gemma because her height did not complement high-heeled shoes. Gemma gulped down a quick cup of coffee and then took one into the bedroom of her Manhattan apartment.

Gemma's latest conquest was, of course, still fast asleep, although consciousness was beginning to register, when she gently presented him with a goodbye kiss.

"Do you have to leave now?" groaned Bertrand stretching out an arm to detain her.

Gemma replied with a positive affirmative. And before further interrogation occurred, she left the flat to start the business of the day.

Bertrand idly supposed that she was off on a job in connection with her work as a private detective. He wasn't quite sure what she did precisely because she was cagey about her cases and the work which she had to undertake for her clients. But he respected this need for confidentially on her part and even admired her tenacity in maintaining it. His main interest in her was, of course, her body and her ability to lend it to him for sexual gratification purposes whenever he felt the need. With these thoughts in mind he returned into the land of the sand man.

Gemma hailed a cab and made her way to the business sector of midtown Manhattan where she was scheduled to stake out one of the office buildings there from the vantage point of a convenient deli. She ordered a breakfast of poached eggs, sausages, baked beans and waffles lavishly coated in a chilli pepper sauce. A pot of real coffee also accompanied the feast. This meal would certainly occupy some of the time which she expected to spend on surveillance.

She read the *New York Times* virtually from cover to cover and then spent the rest of her waiting hours sending emails and surfing the net from her Apple Mac laptop. After a few phone calls, which ensured that she kept the pot boiling at the office while she was away, Gemma calculated that it was time for action because her mark had made an appearance in the street.

She followed the target of her interest discreetly yet diligently into a nearby department store where she could easily monitor her movements.

The trip round the department store, therefore, took Gemma to female underwear, toiletries and soft furnishings. At last the Market Bazaar Restaurant beckoned and Gemma followed her quarry into the lunch section of the dining area as opposed to the cafe which only served mid-morning coffee and pastries. The tables were small, mostly seating two people, in anticipation of the lunchtime trade.

Gemma selected a table near to her prey and perused the menu in a leisurely fashion. She didn't really feel hungry after her huge breakfast but needs must.

Now for the opener.

She brushed her shoulder-bag from the back of her chair on to the floor and left it there. The mark took up the invitation for assistance and picked up Gemma's shoulder-bag and returned it to its rightful owner.

Gemma went overboard with her thanks and insisted on sharing a bottle of wine with the altruistic stranger.

"You must let me recompense you for such chivalry, Miss," Gemma proclaimed in earnest.

Although her offer was rejected it did, at least, start up a conversation in gregariously American style about the excellence of the service at the Market Bazaar, the varied menu, the state of the economy and the heat at this time of the year. Gemma managed to prolong the exchange until such time as the two ladies joined forces at the same table.

The quarry had now been ring-fenced. Gemma was triumphant.

The pair talked about their work and Sally Plumley was fascinated to hear that Gemma was a private detective. Obviously, Sally wanted to learn all about this kind of work but her companion managed to make it sound very mundane and rather hush-hush and so the conversation on this topic dwindled rapidly.

"It's not at all exciting. That's a misnomer. Just finding stray pets, errant husbands and long-lost relatives. All very tedious."

Sally then explained that she worked for a medium-sized pharmaceutical company as a personal assistant to the chief executive. This topic of conversation was, therefore, one which could be expanded and examined in some detail. Sally was delighted to perceive that her new friend was really interested and genuinely impressed by the authority of her position in the organisation. Sally, however, confessed that the corporation was not doing all that well and that they would possibly be swallowed up by another larger corporation in the not too distant future.

Gemma questioned Sally about whether she was afraid of losing her job but Sally assured her that her position would be safeguarded for the future because she worked in such close proximately to the head honcho.

This conversation was much more than polite chat, however, and, as the meal came to an end and the clock ticked towards the end of the lunch break, Gemma wanted to keep the contact going.

"Look, I know this is a bit short notice but I have been given two tickets to see *Harvey* at the Gershwin Theatre for Friday evening. Would you, by any chance, be free to come? I know it's an imposition but I can't seem to find anyone who is free to come with me. Please say you would like to and that you can."

Sally's face lit up like a Christmas tree.

"I love *Harvey* and I'd love to come. It is one of my all-time favourites," she exclaimed.

The pair exchanged contact details and arranged to meet for a quick bite before the show which started at 8.00 pm.

Sally returned to the office while Gemma hastily rang the Gershwin Theatre to pull a favour from the box office manager in order to buy two good seats at short notice for *Harvey* for Friday evening which she collected on her way home to the flat.

Sally spent the afternoon in meetings with Felix Taynton and his team and their lawyers, Harvey Grimshaw and Jack Siskins from Liarbridge Law, in connection with the ensuing negotiations for the takeover bid proposed by Wyatt Enterprises. Felix, as chairman and chief executive of Grant Houghton, was keen to save the corporation from going under but he wanted, at all costs, to ensure that they got the best possible deal. The pharmaceutical corporation had been his father's business and Felix had learned the ropes from hard graft and bitter experience and he was not about to throw all this hard work down the pan because of a downturn in the market.

Taynton had thus given Sally a special assignment in this regard and this would ensure further success in her already impressive career as a right-hand woman to men in high places.

Sally giggled inwardly when she thought of Harvey Grimshaw as she prepared for her Friday evening date with Gemma. She wondered if Grimshaw had seen the play and whether he was teased about his name.

A shopping spree was in order before Friday evening as Sally wanted to look her best. A new long skirt and a becoming top were thus acquired for the occasion on Thursday evening when the shops stayed open late. As Gemma earned a good salary, and she hoped this was likely to continue, she was unaware of any signs of a credit crunch in her life.

It was a long time since Sally had last gone to the theatre and this would be a special treat for someone who seemed to work too hard for her own good. Sally's adrenal glands mounted into overdrive as the time drew nearer.

COGITATION

Faye was well aware of the fact that Ruth Angell was behaving like a coiled spring on Friday afternoon and wondered whether she would be up for another bout of heart-to-heart in Hatty's Wine Bar.

Perhaps she could get another chapter of information from her about Fetherington or anything else which she might be able to feed back to her old school-chum? Faye considered what more, if anything, Ruth might have yet to divulge but doubted that it would be in any respect substantial.

She had banked her last payment from Calendula but intended to use it for paying off the balance of her MSc fees as a lump sum. This would then mean that she no longer needed to have a substantial bite taken out of her salary each month and she would have some financial leeway for the rest of her last year at LSE.

Faye played her usual game of nonchalance when Ruth had steamed into the office after her meeting with Guy Chaffinch and she hung around at the end of the day when Ruth might show signs of a replay of her outpourings. Faye noted, however, that Ruth did not in any way make the usual overture to her about going for a drink at the day's conclusion.

Faye was also a little more than dismayed when Leonard Fletcher breezed into the office at the end of the day and made straight for Ruth's desk. Although Faye studiously kept her eyes on the PC in front of her and buried herself in her work, she conjectured that a date had previously been arranged between Ruth and Leonard. She supposed that they were going for a drink and that Ruth had now found a new shoulder on which to weep. Hell! Damnation!

On her way home Faye gave this incident and the motives of both Ruth and Leonard some concentrated contemplation.

Why was Leonard somehow appearing on the scene? And why had he made a beeline for Ruth? At that late hour on a Friday evening their only intention would be to celebrate the end of the week and to drown Ruth's sorrows.

Faye concluded that Leonard must be up to something. Leonard was not the sort of man to take any interest at all in someone like Ruth. After all Ruth was not particularly alluring either as a sex-object or as a platonic friend. But there was no accounting for taste apparently. But it didn't ring true. What was Fletcher up to?

Faye knew that young Fletcher was the supreme example of an arse-licker. He would be at someone's beck and call twenty-four seven. He was a crawler and a social-climber. Was he a Capricorn maybe? He must be doing some fishing but who the hell had sent him on his current mission?

Faye was aware that they both served on the ESIDR but they had shown no interest in forming a friendship previously despite the fact that they had both served on the sub-committee for several months.

Faye speculated further. Perhaps Fletcher had got wind of the Ruth-Fetherington antagonism or he was looking into the question of the dodgy Elisian figures? That was it! He was checking up on Ruth's information and her sources. But he must have been sent out like a bullet from a gun by someone else. But who?

Faye trawled through the members of the ESIDR. Daniel Faulkes from Innovative Enterprise? Possibly, but unlikely. Edward Cummings in Global Affairs? Again possibly, but maybe not. Vernon Lee in Finance? Never. The guy was a nerd. Vanessa Hargreaves? Again, never. The inevitable process of elimination took hold of Faye's mind. It must be that wheeler-dealer Simon Risborough. That's it. Got it.

Simon was another social climber who was wanting to make his last days on Planet Tory bearable and he wanted to leave the game with a bang. Risborough would want to find out more information about the possible discrepancy in the Elisian figures so that he could impress the PM. Yes! And he had surreptitiously recruited the conniving Fletcher to do his dirty work. That's it.

Christopher Marlowe was suspected of being a government spy so why not young Leonard Fletcher? The US communists, Ethel and Julius Rosenberg, had likewise traded secrets to the Russians. And there were others whom Faye could have named. It all fitted into the jigsaw puzzle very neatly. The game was afoot.

Faye started her surveillance campaign on the following Monday morning. She observed Ruth's movements. She found a way of glancing into Fletcher's office on her several trips to the loo or to the staff restaurant throughout the day. This way she could keep track of both of them simultaneously.

By Tuesday midday Ruth was beginning to show signs of wear and tear. On Wednesday Ruth was scheduled for another meeting with Chaffinch and, therefore, Faye merely waited for the balloon to go up after this encounter. And sure enough Ruth delivered the goods appropriately. Ruth came out of her meeting with Chaffinch like a bull on heat.

What would she do next? The ever-watchful Faye was seriously wondering and waiting.

Faye's patience was soon rewarded when Ruth picked up the phone.

"Do you fancy a quick jar tonight?" Ruth said when the phone had been answered.

Faye decided that now was an opportune moment for her to visit the loo so that she could have a sneaky-peeky to see if Leonard was also on the phone. And, sure enough, he was.

On her way back from the cloakroom Faye gazed once more into Leonard's office. He was no longer on the phone. He was, however, looking slightly embarrassed but also relieved. Faye wondered what had transpired but vowed that she would find out sooner or later.

When Faye returned to Research Central, however, she observed not a jubilant but a dejected Ruth.

Faye engaged in another round of speculation. Had Leonard turned Ruth down and why? Had Leonard got a previous engagement? Had they rearranged the drink-up for another evening? Not very likely by the expression on Fletcher's face once the call had been terminated. Had he rejected her advances outright perhaps? This scenario seemed the more likely of the two.

Faye decided that she would do a bit of probing first hand.

"Who are you going for a jar with tonight then?" she said airily.

Ruth grunted. "I wanted to meet up with Leonard Fletcher this evening but he seems reluctant somehow."

"Perhaps he has another date," suggested Faye. "But you can discuss business with him anytime," she added.

"No, I just wanted a casual drink. I don't suppose that you are free after work, Faye?"

"Sorry Ruth but it's my night to go to the LSE and I have to be there by 6.00 pm and so I must leave work promptly today," replied the other.

Actually Faye had no intention of going to the LSE but she could always, at any time, use her degree study as an excuse for getting out of something which she didn't want to do. And the thought of another evening with bloody Ruth was intolerable.

"Can you arrange a date with Leonard for another evening?" probed Faye. She wanted to get the whole picture.

"He seems very evasive and I don't feel like asking him again," said her colleague in a rather truculent vein.

This was typical of the spoilt child when she did not get her own way. But Faye had now got the complete picture.

Faye promised herself that she would try to find out some more about the situation from Leonard if she could but this mission might be less pragmatic because she hardly knew him.

Faye concluded her conversation with Ruth by suggesting that she try Carol or someone else with whom to have a quick drink. But Ruth merely wanted to retain her sulky mood.

The day began to draw to a close and Faye remembered to leave promptly so as to maintain her fictional story about going to the LSE. She stopped on her way home through Hyde Park in order to contact Calendula, to update her on events and to mention her speculative conclusions. She was a researcher after all and, therefore, drawing an inference from the evidence available was not a foreign activity for her.

Faye reported on Ruth's drinking bout with Leonard last Friday and his subsequent refusal to go with her this evening. Faye believed that Leonard had probably obtained all the information which he desired and, therefore, he would now be in a position to report back to Simon Risborough.

Calendula was grateful for this information and when she had put down the phone, with a promise to recompense her friend in due season, she turned to Barrington and gave him the ultimate go-ahead on the next step of the journey with the suggestion that it should be the sooner the better.

CAPTIVATION

A totally downhearted Ruth Angell flounced into her favourite wine bar by St James's Park on Friday evening after work. She was greeted by Joe, of course, who noted that her demeanour appeared even more sullen than usual.

Nothing could uplift her spirits. The view of the park, the enchanting lake with its crab-claw vista and, in the distance, The Mall, which ran from Buckingham Gate in the West End in an easterly direction towards Trafalgar Square, had no effect on her sour mood. And, indeed, Ruth chose the large round table in a dimly-lit corner away from the window which reflected her dark and despondent disposition. Hatty's was beginning to become crowded and Joe was disappointed that she had chosen a large table but, because she was such a good customer, he did not demur. Joe, in fact, supposed that some of her friends might join her soon by way of cheering her up.

She ordered a bottle of claret and sat sulking over it. Ruth sank her head into her hands. She was just about fucking fed up with working in politics. She hated the male chauvinists to whom she had to kow-tow. She hated having to obey orders. She hated having to compile those stupid reports. She hated being told to manipulate statistics, And, more importantly, she hated being powerless to seduce the man she wanted so desperately. Why didn't she jump into that bloody lake? Why didn't she simply hand in her notice and get a job where her talents would be appreciated?

Ruth mulled over her state of mind and working dilemma. She was well qualified and she had built up a mass of useful experience. She had worked her way up to an enviable managerial position from which she would be well sought after by other appreciative employers, surely? She could even become self-employed as a business consultant or she could work for a research consultancy somewhere possibly? But as she was so depressed, she didn't have the energy or the courage to apply elsewhere. And she had come to rely on her salary, of course, to sponsor her drinking habit. But if she were not so frustrated by her job then, perhaps, she would dry out naturally? Her thoughts jangled around in her mind until she wanted to scream. Oh, if only an angel would descend from the firmament and rescue me.

A man, who had previously been sitting at the bar, approached her table.

"May I join you?" he enquired in a soothing voice.

Ruth became slightly embarrassed because a tear or two had already trickled down her cheek but she did not feel that she could refuse this request. She brushed the side of her face and nodded in agreement.

The distinguished stranger sat down opposite her and continued to read his newspaper.

Ruth still felt like death warmed up. She tried to avert her gaze from the stranger but, somehow, he felt just like a true friend. The stranger then suddenly put down his newspaper and turned to Ruth as if he considered it impolite to read in her presence.

"Do you know this part of London well?" the stranger enquired after an embarrassed silence, "I am just here for a couple of weeks, down from the north, and I don't really know this part of the world at all."

Ruth was a bit startled. She had not expected the newcomer to start up a conversation. She knew that, as a single woman, one did not normally talk to a total stranger in a public place. But perhaps this man was different? If he was not a Londoner, then he may not be used to the ways in the big city. Or maybe he was just being friendly?

"Well, I work just round the corner," she stammered.

"I have just been for a walk in that beautiful park across the way and I wanted to have a drink and get a bite before returning to my hotel."

The conversation was beginning to sound a bit asyntactic. But Ruth felt that she could do with some light chit-chat as a means of passing the time. Ruth also noticed that she did not want to drink so much when talking to this man and so she decided to join in the conversation rather than simply replying to his questions.

"Yes, St James's Park is very beautiful with its views of Buckingham Palace, The Mall, Horse Guards Parade and Birdcage Walk. It adjoins other parks – Green Park, Buckingham Palace Gardens, Hyde Park and Kensington Gardens. Have you visited any of them?" Ruth was beginning to feel her soul revive.

"No, I haven't and, as I shall be returning home at the middle of next week sometime, I may not actually have enough time to fit in any more walks. Over the weekend and early next week I shall be required to do some business entertaining and that may take up most of my time," replied her new companion.

"What a pity," was Ruth's rather lame response.

"I do hope to do a bit of sightseeing on my last evening here, however," he replied. "I was wondering about doing the London Eye, for instance. Have you seen it as you work so near?"

Ruth admitted that she had never really got around to patronising this high-pull London attraction.

"Could we go together, perhaps?" he said.

Ruth did not know whether to be delighted or to be cautious but, before she could reply either way, the stranger corrected himself.

"No, I am sorry that was so presumptuous of me. I am so sorry," he said.

"Not at all. But ... perhaps if I knew you better, it would be nice. And also the Eye gets very booked up," she floundered.

"Well, let me introduce myself then, my name is Keith Viner and here is my card," the newcomer proffered his business card from which Ruth read his particulars.

Ruth studied Keith's business card and she was very impressed with what she held in her hand. And she glowed inwardly to be in the company of such an august presence.

Keith Viner
Architectural Consultant
RIBA Chartered Practitioner

Ruth thought that architect sounded impressive and that he looked very nice. So maybe she could relax.

"I'm Ruth Angell."

"You truly look like an angel," said Keith in his most sincerely flattering tone.

Ruth smiled.

"I thought you were looking very upset when I first came and sat here but you seem to be smiling now," he added.

"Work was getting me down, that's all," she replied, "I need to look for a new job but sometimes I feel as if I don't have the strength after a day like this."

"Listen," said Keith, "if you are a bit down in the dumps, then would you do me the honour of allowing me to buy you dinner here?"

Ruth was taken aback but the idea greatly appealed. Before she could make an attempt at protesting Keith had called for the menu. Ruth also felt that it was a long time since lunch.

"Shall we have some more wine, what are you drinking? Claret? Or would you like a change?"

Again Ruth hesitated and then plucked up the courage to reply in the affirmative. Well, why not? "Yes, that would be nice. Claret will do fine," she found herself saying.

Ruth ruminated for a moment about her life and her work while they studied the menu. She deserved a bit of good fortune. She worked hard against impossible odds and it was certainly fraying her at the edges. She drank far too much and ate far too little. And here was this refreshing stranger on her patch showing her some kindness. Her guardian angel had arrived to help his Ruthie Angell. The spelling and the pronunciation of her surname differed slightly from the popular icon but the sentiment behind her thoughts was the same. She was special but no-one except this total stranger seemed to appreciate it. And, no doubt, he was respectable because he too was a professional who was able to acknowledge her status and value in the world.

Ruth ordered the halibut steak with tomato and basil sauce, green beans and potatoes coated in minted yogurt while Keith chose the escalope de veau calvados with French fries and garden peas.

Keith told her about his work as an architect and how he was visiting a London client who had commissioned him to organise the refurbishment of a building which he intended to use as office space in the East End of London. Keith had also been asked to design a seven-bedroom house which was to be built in the north of England. Keith's client was a computer-software designer who owned a flourishing business in the capital but spent most of his weekends at his home in the north where his new dwelling was to be situated.

Keith was based out of London but it was more convenient for him to visit his client down here than to travel to his home in the sticks. And, besides, the building in the East End had to be inspected several times before plans could be submitted to the local authority.

Ruth noted, with a degree of almost ecstatic delight, that Keith would be in her neck of the woods quite frequently in the next few months. How convenient.

When their meals arrived the conversation turned to her work and Ruth explained what she did in the parliamentary offices in Whitehall. Keith seemed very impressed but she had to explain that she was not a politician merely a research worker. Keith still remained awe-struck and told her so.

"The fact that you work in the corridors of power is still very impressive – particularly to a country bumpkin like me," he decided.

After their meal Keith suggested a walk in the much-talked-of St James's Park as the evening was still light and warm and Ruth now felt carefree as never before. They explored the lake, walked round it twice, and admired the wildlife. Ruth imagined that this view was second nature to a country yokel as Keith had described himself.

He gallantly offered her his arm and, in an uplifted mood, she gladly accepted. Ruth noted that gallantry was obviously still alive and kicking in the rural areas of the country.

"If I can manage to get tickets for the London Eye for one evening next week, would you like to come with me. My treat?"

Ruth noted that he had insisted on paying for the meal and, therefore, she offered to pay for the London Eye trip as her contribution but her chivalrous and generous host again had pressed his suit and she was powerless to refuse. She agreed to his getting tickets for one evening next week and she gave him both her mobile number and her office number so that arrangements could be finalised.

Keith saw her into a taxi for her homeward journey and paid for the privilege. Ruth made her way home to her north London apartment as a much happier woman than she had ever expected to be when she had left the office that evening. Ruth had something to live for now and he occupied her thoughts for the rest of the night.

SPECULATION

"I, err ...," he hesitated fractionally, "had a drink with Ruth Angell on Friday."

Simon Risborough's ears pricked up attentively like a well-trained foxhound. He detected the scent instantly but remained impassive even as the aroma was saturating his nostrils.

They were strolling along to the House, from Whitehall to the Palace of Westminster, on Wednesday morning in time for Prime Minister's Question Time which was scheduled to start at noon. This was often a time when pairs or groups of MPs would have a secret tête-à-tête because they needed to be assembled together promptly at the appointed hour. Yet their words would not be recorded in perpetuity in Hansard during the walk from their offices to the Houses of Parliament for the constitutional convention of Questions to the Prime Minister which all MPs were expected to attend.

Simon murmured encouragingly as a means of prompting Leonard to elaborate.

"Well, I thought you might be interested to know that Ruth is not getting on very well in her dealings with Guy Chaffinch," said the junior. Leonard thought he would start off with this tiny innocuous morsel in order to whet Risborough's appetite.

Simon was not really interested at all in this bit of tittle-tattle but he waited for a tastier fragment to fall his way. He waited like a beggar expecting arms from an obliging benefactor. Risborough, therefore, gave another murmur of encouragement.

Fletcher responded accordingly.

"She also told me of a long-standing war of the worlds with James Fetherington."

Again Fletcher was not telling Simon anything that he didn't already know and cared not a whit about. But Leonard was revving up the engines for the Hiroshima bomb.

"She did, however, say," Leonard added, "that, although she may be winding Fetherington up, she does definitely disagree with the figures for the Elisian business."

Get on with it for God's sake! But Simon still retained his poker-face.

"However, the fact is that Ruth admitted that she had obtained her information about the figures from an outside source."

Simon was certainly listening intently now and savouring every word. Perhaps they could walk more slowly? Could he buy a newspaper to slow the pace of their walk? No, better just to wait and see what transpires.

"Ruth admitted to me that she had received her information from a journo who had infiltrated the ranks of the Elisian government." Leonard continued trying to appear matter-of-fact.

Simon was on the point of having an orgasm. And Leonard was aware of this but affected no reaction. Both of them should have been professional poker-players.

"Really?" said Simon. "You don't say?" Simon was prone to using archaic language because he was, in truth, a bit of a relic anyway.

I do say. But aloud Fletcher said, "Yes, the newshound believes that the payment was a backhander which Finkelbaum paid to Gregory Tranter in exchange for Jepherson's public support for the Elisian government. The backhander arrived, of course, just before our general election and while Finkelbaum was campaigning for his."

Simon smiled the smile of the cat who had got the cream. Like the falcon who had stalked its prey for days before its final and decisive pounce. Like the computer-hacker who had been trying to access the Bank of England's slush fund for decades and now had finally cracked the code.

"Not sure whether this, in fact, rings true," said Fletcher who was, of course, guarding his own back, "but that's what I heard from Ruth. Not sure whether this would be of any use in the investigation of the matter." Leonard carefully neglected to specify who was actually initiating the investigation.

As they were now nearing the House, Simon felt that drawing this particular conversation to a close would be appropriate.

"Well," said Simon, "there may be some foundation to your assertion and I will bear it in mind. But, thank you."

Fletcher felt triumphant. He could easily see through Simon's well-tempered nonchalance. He knew that Risborough was over the moon with ecstasy. And he, too, felt that he had done a whole year's work in five minutes. They entered the House and took their places on the front and back benches respectively.

PMQ (Prime Minister's Questions, to you) was not today an electrifying occasion although both Risborough and Fletcher felt uplifted throughout. Simon felt that he had obtained the golden bullet which would secure his favour with the PM and Leonard felt the pungent bouquet of sweet success. Both listened to the proceedings of PMQ with only half their vestibulocochlear nerve (you can look that one up) engaged.

Jepherson reported on his forthcoming engagements and was then asked to clarify his thoughts on such things as election policy, foreign trade and international relations. He fielded his questions with his usual aplomb and sophistication. The House was, as always, only partially satisfied by his replies but all agreed to play the game of politics for the television cameras. Only one man stood up for a supplementary question but he failed to catch the Speaker's eye and this fact went on the worldwide news accordingly.

Simon was anxious for this event to be concluded so that he could be alone with his thoughts before the busy afternoon commenced. He decided to treat himself to a spot of lunch in a nearby pub and, therefore, he wended his way to the White Hart on Victoria Street which he knew not many of his colleagues would usually frequent.

At the White Hart he ordered a shepherd's pie and a half pint of Bass after he had fought his way through the crowd to the bar. He then managed to get a seat on a high bar-stool facing the window. This way Simon could look out on to the street and be lost in his thoughts without arousing any suspicion from anyone who might recognise him as a politician. Also, if he kept looking out of the window, he would not be obliged to talk to any other loners in the joint.

Simon wondered whether the information he had gleaned from Fletcher was worth feeding through to the PM. After all, if it was only a rumour, then he would be accused of being a scandalmonger or a troublemaker. And that would not promote his cause. He would have to take a just-in-case-you-need-to-know stance, in any case, if he did decide to go to Jepherson.

Simon also realised that he could not challenge Ruth directly about this matter because he would then have to reveal his sources or she would guess them. He also wondered why Ruth Angell would be talking to a pressman and what she had done in exchange for her snippet of information. Had she sold any government secrets in exchange? And if so, what had she told the journo? And what would be the consequences? Had she finally found someone with whom she could share a bed? And were more things likely to leak out? Confusion and indecision rained on Simon's consciousness.

Should he tackle Fetherington directly then on a man-to-man, old boy basis? Fetherington then might send him away with a flea in this ear and he would have made an enemy in the camp. And, again, how could he admit that he had sent Fletcher out on a fact-finding mission? Oh, Christ! He would have to sleep on this one for a very long time.

Could he get Leonard Fletcher to find out the name of the journalist perhaps? No, that would probably make matters ten times worse.

Deadlock.

Simon's shepherd's pie was beginning to get cold and so he gobbled up the remains at speed, and at the risk of indigestion, and turned to finish his drink.

Simon decided that he would have to find yet another way of verifying the truth of the situation before he ever took steps to approach Jepherson or anyone else for that matter. Or perhaps, just perhaps, he could recruit A N Other to tell the PM and mention that the knowledge had emanated from his grapevine? And even if it turned out simply to be a rumour then, at least, he would not be implicated as a scandalmonger. Yes, that might do it. But who? Who had the ear of the PM right now?

What about Charles Maw, the deputy PM? Or Mr Moneybags, the Chancellor of the Exchequer? Yes, he would be the cookie. I know his wife. I was at Oxford with her. Bingo!

Simon recalled how he had met Geraldine Cluxton when doing his degree in Economic History at Oxford and the way in which they had become platonic friends. Geraldine was in the same year as Simon and they had arrived together, both rather tremulous at the prospect of being at the world-renown University and both confessed later to feeling very insecure on that first day. She had subsequently married David Dulchester, who was, in fact, several years ahead of them at Oxford, and working on a scholarship because he was a bright chick. David then propelled himself up the greasy pole to Chancellor of the Exchequer but he, Simon, had not yet lost touch with Geraldine.

I could ring Geraldine up and whisper into her shell-like ear. Simon Risborough felt that he could breathe again. He walked back to the office well prepared for a good afternoon's work.

OBSERVATION

Stuart McGill was still feeling a bit jaded after the setback with his boss, Ronald Turner, the Chief Political Editor at *The Guardian*, the week before.

Stuart had proudly presented his report about what he had overhead from Beryl Wainwright and Belinda Forbes with regard to James Fetherington's sexual exploits and yet Turner had pulled the rug from under his feet by admitting that he already knew the facts. And, moreover, Turner even got cross with him for not knowing who the target of Fetherington's interest actually was.

Stuart wondered how the hell Ronald could have known. But decided that it was no use crying over spilled milk. His function now was to find out who? Who? Who? The word was still ringing in his ears as it had been shouted at him by Ronald.

I must do some further digging, Stuart concluded. But how? How? How? Oh, God!

McGill decided that a stalking campaign was probably his best bet. He tailed James for over a week after he, Stuart, had left the office. But James Fetherington seemed to lead a fairly monotonous life. He left the office late and simply went home. Once or twice he went to a place called Harmony Holistics but that was all the evening excitement in which the MP appeared to indulge.

Stuart was also beginning to tire of having to stay up so late every evening himself. While he was no stranger to late-nights, every single evening was getting a bit much for very little result. McGill had been on the surveillance job now for over a week, his patience was not really being rewarded and he was very short of sleep which was affecting his daytime duties.

Stuart, consequently, decided to change tack. He would try stalking Fetherington while he was at work in order to see if anything transpired from that quarter. James seemed more active around lunchtimes. Stuart noted that he went to the supermarket to do a weekly shop or he collected his dry-cleaning or he had lunch but usually on his own or with an innocuous colleague and they simply talked shop.

How am I going to spring the Venus flytrap? McGill was despondent. Patience, Stuart reassured himself when the chips were down.

The bad news first. Unbeknown to him, James Fetherington had already had lunch with the mouth-watering Verity Baxter while Stuart was on his evening stint of surveillance.

The good news now. Stuart tailed his quarry to Worldwide Frontiers, a travel agent near Fetherington's parliamentary offices, towards the end of his second week on sentry duty.

Fetherington seemed to spend quite a bit of time at Worldwide Frontiers and Stuart, therefore, decided to investigate nearer his mark. He sauntered into the travel agency unobtrusively and began leafing through some of the brochures to exotic places. Spend a week in beguiling Bali with a one-night stopover in exotic Hong Kong.

Explore the ancient hillside remains in Peru and visit the Colca Canyon and climb to Condor's Cross. Pass five nights in the Atlas Mountains of Morocco. A water-sports holiday here. A makeover at a health spa there. An exciting beach holiday somewhere else.

My God! What a life. Stuart was, by now, almost penniless and severely sleep-deprived. All right for some.

James was sitting at a desk negotiating intensely with an agent. He was obviously off on his travels.

The newshound edged nearer to the negotiating table, feeling that he was about to get a breakthrough in his investigations. He idly leafed through some more brochures with his back to the MP.

"Can I help you at all or are you just browsing?" enquired one of the agents.

Stuart resented the interruption but was polite in his refusal of assistance.

"What flight times are available for tomorrow evening?" asked James.

Tomorrow? Friday? Blimey where's he off to? Stuart's ears pricked up again when he heard talk of Paris. James was obviously off to Paris for the weekend. McGill listened more intently.

It seemed that James was booking a weekend in Paris and that he would be staying at the Les Patineurs on the Left Bank on the arty-farty side of the Seine. Perhaps the hotel would constantly be playing Émile Waldteufe's music? Stuart prided himself on a rudimentary knowledge of classical music (if you don't get this reference, then try the Internet).

Stuart wondered whether James wanted to stay here for the culture or whether he wanted to remain incognito by avoiding the upper crust Right Bank? Or was it just that prices were a bit cheaper on the southern side of the river and, therefore, he could get a better last-minute deal?

Fetherington then spent some time in booking a late-night Friday flight to Paris and getting some currency.

McGill took silent notes.

After Fetherington had left the shop armed with brochures and travel documentation, Stuart sat down at the desk of the agent who had attended to the MP and turned on the charm-offensive.

"What do you have in the way of weekend trips to, say, Paris or Munich, for this weekend?" he enquired of the agent.

Stuart then had to sit through the rigmarole of pretending to consider Munich and Vienna but, when the time came, he focused his attention on Paris. It seemed that there were flights leaving at around 10.00 pm or later tomorrow evening. The agent divulged that the previous customer had taken the last 10.22 pm seat but that an 11.25 pm flight still had several spaces available.

Stuart was tempted to book his passage but, obviously, did not want to spend any of his own money and certainly not go more overdrawn in the process. He would have to consult the big white chief first. Stuart took down all the details of the flight, a number of possible hotels on the Left Bank and a note of prices, including car hire. Stuart then told the agent that he would get back to her soonest.

McGill left Worldwide Frontiers like a rat out of hell. Stuart felt that this had been a very worthwhile mission as he had obtained more information than he had expected. And he believed that this level of detail would really impress the big boss.

On returning to *The Guardian* offices in King's Cross, Stuart made another beeline for Ronald Turner's desk but again he was kept waiting while the old toper returned from lunch.

Stuart thought it more expedient to ring rather than to request another audience and so the junior reporter kept trying Turner's number after about 3.00 pm until the phone was eventually answered.

"Turner," said a surly voice at the other end of the line which made Stuart blanche.

"I think I have some more gen on Fetherington's activities," said a tentative Stuart.

"What do you mean 'think'? Either you've got a lead or you haven't?"

Stuart quaked a bit more. He realised, of course, that he actually had no information to go on other than the fact that Fetherington was going to Paris for the weekend. He had better start fabricating some data or lose his credibility utterly or even his job. The Stuart who could invent facts was at this instant born.

"I have discovered that Fetherington will be going to Paris for a dirty weekend," Stuart said bravely. "And I wondered if I should tail him there? I have made enquiries about flights and hotels and so on."

Stuart began to grow in stature. He believed that he alone had ferreted out an important nugget of information and that he would, in the absence of his immediate superior, Graham Fifield, who would normally be assigned to such an important task, be asked to follow it up immediately. And a free trip to Paris for the weekend would be chucked in for good measure. Brilliant! Stuart preened his plumage.

Then the crunch came.

"I know," said Ronald Turner. His voice was bland and he sounded a bit irritated by this upstart McGill who had been wasting time following up trails which had already gone cold.

Stuart was rooted to the spot. All his covert late nights and tedious surveillance activities were all time wasted rather than well spent yet again. He had not, furthermore, impressed his high-level superior but, in fact, he had only succeeded in irritating the bastard. And, indeed, when Graham Fifield returned on Monday, no doubt the junior reporter would be put back on menial duties, such as reporting on Prime Minister's Question Time or writing about local constituency matters.

"When are you going to come up with some interesting facts?" enquired Turner in an uncompromising tone.

Stuart had no answer to provide which could possibly save his face with Turner. Stuart wanted to shoot himself. But he could not afford a gun.

"I know Fetherington has a sex-interest and I know who it is. Thank you!" barked the grumpy voice at the other end of the line.

Stuart was even more astonished. Turner actually knew who Fetherington was shagging? Thanks for telling me. If Stuart had not been housed in an open-plan office, he might have kicked the desk but the staff around him were an effective deterrent.

I will buy that gun. Stuart felt wretched in his inner thoughts.

Turner abruptly terminated the call but chuckled to himself at poor Stuart's predicament and his own insider knowledge. Poor sod!

VISITATION

The time had arrived when James was required to make a brief but necessary appearance in his Throxfield constituency. He usually rocked up about once a month, although he sometimes managed to avoid it by claiming pressure of work but not on this occasion.

James was due to open the new forty-million-pound university library complex at a champagne celebration as the guest of honour. He, therefore, would have to cut the tape, listen to a few inane speeches, shake a few grubby paws and kiss a few babies. This was the aspect of politics which he most loathed but it had to be done.

On the Wednesday following his lunch date with Verity, therefore, he threw some essentials into his suitcase, checked his briefcase and headed for his out-of-town home in Brackendew Beacon. James had felt it expedient to purchase a property in the area and he had opted for the convenience of a new-build, five-bedroom detached house on a reasonably up-and-coming development in Brackendew. It had all the up-to-date ease of a new property and could be easily maintained in his absence by Country House Carers, a home-maintenance company which kept the place clean, tended the garden, did the laundry and generally acted as a watchdog against intruders and vandals. He had rung Rita Trundell, of Country House Carers, in advance to warn her of his impending visit so that her team could get the place ship-shape in time for his arrival, make up his bed and stock up the fridge.

Fetherington was due to be met by the mayor of Throxfield, Councillor Bernard Mason, at 12.30 pm in time for the opening ceremony followed by a buffet luncheon. James, therefore, decided not to go first to his house in Brackendew Beacon but instead to go straight to the festivities and get the affair over and done with in the shortest possible time without causing any offence. He did not want to be late for this event but he also did not want to be there at all.

On his drive down the M4 to his west country constituency James allowed his thoughts to stray on to non-work-related topics. His lunch with Verity at Chai Chillia last Friday was still warm in his memory. And he longed to see her again.

James decided that he would make an approach to Verity and wondered about taking her to *Der Rosenkavalier* at Covent Garden at the weekend. She had made her interest in opera clear to him and so this would be a definite enticement to get her to meet for an evening date. Perhaps with an after-show supper followed by an after-show entertainment of a different sort?

James knew hardly anything about opera except that he could tolerate it in only very small doses but maybe this dose would be worth the interest he would have to feign. He had never seen *Der Rosenkavalier* before but he did know that it was by Richard Strauss and that some bloke comes in and waves a silver rose about to quite nice music and there is a lot of bed-hopping involved. And so maybe it should not be too unbearable to sit through. He would enquire about tickets after the lunchtime do.

The ceremonial opening of the library complex went off without a hitch much to James' relief. Bernard Mason was very attentive, albeit a boring pedant, but his wife, Lynnette, was certainly a welcome distraction. Bernard Mason was a bit of a pompous ass but one whom James had to stomach for the sake of his career. Lynnette was much more the sort of woman with whom he could spend any amount of time. Why was she married to such a buffoon? But he was not in the business of causing a scandal on his own stamping-ground by chatting her up overtly.

James duly made his speech in which he thanked all and sundry and then wanged on about the importance of higher education and opportunities for the future working generation in Britain so that they could forge ahead in shaping the country. And he made a joke about Throxfield University as perhaps being a breeding-ground for one of tomorrow's top-flight politicians. James believed very little of what he said, especially the bit about generating tomorrow's politicians, but it had to be stated all the same.

James then chatted a bit to those dignitaries who warranted his attention, such as the Chancellor and Vice-Chancellor of the university and the senior members of the local council. He also helped himself to a couple of smoked salmon and cream cheese sandwiches and gulped down a glass or two of the champers. James, of course, made a point of speaking to Lynnette as she was easy on the eye but he managed to escape from Bernard, who was droning on about some local affairs and how the nation was going to the dogs, in record time.

James then tendered his excuses about another pressing engagement and, his apologies having been accepted by the assembled company, made his way with much relief off the premises. Often leaving early would give the impression not only that James was very busy, and, therefore, they were privileged to have had a snippet of his time, but also that he was not so greedy as to want to down too much champagne and all the posh sandwiches. His profuse apologies for an early retirement from the event were accepted, he thought, at face value and much to the relief of those who wanted to finish off the eats and drinks themselves. And to loosen their ties physically and metaphorically.

James arrived home in the late afternoon after picking up a few provisions from Sainsbury's and delivering his car to the local garage for servicing. He made his way home on foot as it was only a short walk from the mid-town garage to his home. The house stood on a hill overlooking the fields with the Beacon in the distance. The house had been fully carpeted when he had purchased it and he noted with satisfaction that Country House Carers had efficiently earned their keep as usual.

Once at home, and with a feeling of liberation, he settled down on his angular sofa in the spacious lounge to see about getting tickets for the opera. A search on the Internet and a call to Covent Garden established the fact that a few very high-priced tickets were still available for both Friday and Saturday evening.

James licked his lips and rang Verity. She sounded delighted to hear from him and even more overjoyed to learn about his proposal to take her to the opera.

"Darling, I would love to see *Der Rosenkavalier*. I cannot make Friday but, if they still have some tickets for Saturday evening, I would love to come with you."

James noted the use of the affectionate term and his loins responded accordingly.

"I'll ring you back to confirm," he said.

He then booked a box at the Garden for Saturday coming, arranged to meet Verity in the foyer before the show started and felt the day had been productively spent.

Next James put a lamb casserole into the oven from the provisions left in the fridge by Rita (he actually liked his own home-cooking sometimes) and settled down to listen to the early evening news and to skim-read some of the documentation for his meeting at party headquarters scheduled for early tomorrow.

He checked in at the office but Beryl seemed to have everything in hand at the London end. Diplomatically he also sent a text to Rita Trundell which thanked her for her housekeeping duties.

James was now free to relax for the rest of the day. His mood was one of optimism at the prospect of, at last, enjoying a night of bliss with the lovely Verity.

Fetherington took a taxi to the party office the next morning. At his meeting with Erica Higsmith, the chief official at party HQ, they discussed plans for boosting his profile in the community and the new planning applications currently being sanctioned which would positively affect the life of the district. There was some opposition to these plans but these objections had been successfully deflected because the locals had generally supported the idea.

A new shopping precinct, with extensive car parking facilities and some town-centre housing, was to be erected in the main part of Throxfield which would regenerate a rather run-down part of the town and attract many visitors. This move could only be regarded as a great improvement for the area and, because the project had his officially declared seal of approval, it could only do his standing good in the community.

A working lunch was provided for James and Erica, who were joined by a number of other party-workers, at noon.

The meeting discussed James' perceived profile in the area and his need to make more of his rare appearances there. James protested that his London-based work as Under Secretary of State precluded him, regretfully, from maintaining more of a presence in Throxfield. Erica and one or two others found this a lame excuse but it was a fact which could not probably be altered by arguing with the MP.

The party-workers then went on to discuss their various active promotional campaigns for high-profiling the Tories and making contact with the people and James made the appropriate congratulatory noises of encouragement. By 3.30 pm James had had enough. He made his excuses, more lies, and left by taxi in order to return to the garage to collect his newly serviced and freshly valeted Porsche.

James often took advantage of being in Throxfield to visit his children, one of whom lived with his ex-wife Glenda, in Upper Throxfield.

James' daughter, Celina, lived at home when she was not at Cambridge University studying history and modern languages. James was, of course, a bit sorry that she had not applied for Oxford but, he reasoned, that it probably would do no real harm in the long run because she wanted to work in public relations as a translator. And Cambridge seemed to be topping the charts these days actually. His son and heir, Reginald, had become a property developer who worked and lived in the Midlands.

James had rung Glenda earlier in the week to enquire whether Celina would like to come out to dinner but he was told by his frosty ex-wife that their daughter was already booked by a local boyfriend.

And so James returned to London. He arrived home at his Mayfair flat quite late having hit the rush hour at the London end. He then ordered an Indian take-away and watched the box for the remainder of the evening in order to catch up on news and gossip – the knowledge of which might prove to be essential sometime.

INSTIGATION

As a well-heeled, semi-aristocrat, David Dulchester lived in a large abode in Chelsea and Simon Risborough knew this fact and its address. He had visited socially many times.

When he knew David was visiting the provinces, Simon felt that late Saturday morning would be an appropriate time to call in on Geraldine.

"Simon, how lovely to see," said Geraldine kissing him warmly on the cheek, "but his lordship is not in residence just now. Didn't his secretary tell you?"

"Yes, that's why I am here," replied Simon enigmatically.

"I didn't know you cared, Simon," she jested as she showed him into the Edwardian mini-mansion in which she and her husband resided.

Simon stepped into the hall and then followed Geraldine into the lounge off to the right.

"Would you like a drink?" she said moving to the small home-bar at one end of the room.

"No, too early for me," responded the sober-socks MP.

"A coffee then? I have just percolated some fresh brew."

"That would be wonderful," he replied following her out, through the connecting door, into the kitchen-diner, the room where everyone sooner or later congregated, particularly old friends.

The coffee was poured, milk, cream, brown sugar and a dark-chocolate mint biscuit offered and then they sat down on the easy chairs in the conservatory-like part of the irregularly shaped kitchen-diner.

They chatted inconsequentially for some time about family matters and holiday arrangements but both carefully avoided the hot topic of politics by mutual consent. Geraldine and David's children had all left home. The eldest was an academic archaeologist who was currently on a dig in Africa somewhere. The middle daughter was working for a little-known film company as a dogsbody, despite having obtained her degree in Media Studies from an eminent university. The youngest girl had only just left university and was searching for gainful employment in Manchester but she was threatening to become something of an embarrassing dropout from society. Simon listened with interest because he had followed the progress of the children for some years.

Simon, a widower, said very little about his personal life because there was nothing to tell. Nothing went on in Simon's life since his late-wife's death because he had tended to run downhill once he had lost his favourite companion.

Finally Geraldine began the serious topic of the day.

"Well, what can I do you for? Or is this a purely social call?" She knew, of course, that it wasn't.

Simon came straight to the point. He had no need to pussyfoot about with Geraldine.

"I wonder if I could have a word in your shell-like ear so that you could have a word in his?"

"Tell me more," was her reaction, although curiosity did not show on her lips.

"It has come to my notice that some figures for the recent Elisian delegation trip may be ... shall we say ... somewhat misleading."

"Someone's been fiddling the books again?"

"Not exactly but I think there is a cover-up of some sort which the PM should know about and I am disinclined to tell him directly myself."

"And you thought David could do the damage and mention you in despatches."

Geraldine was very used to the back-street approaches of politicians. She knew the ropes, in many respects, better than the so-called professionals. A nod was as good as a wink to a not-so-blind horse.

Simon went on to sketch the matter in some detail – the implications, those involved and the possible consequences if the news hit the press. As he spoke Geraldine nodded her complete understanding. She had a good grasp of the facts and promised to speak to David as soon as he surfaced. Simon felt satisfied that he could rely on Geraldine's discretion and David's loyalty to the party. Things were now set in motion and all should pan out to his satisfaction. Simon smiled inwardly with pride.

Geraldine, hospitable as ever, offered a scratch lunch and Simon readily agreed after the usual ineffectual platitudes about putting her to too much trouble and taking up much of her precious time all of which she brushed aside with a knowing smile. Homemade parsnip soup with crusty bread rolls and then ham and egg salad went down well with Simon who was nowadays not at all used to home-cooking. How he wished that someone like Geraldine was able to cook for him permanently as his late wife had done.

Simon left mid-afternoon with a degree of confidence and satisfaction not only because of his most enjoyable lunch but also because of the seeds which he had so productively sewn.

He returned home to his bachelor pad in cosmopolitan Stratford in east London. Stratford was quite a lively and trendy place, which was why he had moved there after his wife's death, but this was, in fact, all lost on Simon.

Stratford had housed the 2012 Olympic and Paralympic Games at the Queen Elizabeth Olympic Park, from which time it had mushroomed and erupted like a cantankerous volcano. It now had its own Westfield Stratford City business and shopping park, with its own casino for those who liked to speculate and lose. Stratford was also well connected in terms of travel-links for underground, high-speed above-ground trains and Docklands Light Railway to name by a few. And London City airport was not too far away. Stratford boasted nearly 100 restaurants and pubs, numerous hotels, East London University and it even had its own famous Theatre Royal in Stratford East which presented a stimulating mix of concerts, dance, drama, comedy, musicals and pantomime.

Simon, however, seldom made use of Stratford's leisure facilities and, in fact, he bitterly regretted having moved here because he felt even more alone in such a flourishing community. But it was, at least, a London bolt-hole. And Simon could not envisage buying out of the capital.

Simon's flat was not a new-build, as many around him were, but it was fairly modern in design and fairly pleasing on the eye. Although the flat was pleasant enough it was always a reminder of the woman whom Simon had lost, his beloved Betsy, and the crevice which it had left in his existence. Now Simon had no-one in whom to confide, no-one to cook his meals, no-one to spend his leisure hours with and nobody to soothe his troubled brow in times such as these. His flat was simply a reminder of his interminable loneliness and staring at its four walls was only tempered by his need to invest all his efforts into his work.

Simon did have a son, Kenneth, who lived in Japan, working for a merchant bank out there, with his wife Felicity but he rarely saw them in the flesh. So this didn't serve as a means of overcoming Simon's feeling of being isolated from the world, if anything it added to his dilemma because he was so far from his son and his grandchildren. And a holiday in Japan once a year, enjoyable though it might be, was little consolation.

Simon had tried a couple of holiday packages for single people but this only worsened the situation because the women whom he had met were either too lonely and desperate themselves or too lacking in intelligence and understanding to be a politician's wife or partner. He did not really want to remarry but still living an isolated existence was a severe ordeal which could not be avoided.

He wondered about going out to see a film or going to a local restaurant that night but he decided that he did not have the inclination and the effort would be too much for him. He settled for a pizza which was languishing in the fridge and needed to be eaten up quite soon.

Simon's thoughts turned to David Dulchester and Ian Jepherson as he idly watched a film on the box. Would Dulchester ask him for further details about Fetherington and Ruth? Would he be made to provide Dulchester with more evidence? Would he need to mention that Fletcher had been his spy? Would he be expected to have the figures re-examined in detail? What would Dulchester's reaction be to his being a mole? How would Dulchester present his knowledge to Jepherson?

Would the PM really appreciate Simon's efforts? Or would he simply dismiss the accusations as meddlesome and malicious? Did Jepherson already, in fact, know the score? And would he want it covered up therefore? Would the PM actually place him, Simon, on the backburner as a result of his clandestine investigations?

Simon's thoughts became a raging panther inside his head. But there was nothing he could do about it now. The dye was cast. There was no going back. Poor old Simon!

After a restless night, Simon decided to go back to the office and have another look at Fetherington's figures in order to see if he could come up with another juicy nugget of information. The office was often populated, albeit sparsely, on a Sunday but those who were about only had a nodding acquaintance with him. Even though there was virtually nothing pressing, he felt that it was better than staying at home.

Simon reread Fetherington's draft documentation in his office and glanced once more at the figures which, merely on the page, gave nothing away. He decided that nothing extra could really be gleaned from the information before him.

The staff restaurant was not open on a Sunday but a vending machine furnished him with a ham and tomato sandwich and a cheese roll for lunch.

An aimless afternoon walk through nearby James's Park and Green Park still did nothing to lift his spirits or to assuage his loneliness and lack of purpose. He ate his lunch on a bench in the park and spoke to no-one.

Simon then took the tube home from Green Park station on the Piccadilly Line before changing on to the Central Line for Stratford. He often took the underground home rather than taking a taxi because his journey would then take longer and so he would put off the inevitable time when he was saddled with his own company once more.

PREOCCUPATION

"Are you free to talk now?" said the text message.

"Yes," was the response.

Ruth's mobile sounded and she picked it up immediately.

"I've got tickets for the Eye on Wednesday evening at 6.00 pm. Will you join me?" he said.

Ruth felt ecstatic when she heard Keith's voice and she agreed readily to meet him in Jubilee Gardens between 5.30 pm and 5.45 pm by the International Brigade Memorial erected to commemorate the causalities of the Spanish Civil War.

Barrington had contemplated hiring Cupid's Capsule of the London Eye for the occasion but he felt that this would be an unnecessary business expense because he could probably achieve his aim for a tithe of the price of the personal love-capsule. Instead Barrington opted for the Champagne Tasting Experience. This package provided for the sampling of five varieties of champers, the much sought-after fast-track entry and access to a four-dimensional camera experience (whatever that meant – but they would soon find out).

Ruth felt so excited that she had met someone like Keith and she now simply had no desire to shell out in Hatty's this evening, or any other evening for that matter, in spite of any crap which her colleagues could dish out to her today or any other day. She had spent most of the weekend dreaming about her new admirer and willing the phone to ring. She knew, of course, that he was on business that weekend but she had fervently hoped that he would make contact once she was back at work. And indeed he had done so late on Monday morning as if he couldn't wait to speak to her.

While pretending to read the report which Faye had submitted for her approval, Ruth engaged in a protracted reverie.

Keith would come running up to her in Jubilee Gardens and they would embrace long and hard. He would stroke her cheek and her hair and plant a kiss on her lips. He would take her by the hand and together they would skip towards the London Eye. Keith would hug her as they admired the 360-degree view of London, particularly the Houses of Parliament and Downing Street from the God's eye vista. But they would also note the sweep of the Thames from the top of the Eye, sandwiched, as it was, between the two nearby bridges of Westminster and Waterloo. They would spot the BT tower, Buckingham Palace, the Royal Opera House, the British Museum and Centrepoint. It would be as if they both sat on top of the world ... their own personal universe ... and floated upwards in their dreams submerged in their undying love for each other. Keith would be hers, she believed, forever. To have and to hold from this day forth maybe?

Perhaps when Keith was next in London, they would take a river cruise, a special dining experience for ardent lovers. They would sit with their bubbly on the wooden benches by the side of the boat, while the awning flapped in the breeze, and listen to the strains of enchanting chamber music before partaking of a superb French cuisine prepared before their very eyes by the on-board chef. They would view all the famous Thames landmarks, such as St Paul's Cathedral, Big Ben, the Tower of London and then pass under Tower Bridge, which would lift especially for them, as they glided through locked in each other's arms on their way down to Greenwich for the round trip.

Then they would retire to a luxury hotel where they would symbolise their adoration for each other in a blaze of unbridled passion ... reaching the heights and delights of heaven as they had never experienced it before. Lounging in their personal Jacuzzi and sinking into the silken sheets of the four-poster they would envelop each other in their love. Ruth's mind was in a whirlwind of bliss.

"What do you think of the report?" came a voice from out of nowhere. "Do you think it is yet suitable for submission? I am being hassled by James Fetherington to deliver the goods."

Ruth was rudely jolted back to reality instantly. But she was still flustered by this insensitive interruption to her musings.

"Sorry?" she said, "Report?"

"Yes, the report on *Voting Trends and Preferences*," replied her colleague, "which I gave you first thing this morning for a final read-through. Fetherington is nagging me like hell for it. And, no doubt, Gregory Tranter is on his back too," said Faye.

Ruth was propelled back to cold and nasty reality. Fetherington, that bastard. Well, I don't give a stuff whether he lives or dies now. Now that I have my Keith.

"I'm just finishing it now. Give me about another ten minutes," Ruth replied.

Faye knew that clearly Ruth wasn't anywhere near finishing the thing but, hopefully, she would just simply scan it and then give it her seal of approval. That way Faye could meet her deadline and, if there was any comeback, then Ruth would take the rap. Perfect.

As the clock ticked nearer to 5.30 pm on Wednesday, Ruth assumed the role of a cat on a hot tin roof and Faye noted this uncharacteristic trait. Ruth had come to the office dressed in her Sunday best it seemed. She wore an understated grey suit with a pink-and-white striped top. Ruth's make-up was immaculate and it looked as if she had been to the hairdresser at lunchtime.

Faye pondered. I wonder what time her interview is? Will she be getting another job so that I will be promoted perhaps? I didn't think she was looking for a job but maybe she is now that Chaffinch and Fetherington are driving her insane? But Faye finally decided that it must be a man by Ruth's uplifted spirits.

By 5.20 pm Ruth could contained herself no longer. She threw down her papers, stuffed them into her desk drawer, locked it up and bustled out of the office. No doubt to touch up her make-up, concluded Faye, before the hot date.

Faye wondered also where she might be heading but, as the report had now been rubber-stamped by Ruth and despatched, she was little interested. But Faye had decided conclusively that Ruth was off on a hot date because of her spring-chicken act, interspersed by day-dreaming episodes, which she had adopted for most of the last few days.

Ruth walked on air as she neared Jubilee Gardens. Keith was not actually there, however. Only a slight setback, of course. But, in any case, it was not quite 5.30 pm yet. She glanced affectionately in acknowledgement of the enormous ferris wheel as if to give notice to the beast that she and her new lover would grace it with their presence just as soon as possible.

She decided on a circular walk on the grass of the inner circle where she could admire the flowerbeds. That way she would be able to spot him the moment he arrived. The gardens in summer sported a blaze of colour with both flowering plants and perennial evergreen shrubs. The weather, which could be inclement even in mid-summer, was favourable and Ruth saw this as a token of her own good fortune.

"According to my information, which I gleaned from a local gardener, this year you can see acanthus, praecox, gladioli, lilies, irises, paeonias and alliums," came a deep voice from out of nowhere.

Ruth swung round. They hugged, delighting in each other's presence. As there was still time, they walked around the compound, arms linked, chatting, talking, laughing, smiling and gazing occasionally into each other's glazed eyes. Ruth gazed appreciatively into Keith's eyes as if all her troubles had vanished in a nanosecond.

Barrington felt that this job was going exceptionally well.

They read the inscription on the International Brigade Memorial which stirred their deepest emotions and their patriotic instincts. They noted how 2100 men and women, 526 of whom had lost their lives, had gone to the aid of the Spanish people who were struggling against Fascism between 1936 and 1939.

The London Eye did not disappoint. It was a supreme and awesome experience. The champers and the mouth-watering canapés only added to the magnificence of the unforgettable occasion. They sampled caviar and pâté de foie gras on bruschetta-style toast, prawn and asparagus vol-au-vents, savoury tartlets, Asian spring rolls and smoked salmon roulades.

And Ruth felt that all her troubles, and those of the people on the ground too, had vanished the moment she and Keith had stepped aboard the capsule. It was so unreal that everything, which was normally quite large and daunting on the ground, became so small and insignificant from above. The queue-hopping cars, the red London buses, the tooting taxis, the colourful boats and the people appeared like ants as they reached the top. This was majestic London steeped in all its glory and chequered history.

The sun glistened on the metal of the wheel, on the clouds, on the river and on Keith's affectionate smiles and warm embraces. Even Big Ben and the Houses of Parliament, which would normally remind her of her daily toil and frustration, had no power to faze her.

Once back on the ground they hugged with delight at the memory of the occasion and Ruth believed that life would never be the same again. They watched the next batch of people boarding the Eye and waved them goodbye as they left.

"There is a little French restaurant just down the road from here. Will you join me for dinner?" enquired Barrington.

"Thank you, Keith, that would be marvellous." Keith was so gentlemanly and polite.

They strolled along to L'Auberge du Troyes, just further along from The Queen's Walk in the direction of the Golden Jubilee Bridges. This walk allowed them to further admire and comment on the view from the South Bank.

At L'Auberge du Troyes Ruth choose the lobster thermidor starter and the goat's cheese with figs and pumpkin seed salad as a main course. Barrington ordered a Vichyssoise and a steak tartar platter. They both shared a bottle of Premier Cru Chablis – not an imitation Keith told her when he placed their order.

They consumed their starters and reminisced about the Eye. Ruth felt that she had never tasted anything so delicious in such a fine-dining restaurant.

"Last time we met," Keith reminded her, "you seemed a little dismal. Do you want to talk about it?"

Now the game was really afoot.

Intoxicated by his solicitous attention, Ruth told of her troubles with James in vehement terms, omitting the bit about her former sexual attraction to him, of course, and the way in which he was constantly winding her up. And the fact that she desired to wrong-foot him because he was such a scoundrel. Ruth poured out all the trade secrets believing that Keith had no interest at all in politics. She spoke of the journalist from whom she had traded some information in exchange for learning of Fetherington's dirty-tricks. She knew that Fetherington was hiding something and she was, therefore, sure that a scam had occurred with the Elisian government. Ruth also mentioned that the journalist had infiltrated the Elisian government's ranks and was party to some insider information. But Ruth could not actually prove any of this in order to discredit James which was even more frustrating.

Barrington, therefore, had gathered nearly all the information which he wanted to obtain from this evening's jolly.

"A journalist?" he gasped, "Who? Do you know his name? Can you get him to publish his findings? So that you can expose this Fetherington person once and for all?"

"Well, I know his name is John and that he works for *The Times*," said Ruth, "but that is all."

That was all Barrington needed to know.

"And what did he tell you in exchange?" continued Barrington.

"Oh, only that one of the MPs was on the verge of resigning, which is common knowledge now anyway, because he left some weeks ago."

Interesting. Very interesting. So John somebody had told her nothing special but she is now sitting on a time-bomb. Barrington could definitely chase this one up, put two and two together and certainly make five.

Should he invite Ruth back to his make-believe hotel? No. I want to go home to my poochie.

Barrington told Ruth that he had to drive to Yorkshire there and then but he asked to see her again when he was next in London. The disappointment was visible but Barrington consoled Ruth with a lingering kiss when they parted.

REMONSTRATION

She saw before her a majestic creature wearing full-length diaphanous robes in black silk shot through with filaments of silver and gold. Some of these precious metal threads trailed on the floor behind her as she moved. She had flaming red hair radially splayed out like a halo and encrusted with dripping rubies and emeralds, dark skin and penetrating green eyes.

The creature beckoned insistently to Sandra who felt powerless to disobey and was transfixed. The unearthly being tossed her head and half turned as Sandra was mesmerised by the spell under which she had fallen. Keeping her eyes fixed hypnotically on Sandra, the omnipresent being walked away. Sandra, apparently not knowing the direction in which she was heading, followed submissively. Sandra was impelled forward by an unknown force.

Then Sandra saw some traffic lights ahead to which she was drawn. The traffic lights were green. She floated on air through space and time to another series of traffic lights which were red when she approached but they had now turned green. And then another set of lights and another ahead which all turned green and indicated 'go now' as she advanced not knowing the way in which she was headed or where she was ultimately destined.

Then the supernatural presence turned into one whose robes were now white and angelic. Her red hair was transformed into blonde locks which were draped about her shoulders and hung down to her waist. She smiled at Sandra with a welcoming visage. She lay down on a white velvet sofa and invited her companion to lie down with her.

Sandra then found herself being uplifted by Rousel ... taken in his arms and kissed passionately. She was aware of the patent evidence of his passionate ardour and this awakened in her a desire which she had not felt for years. If ever.

And then, suddenly, there was a thud across her chest and a violent groan.

"Why aren't you up yet?" demanded an intrusive voice. "I shall be late if you don't get up soon and get me some tea and breakfast woman," he maliciously instructed.

Sandra was still dazed and shocked. So it was a dream? A pleasant dream or a nightmare? A reality or a fantasy?

She obeyed her husband and got out of bed. Not so much because he expected to get his own way, although he usually did because it was easier to acquiesce than to argue, but also because she wanted to be alone with her own thoughts. To mull over the dream. To return to waking consciousness. To take in the fact that it was actually a dream. To come to her senses. And to analyse what had occurred in her private nocturnal imaginings. What was this dream telling her? What was its message? And why had it been so compelling and even violent in the grip it held over her? How significant are our dreams and half-waking reveries in predicting the future or throwing light on current events?

Sandra threw on her dressing gown and made her way downstairs to the kitchen where she hastily made some tea and began cooking Ted's usual heart-attack breakfast. Secretly she actually hoped that one day he would have a heart attack. That would solve most of her problems. But these wicked thoughts she instantly dismissed.

Breakfast was its usual perfunctory ritual when Ted read the paper while she waited on him, washed up and observed the silence and hostility between them.

Sandra's thoughts turned, in contrast, to Rousel. How different life would be with him. How he respected and cherished her and, most importantly, how he valued her as a woman. Ted had never regarded her as anything but a skivvy who should cater for his every need, provide sex whenever he wanted it (which, fortunately, had been not at all for several years) and generally never complain or make any demands on him. She decided that, in fact, she hated him especially now that she had met Rousel who, at least, had shown her that there was an alternative.

Sandra made herself another cup of coffee and settled down on the sofa in order to be alone with her musings after Ted had left for work with the usual grunt — not even a bland kiss on the cheek these days. She wanted to scream from the rooftops and tell the world about how much she hated him.

But then a pang of conscience struck again. She should not be thinking like this about her husband. She had taken vows in church. These thoughts were wrong. But, perhaps, God could see and understand her predicament and sympathise with her plight?

But her thoughts about Rousel were definitely wicked. She may not love Ted but to desire another man, however charming and attentive, was definitely sinful and verboten. God would certainly not approve of her longing for unity with Rousel. Sandra remonstrated with her conscience and decided that she would be strong and refuse to see him today for the scheduled boat-trip.

She recalled the last time that they had met. She remembered the intimate walk in the park which had started out innocently enough but then they had ended up alone lying under the willow tree which draped its hair in the river. Rousel had taken her in his strong arms, caressed her cheek and her lips, fixated on her eyes, stroked her hair and then planted a passionate kiss on the lips which he had admired for much of the time while they were together. He had spoken sweet words of love into her ears and this had become music to her soul. Rousel was aroused noticeably and she was too.

But again she admonished herself for her longing to be united with Rousel. I must ring him to say I cannot make it today. She had made her decision but, somehow, she never got round to picking up the phone in order to cancel their river-cruise date. Perhaps I could pray to God for strength? Perhaps I should take a cold shower? Maybe I should go out to the cinema and just simply not arrive at the appointed time and place? She continued to remonstrate and negotiate with herself but no final decision was, as yet, clear to her.

But what would be the harm in it? It would only be a holiday romance after all? He would be going back to France in a couple of weeks, perhaps? And what difference would it make to Ted if I went on the river with a friend? Would he care? No. There will be others on board the boat and so there will be no chance of any overt sexual practice? And maybe I need a change of scene anyway? Some different company instead of being stuck in the house all day and behaving like a frumpy old house frau.

She hurriedly finished the washing up and made the stale communal marriage bed.

She then took a long lingering bath, washed her hair and sprayed herself with the perfume which she had secretly bought the other day and put on the new dress which she had picked up in a sale recently.

Sandra made her way to the park as the appointed meeting place and behold there he was. Waiting patiently and expectantly for her ... and for her alone. Such dedication. Such gallantry.

Rousel bowed low and presented her with a delightful bunch of carnations and fuchsias. Sandra was thrilled to receive such a wonderful gift in such contrast to her husband's behaviour towards her even in their courting days.

He took her face in his hands and kissed her lovingly on the lips. Then he took her hand, kissed it while gazing into her eyes and led her to the riverside boat which he had hired.

Sandra was aghast. She had imagined that they would be taking a river-cruise with other people. But this was a small, yet luxurious, motorboat which was intended only for the two of them. And it had a cabin in which they could retire from the onlookers of the world. She simply dared not look down into the cabin in order to inspect the accommodation.

She hesitated momentarily but Rousel propelled her towards the boat and lifted her into it effortlessly. Again she beat her bosom. But I did not agree to be alone with him on the boat. Anything could happen on this boat. He might even try to seduce me. No, he was a gentleman. But a Frenchman. They had different values from our own, surely? And what if she could not be strong? What if he overpowered her? She would remain on deck throughout the voyage and not venture into the cabin below. Sandra tried to take comfort in this self-assurance. As the weather was beautiful, she would not have any need to enter the cabin in any case.

Maurice started the motor and proclaimed that he would be taking her along the water for lunch at a riverside pub.

Oh, well, that would be OK then. I cannot come to any harm if we just have lunch. She relaxed slightly.

He drove the boat gently downstream towards their luncheon venue, glancing at her regularly and blowing her the odd kiss.

They waved at passers-by on the towpath and to other boat-trippers. A passing river-cruise boat afforded a great sense of fun when all waved joyfully in both directions. Sandra and Rousel laughed heartily at this encounter. Sandra was not sure whether she would have preferred to be here with him alone or in safety on the passenger-laden vessel.

At the Crossways Tavern they ate homemade vegetable soup and macaroni cheese washed down with a bottle of house white. Sandra thought it was strange that a Frenchman should opt for an Italian dish but he told her that he had chosen it because it was one of her favourites. She blushed at the compliment.

They returned to the boat after lunch and Sandra expected them to return upstream but Rousel instead continued downstream towards more desolate terrain. Sandra was a little disconcerted by this move but, as she was not pressed for time, she considered that a little more time in the boat would not do any harm at all.

In England the weather is predictably unpredictable. And it turned, in an instant, from brilliant sunshine to pouring rain. Sandra was now certainly in a quandary.

Rousel, as always, manoeuvred the situation skilfully. He steered the boat into the bank, tied it up, took her hand and led her down into the shelter of the cabin below.

Sandra's knell was rung. There was no going back now. She noticed the sofa-bed as she entered the cabin and she knew exactly what was coming next. Her conscience would not save her now indeed. Her dream might have had a predictive quality after all.

Maurice pleasurably thought of the money he would collect from this one.

REGENERATION

Sally Plumley dolled herself up in her new glad rags and made her way to the Café du Parc on Fifth Avenue where she excitedly awaited the arrival of her new associate Gemma Gallagher.

Gemma soon arrived and apologised for keeping her friend waiting for an instant but she was assured by Sally that no undue delay had occurred.

The pair called for the menu from which Sally selected a consommé starter and scampi Provençale for the main course. Gemma chose a smoked mackerel salad starter followed by venison cutlets with red cabbage, game chips and onion gravy. The meal went down a treat with both parties as a sublime precursor to a scintillating night at the theatre.

A taxi transported them to the Gershwin Theatre on Broadway and they seated themselves in some very comfortable and obviously pricey seats near the front of the stalls. Gemma had obtained the tickets but not at the advertised price because of her connection with the box office manager but she failed to mention this salient point to her compatriot.

Harvey is a play which was written in 1944 by Mary Chase who received the Pulitzer Prize for Drama in 1945 for this ingenuous work. The plot traces the antics of the eccentric Elwood P. Dowd with his imaginary friend, called *Harvey*, who is an invisible six-foot high rabbit.

Sally and Gemma laughed throughout at the production, which was played for its comic aspects brilliantly and, of course, was much appreciated by the audience.

During the intermission they talked jovially to fellow audience-members and a good time was had by all.

When the show was over, however, a dilemma occurred. Where to now? Sally wondered about this one. And so did Gemma.

"Do you fancy a nightcap?" asked Gemma tentatively.

"How delightful," followed Sally who was angling for more of Gemma.

Gemma knew that she could not offer her flat in case there was too much evidence of Bertrand still, despite the fact that she had told him that she would not be available for a couple of days because of business commitments and, fortunately, he had accepted this untruth without question. She had got him well trained. So she was in a bit of a predicament. Her pause for thought, however, had the desired effect.

"Would you like to come back to my place then?" enquired Sally who had not been allowed to pay either for the theatre tickets or for the pre-theatre repast and so she felt she was obligated.

"That would be splendid," replied Gemma with relief.

The rest of the evening then took its natural course.

Gemma woke the next morning to a day which greeted her with a pleasing hue of light. She wondered about her next move. Should she suggest another date with Sally? Should they plan the weekend ahead? Where would she like to go?

Sally turned over in bed and outstretched her arm which Gemma took and kissed seductively as if to invite some matutinal sexual activity as a perfect supplement to the night before.

"What would you like to do today, honey?" asked Sally a moment later. "Shall we do an island cruise? My treat this time."

This seemed the perfect answer to Gemma's previous wonderings.

Sally booked the tickets online for a two-hour all-you-can-eat buffet lunch cruise which started at noon. The cruise offered breath-taking, panoramic views of the New York skyline and took in both the Hudson River and the East River on either side of lower Manhattan.

A taxi was then ordered for Chelsea Piers on the west side of Manhattan so that Sally and Gemma could board the cruiser at 11.30 am. From the tour of New York Harbour the couple became tourists for the day in order to view Battery Park City, South Street Seaport, Manhattan Bridge, Brooklyn Bridge and the Williamsburg Bridge. The various small islands were also explored on the cruise, such as Liberty Island which houses the much-loved and spectacular Statue of Liberty, Governor's Island and Ellis Island. Other sights included the One World Trade Center and the Empire State Building as well as a view of Brooklyn and New Jersey.

The girls hardly needed to be reminded by their on-board guide that Lady Liberty, as the beacon in New York Harbor, was donated as a friendship gift from France in 1776 in order to celebrate America's Independence Day and to welcome immigrants to the States. It was finally erected in 1886 and French sculptor-designer Frédéric August Bartholdi (1834-1904) was instrumental in bringing the project to fruition. The construction was coated in copper which, once oxidised, became green rather than the original brown. The internal structure, of course, was created by the engineer Gustave Eiffel (1832-1923) known most famously for designing the wrought-iron, lattice-work Eiffel Tower in Paris. Symbolically Lady Liberty holds the torch of enlightenment and her seven-pointed crown depicts the seven rays of the sun, the seven seas and the world's seven continents. This statue has, therefore, become the iconic symbol of freedom and the American dream.

Gemma and Sally, however, both thought that it was fun seeing their residence and their life from a different angle and the pair giggled like schoolgirls in appreciation of their expedition. Both also treasured time-off from professional duties which rarely occurred in their hectic lives.

The buffet menu consisted of various salads, couscous, rolled and stuffed sole fillets, chicken roasted with honey and sesame seeds, baked ziti, French fries and chocolate gateau with ice cream to help it all down nicely. And all this while a DJ did his stuff for the guests.

A stroll through Chelsea Waterside Park was then the order of the day for the happy couple who wanted to stick with the riverside theme in order to prolong their cherished memories of the cruise experience. Watching the kids playing and being al fresco further lightened the mood of the participants on this unique occasion. They sat down on the grass and listened to the sounds about them as if in a therapeutic group meditation. Traffic noises, blended with both birdsong and children's games, added to their hearing.

It was now time for Gemma to ply her trade by gently encouraging Sally to open up. Sally certainly had a shedload of garbage on her mind of which she wanted to divest herself and her new mate had the kind of listening ear which made way for such unloading. Sally spoke of the way in which her boss Felix had been stressed out with regard to negotiations over the takeover bid and how she had been requisitioned to offer the lawyer acting for the other side a sweetener.

Sally knew, of course, that engaging in such a practice would open her up to the end of her career, at best, or prosecution, at worst. Gemma suggested that she got out of her current job bloody quick. The theatre and the river cruise had enabled Sally to let her guard down and to dispense with the pretence that everything was hunky-dory at work.

"Why get mixed up in doing someone else's dirty work?" demanded Gemma vociferously. Sally, of course, could see the logic of such an argument when the implications of her actions were explained to her so forcibly. She came face to face with reality. Sally felt the relief of unburdening her soul but she also trembled at the consequences of her former actions.

"But I might have difficulty getting another job," protested Sally.

"But you might be on the scrap-heap forever if you continue to go along this road." Gemma was on the point of shouting at Sally and shaking her violently.

Sally agreed to resign on Monday once Gemma had put her point across so persuasively and she had given her the name of a recruitment agency which specialised in placing executive women who had been exploited by their employers.

The rest of the weekend was concerned largely with discussion about Sally's parlous position and then planning her future. With each dawning day Sally grew stronger and more resigned to resigning. The result was that first thing on Monday morning Sally quit her job and more or less walked out there and then. When Felix protested, however, a blazing row ensued.

Sally told Felix that she had been exploited and compromised.

Felix threatened to sue her.

Sally countered with the fact that she would tell the press if he dared.

Felix decided not to dare. Takeover had now turned into take cover.

A deal had been struck over the acquisition and this was all that Felix really cared about. The takeover bid was now going ahead at a price which he found more than acceptable and so he would let sleeping dogs lie. He thought that he could easily get a replacement for the turncoat traitor. Felix contented himself with this knowledge as Sally walked out triumphantly.

PROGNOSTICATION

"Poppy, my darling, I wasn't expecting you home tonight. What a delightful surprise."

"Well, I may have got all the gen we need from Ruthie, buttercup."

"Then don't keep it to yourself."

They poured out some drinks and the Director's Meeting of the Medici Squadron commenced in Vauxhall. Barrington had been too busy today, however, to make his usual consignment of mulled wine and cheese straws.

Barrington then related the facts which he had obtained from Ruth Angell.

He gave Calendula the low-down about Fetherington and about Ruth whom, he suspected, had the hots for Fetherington despite her efforts to conceal it. He spoke about Ruth suspecting Fetherington and wanting to put one on him. Barrington also stated what Ruth knew but couldn't prove – namely that Fetherington was maintaining that the figure in the accounts for the Elisian delegation's trip was a backdated import duty. But Ruth suspected that it was a high-level, undeclared, bribe from the Elisian Prime Minister.

Barrington then told Calendula that a journo named John from *The Times* had obtained from Ruth some information about a politician who was about to resign in exchange for telling her that he had infiltrated the Elisian government offices where the double-dealing was discovered.

They then speculated about who Fetherington was covering up for and both Calendula and Barrington concluded that it must be Gregory Tranter, the Secretary of State for International Development. Tranter must have then put pressure on the PM to back Finkelbaum's campaign in Elisia for their general election.

"Could that journo be John Fanshawe, do you think?" Calendula asked.

"Fanshawe is not really a political newshound. His stuff is more general," added Barrington.

Calendula then thought a bit more after making this statement as an element of doubt had crept in. "No, it must be John Griffiths because he's on the political circuit and he has been out of the country, in Europe somewhere, for some while. I wondered if we could find out whether he might have been in Elisia recently?"

"That answer could simply be a phone call away, poochie."

"Well, get on with it then, panda," demanded Calendula playfully.

Barrington rang one of his contacts at *The Times* and, indeed, it was confirmed that John Griffiths had been in Elisia for a longish period and that he had only returned very recently.

Calendula now began to plan their next move.

"I think what we need to do is find out the sum involved and get sight of the actual accounts which show the figures. The press would easily be able to make something of it even if it turns out to be a genuine backdated payment."

"And we ought to also review the Elisian end of the equation in order to verify the facts and the reason for the bribe," interjected Barrington. "Maybe our man could succeed where John Griffiths has failed and then we could sell our story to *The Times* as well as *The Guardian*. A nice double scam here would certainly reflect well in the balance sheet."

Calendula changed the subject slightly by asking another question. "How did you leave it this evening with Ruthie?"

"I said I would ring her when I am next in London but I didn't specify when. I thought it better to talk to you first and then see what could be done. She's certainly more than up for it. Perhaps I could get her to make a copy of the relevant pages of the accounts?"

"No, far too risky, if she's a bit neurotic," warned Calendula. "And she would instantly suspect you, lion cub, when the news broke. And might seek revenge on you then."

"Well, I can just keep her on ice, if necessary, for a while and then do my disappearing act."

"Yes, just keep the pot simmering in that department. We might need her later on. But I think I can put Faye to good use here and then we shall have to get her out of the place pronto."

"I agree," conceded Barrington.

Calendula, true to her word, rang Faye Windsor-Harris.

"I have another little job for you, sweetie," she said.

Faye was very pleased to receive this news. Now that she had paid off her student loan from LSE for her final year of the MSc, she felt that even more extra cash might come in really handy right now. She could replenish her wardrobe perhaps? Take a holiday? Buy a new kitchen maybe? Move somewhere more salubrious even? She could certainly put the dosh to good use somehow.

Calendula interrupted Faye's financial forward planning.

"Can you also get hold of a copy of the report which gives the Elisian figures in which the discrepancy was found?"

"Unfortunately Ruth always keeps her important papers locked up in the desk-safe. And I don't even know the combination. God knows what would happen if she got run over by a taxi someday?" replied Faye.

"And you have not yet perfected the art of the hairpin routine?" joked Calendula.

"No, sorry," was Faye's reaction.

"Well, I think we can overcome that little sleeping policeman as long as you are able to take a visitor into the building at some point. Say at the weekend rather than during the week when not a lot of people are about. Could you fix that?"

"I should think so," said Faye.

"Then here is my plan," replied Calendula who accordingly gave Faye an outline of how they could get into Ruth's desk-safe undetected. Both ended the call satisfied with the arrangements.

"Shall we have a shower, buttercup?"

"Definitely! But I must call Foxy first."

Calendula rang Foxy Ferguson but, when she reached his voice mail, she simply left a message.

Barrington turned on the power shower. Then he undressed his beloved and they luxuriated in the warmth of the cascading waters. The Medici Squadron director's meeting, therefore, decanted to the shower room of their apartment for a short interlude.

"It Ain't Necessarily So" reverberated in the lounge. But both Calendula and Barrington were otherwise engaged on a job which needed to reach a climactic conclusion. And so a return message was recorded.

"How's Maurice doing, by the way?" wondered Calendula when the comfort-break was over and the shower and the heat of the moment had died down.

"Wonderfully well, I gather," answered Barrington. "He's certainly hit the jackpot and his out-of-pocket expenses are not too terrible either."

"Has he got anything to go on?"

"Well, Mullingar is certainly on the brink of defection. She's utterly disenchanted with the Tories and with working in their constituency HQ. But how could we put her to some real use, I wonder?" remarked Barrington.

"Well, she works on Helena Dartfield's patch, doesn't she? So maybe Sandra could be persuaded to pump Dartfield for some information," concluded Calendula.

Barrington grabbed his laptop. "Yes, and I think Dartfield had a ding-dong with Fetherington, if I am not mistaken." He checked the database which confirmed his recollection.

"Well, we certainly could make capital from that, poppy. Tell him to keep at it."

"As ex-gigolo Maurice has an insatiable sexual appetite, I don't think that would afford him any problem at all."

They both chuckled. Such was the way of the world which they exploited whenever money and intrigue would be the result.

Calendula called Foxy back.

"Foxy," cried Calendula when Foxy had answered his phone. "Got you at last."

"Miss Calendula," replied Foxy. He always called her 'Miss Calendula', and sometimes 'Miss F-B', because 'Miss Fortescue-Bligh' was a bit of a mouthful for a cockney. And he was too polite to address his employer just by her first name.

"We have a little job for you, Foxy dear," began Calendula. "One which only you can do."

"Flatt'ry always gets the goods, Miss," he responded. "Anyfink you like. Foxy will fix it."

Calendula explained the mission which she wanted Harry Ferguson (known as Foxy to all his friends) to undertake.

"Nuffink simpler for o' Foxy, Miss Calendula."

Foxy, a sometime bigtime safecracker and not-so-recently an ex-jailbird had given the impression to the law that he was now a so-called changed man. But even a reformed citizen does not turn his snout up at a bit of cash on the side particularly when he believes that he can get away with it under the umbrella of the Medici Squadron.

Barrington also rang Maurice for an update and informed him of the link between James Fetherington and Helena Dartfield. Maurice brought Barrington up to speed on progress with the Sandra Mullingar project and agreed to put plan B into action.

"I also think we should plant someone in Elisia," said Calendula.

"That's what I said some time ago," protested Barrington.

"Well, I have just been cogitating on the question and I have now come up with the answer," she responded.

Calendula explained her strategy and outlined the way in which the pieces of the jigsaw could all fit together neatly.

"Oh, my darling poochie. Buttercup! Darling face! What would I do without you?" asked Barrington.

"Masturbate!"

DEVIATION

"It's always been a match made in hell and damnation. Always! I should never have married the bugger. I really would like to divorce him, you know. But I am not sure how to go about it. And I don't want to pauperise myself," she pondered.

"There would be no need to pauperise yourself. Divorce is easy these days. And if he is loaded with money, and you haven't worked for years, you could easily screw him for all he's worth," her lover replied.

"But how?"

"Well, for starters, I have a friend who's a solicitor and he's very good at clobbering wealthy husbands good and proper."

"He sounds like my sort of guy."

"I'll give you his details. Nothing simpler. Just give him a ring to see the deal through and you should be laughing in no time at all."

"Really?"

"Really."

"But he's a lawyer himself. So wouldn't he know how to wriggle out of it?"

"Not if you knew what he was worth. You can look at his bank accounts. You know his salary, I suppose? Does he have any money squirrelled away that you don't know about, for instance?"

"I think I know what he earns. Roughly. And I am sure he has some hidden reserves but how could I ever find out?"

"Have you gone through his office lately?"

"Well, yes, but his desk is locked and I don't understand how the computer works," she lamely protested.

"Oh, but I do. And I can pick locks like a professional. And it would be a good idea to do it while he's away. Let's do it."

"Let's do it. Now!"

They both leapt out of bed. But decided that office-raiding in the nude was not a good idea. And so they showered in Mariella's en suite shower room, dressed and had a leisurely breakfast.

Nicholas then proceeded to case the office joint.

Piers' so-called library had a desk which presented no challenge and a computer which could similarly be inspected. Nicholas first of all tried a corkscrew on the desk drawer but this was not up to the task. A hairpin was similarly ineffectual. A hatpin eventually from Mariella's dressing table did the trick in opening the bureau.

In the top drawer of the desk were a number of papers which both Mariella and Nicholas scrutinised. From this information it transpired that Piers Wendell had several accounts abroad in which large sums of money resided.

"Take a note of these bank account numbers," he instructed, "and also take a photocopy of these up-to-date statements."

Mariella did as instructed. She did know how to use the photocopier at least.

The rest of the desk was uninteresting and boring legal papers connected with Piers' work at GMC.

Next the computer was attacked.

"Would you know his password?"

Mariella cudgelled her brain.

"Hm. Try his mother's name – Florence."

That didn't work.

"What about Fido. His favourite pet in childhood."

"No. Try again."

"I know. Law, legal, lawyer, something like that."

All permutations of these words were tried and eventually 'legalities' won the prize. They unlocked Pandora's box which gave up its secrets with gratitude and left hope for the future.

They both looked into his spreadsheets and textual documents. Much was discovered. Wendell's emails also revealed much which would hang him several times over.

Mariella was delighted with this find even though she didn't really understand it much. Nicholas was ecstatic. He'd certainly earned his keep on this job.

They printed out all the papers which Nicholas felt were relevant to Mariella's divorce proceedings and a handsome financial settlement.

Nicholas also took a quick USB download of the lot.

"Now we had better get down to the bank, bloody quick."

"The bank? Why?"

"You need to get this stuff out of the house pronto and into safe-keeping until you need it."

Mariella admitted the wisdom of this advice. She and Nicholas, therefore, made their way into town for more raspberry tartlets before heading in the direction of Mariella's bank where the various papers were put in a safe-deposit box for future reference.

In the afternoon Mariella also spoke to the solicitor, Guy Peregrine, whom Nicholas had recommended. Mr Peregrine suggested that she wait until she wished to proceed with the divorce before consulting him but Mariella thought it worth going ahead with making an appointment. A date was accordingly set for the following week. It was yet another way of spending her husband's money which amused her magnificently.

Mariella and Nicholas then decided on a picnic lunch in the out-of-town Henchmead Woods in order to discuss the ploy for her divorce. They went to a nearby Italian delicatessen in Henchmead where they purchased some Tuscany bruschetta coated with sun dried tomatoes and black olives, a selection of naturally cured meats, an artichoke salad, a Mediterranean feta cheese salad together with a pheasant terrine. Some cantuccini (almond biscuits, to you) provided a neat conclusion to the meal. And a bottle of Frascati accompanied the feast which they drank from plastic wine glasses also purchased for the occasion. Mariella, in addition, kept plastic plates, knives and forks in the car and so the occasion was perfect.

They sat on the cedar-wood picnic tables which were very kindly provided by a generous and appreciative donor. And the couple afterwards went for a long walk deep within the woods where they were afforded the type of privacy which they craved just now.

Mr Peregrine, when Mariella met him the following week, asked her for the details of her marriage and why it had so irretrievably broken down. He was such a kindly man that Mariella furnished him with all the data about her dissatisfaction with her spouse and described the way in which they hardly encountered each other these days because of his dedication to his work. She omitted, however, to make any mention of the fact that she had been seeing his friend Nicholas. Peregrine suspected that this was the case anyway but he felt that he would keep the knowledge in reserve.

Mariella was then asked about the financial situation and Mr Peregrine rubbed his hands beneath the desk as she outlined the position, the evidence in her possession at the bank and the size of her husband's salary. The lawyer felt that he could make a killing out of this one which he could feed on for some time as well as gaining a satisfied client in the process.

Peregrine's first step was to relieve Mariella of a large sum of money in order to start the proceedings. And to obtain her authority to access her safe-deposit box at the bank.

Accordingly Guy Peregrine began divorce proceedings by issuing a Divorce Petition to Piers Wendell on the grounds of unreasonable behaviour. This petition, together with a Notice of Proceedings Form and an Acknowledgement of Service Form, were sent to Piers to await his return from the States. An accompanying letter to Piers set out the demands of his wife for financial maintenance and a sum of capital in order to keep her in the manner to which she had become accustomed and another pay-out by way of a financial compensation following the divorce.

Mariella felt it wise to go and stay with her sister for a couple of weeks just before Piers returned home in order to give her husband a chance to read the documentation and the details of a proposed financial settlement without her hovering presence.

Meanwhile, Tom Dryden, alias Nicholas Benson, sent the contents of Piers Wendell's computer to his employer at the Medici Squadron and received a princely sum in exchange.

Nicholas also told Mariella that they should not meet for some time while the divorce was going through and she reluctantly agreed particularly as she was staying with her sister in Norfolk.

Tom, therefore, decided to take a protracted holiday in the north of England where he intended to visit an ex-girlfriend and her partner who were amenable to his company. Vera Clough, alias Dorinda Bright, and her partner Ivan Phelps, also known as Anthony, welcomed Tom for a lengthy and enjoyable stay in their quaint cottage in the Yorkshire Dales.

DISINTEGRATION

James had that Friday feeling again. Especially so because he was due to see that mermaid on the rock tomorrow evening. An evening appointment boded well for his intentions with her.

Fetherington had, as usual, had a harrowing week and, therefore, the prospect of an uplifting weekend ahead was a godsend.

After his trip to Throxfield in order to open the university library there and to sort out matters at HQ, he had been required to attend Question Time in the House as it was his department's turn to face the music. As a level-three minister, he had not been obliged to answer any questions directly but he was, however, expected to supply his senior government minister, Gregory Tranter, with information in support of his answers to the nitpicking questions. Such oral questions were actually designed to undermine the department's position and to generally make all members of the International Development team feel very uncomfortable in front of the television audience who were, of course, the voting public.

Tranter was questioned about the latest published foreign trade figures and any subsequent developments. Gregory managed to field this question successfully because Fetherington had supplied him with a summary of the latest statistical update which showed even more improvement.

A supplementary question was posed by an opposition spokesman about Tranter's attitude to the latest foreign trade results and he was asked to comment on the suggestion that he was complacent about the situation as reported in the press. Gregory had then drawn the House's attention to the fact that a press release had been issued, which had quietened press comment, and he reiterated his true opinion on the matter.

Another tricky tabled question was asked about the way in which the department was helping Britain in terms of its forward-planning policy.

This question, unfortunately, had meant that James had been forced to actually read Faye's 168-page report on *Voting Trends and Preferences: A Predictive Analysis for Forward Planning*, which he had only recently received. He had extracted the important facts but only a verbal summary had been given to Gregory that morning in haste. The grumpy Tranty was not amused by the lateness of the hour or the non-written report summary but Fetherington claimed pressure of work which his superior could not dispute without any known facts.

The Secretary of State for International Development fortunately managed to ride the tide of this policy question exceptionally well in the circumstances by emphasising the depth of detailed research which his department had commissioned and had then undertaken at lightning speed.

Now, after the parliamentary business of interrogation had concluded, all Fetherington needed to do was to have lunch with Gregory in the staff restaurant in order to brief him on the full contents of the voting trends report and later to submit a written précis and abstract of the lengthy document. The two politicians, of course, were also scheduled to conduct a debriefing of Parliamentary Question Time over lunch.

James disliked eating in the staff restaurant because it reminded him of school-dinners which he had found repulsive. But Tranty, who had really enjoyed his school-dinners like the philistine that he was, was always in favour of meeting there during lunch not only to appease his humble palate but also because he did not want to have to bear the expense of an outside restaurant or pub meal. Stingy bastard! And, far worst, James even had to pay for his own lunch. Poor sod!

Tranter was a bit of a bumbling git but he was able to put Fetherington on the spot occasionally by pestering him for information which he, James, did not possess. The lunchtime conference was no exception and, therefore, James was detailed to return to the office in the afternoon where he was actually required to read, rather than to skim-read, some of the reports which normally sat on his desk untouched.

This activity of reading certain aspects of the outstanding reports in detail, and dictating his comments into a recording device, therefore, had occupied James fully on Wednesday afternoon and for much of Thursday and Friday. He intended to work on the report-reading and precis-writing until it was time for him to leave the office and to head in the direction of Harmony Holistics for another massage with Jean Paul in readiness for his weekend.

On Friday morning, however, Fetherington's mobile phone vibrated and this event turned his plans for the entire weekend completely upside down. Fetherington purposefully kept his mobile phone on vibrate so that it could not be heard by anyone in the outer office. Nosey old Beryl could never even hear if he received or made any calls from his mobile while at his desk. That way he retained at least some of his privacy.

"Darling," said a breathless voice, "I am so sorry to have to do this to you but I shall have to cancel tomorrow. And I was so, so looking forward to *Der Rosenkavalier*." She sounded as if she wanted to weep.

James could not believe his ears. This was all his hopes dashed and his soul deflated.

He was just about to throw the latest copy of *The Times Universal Atlas of the World*, followed rapidly by *The International Who's Who*, at the wall when a second statement arrested his intention and defused his rage. James was a fully paid-up member of an amateur traumatic society when the mood gripped him.

"But I have another suggestion to make which you may appreciate more," said Calendula mysteriously. "I have to be in Paris later this evening and I will be spending the whole weekend there. Would you like to join me at my hotel? It would mean that you would have to miss *Der Rosenkavalier*, of course."

James could not make out whether or not she was inviting him to share her room or to book a separate one for himself. He decided to go out on a limb and to chance his arm.

"Do you have a room booked?" he tentatively queried.

"Yes, and it's a double room. Would you like to join me, perhaps?"

"Perhaps, I would," said James.

James slowly replaced the reference books back on his desk. A copy of these reference books always sat on James' desk in order to give the impression of his high international profile.

This was more interesting. James' mind pulsated with speculation. That jezebel is actually asking me to sleep with her, or rather to stay awake with her, and, secondly, he would not have to sit through some boring opera. Fetherington's initial brain-collapse turned to expectant optimism and he reached downwards towards the zip in his trousers.

Calendula then made a feeble attempt at offering to reimburse him for the cost of her theatre ticket, not his ticket as well, he noted, but he nobly refused her kind gesture and agreed to reshuffle his plans for the weekend. Unfortunately, he could not return the tickets for resale and so he gave them away to Evelyn in the staff restaurant whom he knew to be a full-on opera-buff, thereby earning her eternal gratitude in the process.

Fetherington scuttled off to the travel agent almost immediately at lunchtime. The reports were neglected without a second's hesitation. He told Beryl that he would be taking an extended lunchbreak but he deliberately refused to satisfy her curiosity about where he was going and why. Beryl wondered what he was up to but came to no conclusions except that a female would be involved.

James left the office with hardly a glance at the delectable Claire or the buxom Zena.

Worldwide Frontiers was often a reliable port of call when James needed to jet away for an impromptu liaison and so he made this agency his first lunchtime appointment. Business was speedily concluded in that he secured a seat on a late evening flight from Heathrow to Charles de Gaulle airport in Paris and he got hold of some euros.

Now for some shopping.

James bought two new shirts in celebration. He was not sure how many of his playboy shirts, which had been cleaned and ironed, were at home. Mrs Maskell, who did his housework and laundry and some occasional shopping, was certainly up to speed on his business gear but she was not due now until the middle of next week and so much of his leisure attire was still in the laundry basket.

James left work promptly. Taking a few of his reports with him and making the usual lame set of promises to himself about working on them over the weekend.

He cancelled his outing to Harmony Holistics and hurried home eager for the fun of the weekend to begin. James threw some undergarments and his new shirts minus the packaging into a small travel bag together with a couple of bottles of his exotic and erotic male perfume. He would not need any pyjamas, surely? It was naff to even consider pyjamas.

He took a quick shower to wash off the monotony and pressure of the week. The weekend is the time when you throw all your clothes on the shower-room floor with nary a care in the world for tomorrow.

Now it was all systems go as James drove to Heathrow full of optimism and an egg and cress sandwich which he had picked up on the way back to his Mayfair flat. He turkey-gobbled down this snack on his way to the airport.

MISAPPROPRIATION

Jules Axminster had been an exceedingly precocious child prodigy. Now he had grown up and become slightly more obnoxious. And, as such, he was usually a lone wolf on the prairie.

He had taught himself to read by the time he was four years of age which thus opened up the gateway for him to become a self-taught mathematician, multi-disciplinary scientist and general boffin.

Axminster had obtained a degree in Forensic Science from Dundee University by the time he was thirteen. He then took a couple of postgraduate degrees in Mathematics and Electronic Engineering both at Cambridge University where he seemed to settle down for a while until he had, subsequently, gained a PhD in Computer Science only four months after he had left his teenage years behind him forever.

Life was, therefore, hard for Jules Axminster.

He had few friends, job opportunities were limited to the academic sphere and people generally bored him stupid with their inane chatter and brainless remarks. Jules did not ever consider going to charm school. His parents had possessed above-average intelligence and were well educated but he still found them insufferable and so he left home for good once he had embarked on his university studies.

His tutors at Dundee and Cambridge had neither excited him nor inspired him. Jules spent most of his time at university either in the college libraries or on the Internet. Jules, of course, had contempt for many of his relatively stupid fellow-students. Axminister's studies propelled him towards the Internet and he regarded this facility as merely an extension of himself invented in order to maintain his sanity. Indeed, he probably would have invented the Internet himself had someone else not got there first.

Jules had, almost unknowingly, lost his virginity with a very persuasive female when drunk at a party in Cambridge but he had soon decided that his need for physical contact could be satisfied more easily in the comfort of his own home alone or via the occasional dial-up rent-a-bum escort agency.

He finally got married to his laptop computer. One which he had built himself from parts snipped off eBay.

Jules also, at his leisure, had taught himself Latin, Greek, French, Italian, German, Russian, Arabic and Chinese. Axminster decided to skip the rest of the world's languages because he could probably make himself understood or muddle his way through reading any other language which he might encounter.

On gaining his PhD, Jules had taught at Cambridge for a year or two but he had soon found that many of his students were either too stupid to bother with or too disinterested in studying to retain him in the teaching profession for any length of time. Jules, by this time, had also become thoroughly disillusioned with the strictures and inflexibility of the academic system generally.

After working at Cambridge, Jules spent a while bumming around Europe making good use of his languages by swearing at the locals in their own dialects. He then made a study of innovative information technology applications which were employed in the USA and the Far East.

But Jules was unemployed and more or less unemployable. He needed, however, to maintain a certain standard of living and to support his dope habit and so he sought ways of improving his cash-flow which would not involve too much interaction with the great unwashed.

One day, while casually trawling the Internet, Jules discovered that he could peek into the bank accounts of some wealthy people and even detect what the big banks themselves were up to. In order to swell his coffers, consequently, Jules helped himself occasionally to funds which he believed certain people would not even notice let alone miss. Hence Jules became an IT hacker out of necessity but he also found that he could actually market his services to others as a means of improving and maintaining a reasonably comfortable lifestyle.

Jules then made important connections with people who relied on computer-hackers to keep their nefarious business activities or leisure-time pursuits afloat. He had a database of numerous satisfied clients drawn from among the echelons of the gangster world and the criminal demi-monde.

Jules' latest lucrative commission was to investigate the goings on at the offices of the Elisian Federal Government. This was, at present, proving to be something of a knotty little problem and, therefore, it had captured his attention and was haunting his every waking thought.

He was currently residing in Morocco with Hakim, a young man who provided him with shelter in a high-rise flat in Agadir. Hakim supplied Jules with regular doses of subtly spiced beef or chicken tagine with couscous and fresh sardines marinated in chermoula, all washed down with gallons of gunpowder-mint tea, as well as occasional sexual favours. His dope habit was also well catered for in this part of the globe.

Jules was beginning to feel, however, that a move or, at least, a short vacation was necessary and an excursion into the outside world was signalling. And he needed, indeed, to go to Elisia in order to solve his current dilemma of how to extract top-secret information from the Elisian government's files.

Accordingly Jules kissed Hakim a fond goodbye, booked himself on a flight to Vienna, settled into a back-street hotel, explored the low-life nightlife and applied for a position in the IT department of the Elisian Federal Government. With his stunning academic qualifications, together with his wholly duplicitous curriculum vitae, his new business-like wardrobe and his youthful appearance, he soon secured a relatively junior post in the government offices. Actually it suited his purpose better to be a junior programmer, rather than a more senior executive, because he could still hack into the mainframe computer network but was not likely to be suspected as a more senior colleague might. There was also a fringe benefit attached to the job in that Jules could chat up some of the younger members of the team, both male and female, in his tea breaks.

Within hours Jules had discovered the adapted coding language behind the programming of the computer, the internal network architecture connections, the way in which the security system operated and how he could get access to red-hot files from the Prime Minister's office. But Jules bided his time. Besides, the nightlife was pleasing enough to entertain him temporarily and he was on expenses in any case.

One weekend, when pressure of work necessitated it, of course, Jules brought in his own USB stick and managed to download all the information which he required and some more which he could make use of himself personally. Now the woodcock was truly approaching the gin (although the woodcock was by no means an alcoholic). He also transferred some funds from a central government bank in Vienna into his own account just for the sheer devilment of it.

One night Jules was able to ship his findings off to his employer and he received an appropriate payment in return paid directly into his numbered Swiss bank account. Jules reckoned that this tidy windfall would keep him and Hakim rent-free for another couple of years.

Jules became lazy and incompetent in his work for the IT division of the Elisian government and, therefore, he did not survive his probationary period of one month. Jules again found himself on the streets of Vienna homeless and jobless. The back streets of Vienna, however, were a great consolation to Jules for his abrupt loss of employment. And he chuckled all the way out of the office in so-called disgrace, making sure to give one of the messenger boys a quickie in the washroom before he actually left.

Jules checked out of his hotel in the Elisian capital and returned to Hakim in Morocco for some more chicken tagine and mint tea.

Hakim, attentive as ever, greeted Jules warmly as usual. And when Jules handed over a fistful of dollars, he, Hakim, was even more pleased to see his neglectful inamorato. Jules, however, did not deliver to Hakim his usual consignment of sexual favours, having more or less exhausted his supplies of libido while away in Vienna. But he did, of course, eat his fill of tagine with couscous and nearly drank himself to death with mint tea.

Life continued as usual, therefore, in Agadir. And Jules looked forward to his next money-making assignment while he got on with creating a new games programme which he could sell on his beloved Internet website at www.galaxywars.com registered by Inter-Galactic Expeditions Incorporated on his own server.

MYSTIFICATION

David decided that he might try to buttonhole Ian after the cabinet meeting and, if not, to flag up the fact that he wished to have a private word with him.

"Could you spare a moment, Prime Minister?" Dulchester asked.

"A few minutes, yes, of course," came the reaction, "What do you want, old boy?"

Boy, I like, but I don't need a reminder of my fast-approaching old age. But David's thoughts were obviously unvoiced and he trusted that the PM had not been to telepathy evening classes.

"You don't have a meeting with Chaffinch then?" enquired Dulchester politely. David was another consummate liar. He knew perfectly well that Jepherson's meeting with Chaffinch had been cancelled at the last minute because the fact had been recorded in the PM's electronic diary to which the Chancellor automatically had direct access.

"No, what can I do you for, old boy?"

They retired to the PM's office which was slightly more private than the cabinet meeting room in Downing Street.

"Fancy a sherry?"

David hoped that his virtually imperceptible wince would not be detected by his senior colleague. But his obvious hesitation meant that Jepherson recalled Dulchester's preferences and saved any embarrassment all round.

"No, Scotch on the rocks, isn't it?" amended Jepherson.

Dulchester thought that things were looking up for him.

Ian poured out the drink for Dulchester but stuck with the dry sherry for himself. Dulchester thought what a pansy Ian Jepherson was for his alcoholic preference.

"As I said at the meeting," proceeded Jepherson, "I am more than gratified by the way in which your budget predictions have panned out and the way in which the economy is shaping up generally."

Although this remark was music to Dulchester's ears, he did not want to waste time going over formerly trodden territory.

"Thank you," he said, showing some impatience at not being able to broach his own delicate matter. "But I have another matter which I wish to talk to you about, Ian."

"Yes?"

"A slightly delicate matter has come to my ears," said Dulchester, bravely plunging in.

"Hmm?"

"Well," continued David, "I have heard something which disturbs me slightly and I think you should be apprised of the situation."

"Hmm?"

These murmurs were beginning to unnerve Dulchester.

"Apparently there is some dispute about whether Gregory Tranter has ... shall we say ... misread the figures with regard to the Elisian delegation earlier in the year which has led to some speculation. "

"Hmm?"

Jepherson was not about to make things easy for Dulchester.

"It has come to my ears, as I said, that perhaps Fetherington, who is responsible for having the report to the ESIDR compiled, is defending his corner a bit too defensively."

"How did this information come to your ears, then, David?" enquired the PM.

Dulchester was relieved that Ian had stopped calling him 'old boy' and that he had ceased his infernal murmuring.

"Well, I did get wind of it from Simon Risborough, who seems to have his ear to the ground and has been looking into the matter with the help of others, such as young Leonard Fletcher, who is also serving on the committee."

"Hmm?"

Dulchester wanted to start a campaign for a statute which banned the use of 'hmm' from the English vocabulary. Anyone using it would be shot at dawn.

Having started, Dulchester continued. "I gather that at the last ESIDR meeting Ruth Angell raised the matter but it was summarily dismissed by Fetherington. Apparently Fetherington is maintaining that the sum in question is a backdated import duty but Risborough does not believe this assertion following his discreet enquiries. The question was left hanging in the air at the meeting, I gather. Pending an informal investigation, I believe. I am just a little concerned by what I have heard. And I thought I ought to just keep you in the loop."

Dulchester waited, somewhat economical with his outbreaths, and hoped that Jepherson would receive the news in good faith and treat it accordingly. He also trusted that the information would not do him any discredit personally but, conversely, that it would earmark him as a faithful servant of the big cheese. And please don't utter another bloody 'hmm' for Christ's sake!

Jepherson hesitated, adopted a frown of uncertainty and then played the give-nothing-away card.

Before another blooming murmur emanated from the PM, David felt that he ought to play his trump card now.

"Risborough also believes that there is a suspicion that Ruth Angell might have got some of her information from an outsider." David left this statement to permeate the air.

"I will look into it, David," was Jepherson's response to the problem. "Give my regards to Geraldine will you? You must both come round for dinner one night soon," he added dismissively.

Dulchester felt it expedient to beat a hasty retreat now and so he made an excuse about having to get some urgent papers off in the post that day. His cue to exit had been received loud and clear and it was obvious that the PM had reacted dramatically to this final pronouncement.

Both the PM and the Chancellor of the Exchequer were mighty relieved that their informal meeting had now concluded.

Dulchester bustled back to his office hoping that he had not blotted his copybook. He felt that he had acquitted himself reasonably well in the PM's eyes. And he had covered his powder in case anything should come of it. David, of course, suspected that there would be some fall-out from this in the fullness of time.

When Dulchester had first heard the news from Simon Risborough it had also fuelled his general suspicions about Fetherington and Tranter. More than once David had wondered whether Gregory Tranter had not, in fact, had his delicate fingers in the petty cash. Dulchester could trust Tranter no further than the nearest dog-stained lamppost. And Fetherington he would not trust with his grandmother's pyjamas.

Ian Jepherson took in some deep breaths and began to mull over his reaction to this unexpected news which had reached the throne of control.

Jepherson had wondered why Tranter had urged him to support the Elisian first minister's election campaign so vociferously but, at the time, he did not suspect any hidden agenda. But perhaps Tranter had accepted a backhander from Johann Finkelbaum and had then put pressure on him to respond accordingly? And where did Fetherington fit into the equation? Was the source of the trouble Fetherington or Tranter or both? Were they playing a double-blind game? Or were the figures quite justifiable? Were Ruth Angell and Simon Risborough trying to get at Fetherington as an innocent victim? Was Risborough attempting to promote himself by demoting Fetherington or even Tranter? The possibilities were endless. And why had David taken up the cudgels?

The electoral success was, Jepherson felt, based largely on the government's healthy bank balance but, if it was massively augmented by the Elisian government from under the table, the implications could be uncomfortable not only for the government itself but also for his position as the premier.

While backing the election campaign of a foreign power was not, in itself, a crime, it certainly would be if the kickback had not been openly declared and he had then made capital out of it during the election. The Balance of Payments, therefore, would have misrepresented the true position of the economy. And if the press had been down wind of this one, they could have themselves a field-day which would, at least, discredit the Tories somewhat in the eyes of an already sceptical public and a soon-to-be-disenchanted electorate in the wake of election fervour.

Normally Jepherson did not soil his hands with internal politics, the external ones were his main concern, but this time may have to be an exception. The PM continued to mull over the evidence. If rumours of this form of malpractice leaked to the press, moreover, Jepherson felt that he might be in a very parlous position personally.

But, if all this were true, how the hell could it be covered up or explained away? If the suspicion of a number of people outside the International Development Department had been aroused then the ticking bomb would snowball. This particular storm in a tea cup could prove to be a tornado and the repercussions for Ian would be very unwelcome. Jepherson squirmed at the prospect. And it would be extremely difficult to chloroform the press under any circumstances.

Jepherson brought himself out of his reverie because he felt that he wanted to let this one lie on the table before making any decision about what to do next.

> *Now we, who are admitted behind the scenes of this great theatre of nature (and no author ought to write anything besides dictionaries and spelling-books who hath not this privilege) can censure the action, without conceiving any absolute detestation of the person, whom perhaps nature may not have designed to act an ill part in all her dramas: for in this instance, life most exactly resembles the stage, since it is often the same person who represents the villain and the hero; and he who engages your admiration today, will probably attract your contempt tomorrow.*
>
> Henry Fielding
> *Tom Jones*

PART 3
PRINCE PARIS

"Oh, make yourself easy," she continued, laughing; *"however short a time I have to live, I shall live longer than you will love me!"*

Alexandre Dumas fils
The Lady of the Camellias

TITILLATION

James paid off the taxi and made his way up the steps of Les Patineurs on the Quai des Grands Augustin. The hotel was located between the Pont Neuf and the Pont Saint-Michel on the Left Bank of the Seine. As he strode into the hotel foyer, James felt as if he were walking on air with anticipation of a weekend of sheer sexual indulgence. This was going to be a weekend to remember.

Once in the hotel reception area, Fetherington suddenly realised that he did not know Verity's room number nor did he know whether she had booked a room, say, in his name, in joint names or just in her own. Fetherington could not, however, escape the watchful eye of the receptionist who had clocked him on arrival and the fact that he was carrying a travel-bag. So James was compelled to approach the desk rather than to pretend to be a non-resident.

James, however, assumed an artificial air of confidence which he certainly did not feel, acquired through his political training, as he got nearer to the girl on reception. He donned an air of aplomb as if he owned the establishment. The receptionist's welcoming smile, rosy lips and her snugly fitting top did not, of course, go unnoticed by the raunchy politician despite his apprehension.

In his best schoolboy French, he asked authoritatively for Miss Verity Baxter. James, of course, was more accustomed to having a bank of translators at his side for such occasions. The receptionist answered him in his native tongue much to Fetherington's annoyance. He was informed that there was no reply to Verity's line even though the receptionist had tried her number a couple of times.

Fetherington decided to go out on a limb by telling the receptionist that Verity's room had been booked for them both. The receptionist called over another man, who also spoke impeccable English, whom James took to be the hotel manager or, at least, someone similarly senior. These two officials then had a short conference in their native language. James, unfortunately, could neither overhear nor understand the import of their conference. Oh, hell! James glanced down rather crassly at his travel-bag. This situation was starting to become embarrassing. He prayed that the paparazzi were not rubber-necking around here.

Michel Gautier, the Head of Hotel Administration, turned to address James. He confirmed that Miss Baxter had indeed booked a double room but that she had not, as yet, specified the name of her companion. Gautier stated that he was reluctant, consequently, to show Monsieur Fetherington up to Mademoiselle Baxter's room until she had returned to acknowledge him in person.

Monsieur Fetherington was thus invited to wait in the bar for Mademoiselle Baxter's return. James felt that he had no alternative and so he retired to the elegant bar area which looked out on to the river. Fetherington fumed. He sincerely trusted that this degree of humiliation would be worth it. Apparently, Mademoiselle Bloody Baxter had not given any indication of when she might deign to return that evening.

James had made short work of a couple of glasses of gin and tonic while idly reading today's copy of *The Telegraph* which he had acquired at the airport. Uncertain whether to order another drink, James was just about to walk out of the hotel in disgust when he heard a familiar voice at the reception desk. He studiously ignored this voice, however, in his fury and maintained his seat, nonchalantly pretending to be engrossed in his newspaper rather than rushing out to greet Verity like a new-born lamb on springs.

Verity breezed into the bar and regaled him with excuses about why she had been delayed. James felt that her excuses were all pretty lame but he let it pass. She also gave him a warm kiss on his lips which promised much of what Fetherington was expecting of this weekend. He melted like an ice cube on a hot day as it is dropped into a glass of champers on a yacht moored in a Mediterranean marina. James lapped it all up like an obedient spaniel. Poor sod!

"Shall we go for an evening walk by the river?"

James was about as enthusiastic for such a proposal as a fart in a thunderstorm. But, despite his deflation, he nevertheless endeavoured to keep a lid on it and agreed to her titillating prevarication ploy.

Even at this relatively late hour, it was almost midnight, the streets were a hive of activity with street noises, jangling lights across the river and scores of people invested with summer madness.

Verity led James towards and across the Pont Saint-Michel and into the ancient Île de la Cité at the epicentre of the French capital. This island in the Seine was said to be where Paris was founded by ancient Gallic tribes, around the time of Julius Caesar's invasion, explained the knowledgeable Calendula. It was breathtakingly beautiful even though James had his mind on more important things. She did allow him to put his arm around her, as a consolation prize, while simultaneously holding her right hand which he frequently kissed. From this vantage point he could drink in her perfume, nuzzle in her hair, fondle the soft skin of her arms and shoulders and, of course, peer down her cleavage not so surreptitiously.

They wandered in an easterly direction along the Quai du Marché Neuf and down to the Promenade Maurice Carème, named after the Belgian poet, which led towards the Square Jean XXIII and Notre Dame Cathedral. The street lamps, the trees, the river, the boats, the night birds and the night sky gave an atmosphere of mystery and breath-taking beauty which fuelled James' fire even more ferociously.

They sat down for a short repose on the small parapet wall which bordered the river and listened to a busker serenading the tourists.

This adventure, of course, was a real ghostbuster for Calendula who relished the memory of her days as a resident of the city.

"You look worried, my dearest," Calendula suggested when they sat down beside the river. "Tell your Verity all about it, my darling. How's work?"

"Let's talk of something else, shall we?" James attempted to curtail this line of questioning but Verity was insistent.

"No, darling, tell me all about your week. You look exhausted, my poor sweetie."

Such attention from this beautiful creature had an uplifting effect on the politician who talked, in very general terms, of course, about pressures from people in the office and the intrigues which were a constant undercurrent of his work. James outlined, in very scanty detail, his visit to Throxfield, the Question Time episode, his meeting with Tranter and the reports which he was supposed to have read but had abandoned in favour of joining her for the weekend.

Verity affected great concern which went down well with the politician. James was relieved to note, however, that Verity took no real interested in what he was saying, throughout stroking his face and further arousing his longing, and she asked no further probing questions. The conversation about James' work was then dropped.

Calendula carefully noted that James had failed to mention anything to do with Ruth Angell or the Elisian accounts.

A busker began entertaining them with his latest repertoire and Calendula insisted on remunerating him accordingly. But James was still impatient for some action of a different kind. Could we, please, return to the hotel? For God's sake! I could do myself a permanent injury if we dally any longer.

Back at Les Patineurs, Verity engaged in more prevarication by claiming that she wanted a nightcap of Louis Jadot and a Breton crêpe stuffed with mushrooms, asparagus and spring onions laced with a tasty Bleu d'Auvergne sauce which she promptly ordered from the night porter. James admitted defeat and asked her to order for two. Fetherington, however, did enjoy the meal after his hasty egg and cress sandwich, an on-flight packet of biscuits and their walk in the night air.

The crockery, cutlery and wine glasses were, at last, cast aside and James finally decided that it was time to get tough whether the bitch liked it or not. He picked her up and threw her on the bed. Now I will have you, you tantalising dame, if it's the last thing I do. Geronimo! She responded.

And Verity did not disappoint. She gave James all and more than he had expected. And he didn't need any go-faster stripes on this occasion. Their first encounter was something of an over-and-done-with-in-a-trice affair because James could contain his ardour no longer. But their second union was a more lingering and sensually stimulating experience, the memory of which became encrusted on James Fetherington's soul for eternity. And her bleeding mobile phone never rung once!

Calendula, however, was unmoved by the experience but, as a consummate professional, she knew just how to deliver the goods which were designed to please. Calendula merely saw it as a means to an end but she could put on a good performance for the punters.

While James was doing his beached whale impression, she wondered how she might extract that vital snippet of information which she really needed from him. Did he or Gregory Tranter have their sticky fingers in the cookie-jar or were they both above reproach? Unlikely. What did James know which she could extract like a poisonous venom from the arm of a dying man? How would she next raise the subject of politics? Would he need another bottle or two more of Louis Jadot? Would she need to give him another dose of Parisian romance? Or remove him to Rome or Venice? Or could she just complete the job in a London luxury hotel? Or perhaps a country-house venue?

This nut had got to crack for the Medici Squad to make another killing. Calendula was at a problematic crossroads but she knew from experience that she had eaten little boys like James Fetherington for breakfast many times before and she would do it again.

INFILTRATION

Faye dressed as if she were off to an important business meeting duly clad in a smoky blue-green trouser suit with grey lace-up shoes and, of course, her briefcase.

There was not much traffic on the road because it was a weekend. She parked in one of the back streets which usually could supply her with free parking on a Sunday, insider knowledge of the area had secured this prize, and she made her way to the office in order to arrive in good time for a spell at her desk before lunch.

When passing the security guard's desk, she mentioned to Peter, the man on duty, that she was expecting a visitor at around 12.30 pm and she gave his name.

"Working overtime are you, Miss Windsor-Harris?"

"Unfortunately, yes. I have an urgent report to finish," she lied. "But it should not take long and I hope to have completed it by the time my visitor arrives for lunch."

"Don't work too hard then, Miss," warned Peter jovially.

Faye smiled and waved at Peter as she left the entrance hall and made her way up to her office on the third floor.

Faye turned on her computer and began to put the finishing touches to some statistics which she had been preparing for Guy Chaffinch in Innovative Enterprise. Her statistics were to comprise one of the appendices of the latest report for Chaffinch on *British Industry and the Impact of Technological Advancement.* A report of this nature was usually compiled every two years in order to keep abreast of the rapidly changing world of technology and computer software.

Faye's statistical analysis covered the introduction of new systems into the larger UK corporations and the rate of uptake and acceptance of their use. She was also compiling data on whether such changes had benefited the consumer and the employee and how technological innovation would affect the UK's export position. Some of the data had interesting results and far-reaching implications for the future in Britain but she longed for the day when sunnier horizons could be attained beyond her present employment for the government. Finally, when her statistics had been entered into the spreadsheet, checked and double-checked, she printed out a fair copy which she could pass to Ruth tomorrow.

It was now only 11.15 am and Faye had completed her outstanding work in record time.

She then used her time more productively in making some changes and adding some more words to her MSc dissertation, provisionally entitled *A Comparison of Current Trends and Economic Forecasting for International Trading in the First Half of the Twenty-First Century*, and expected to get ahead of schedule by this means. Faye had begun her dissertation with all guns blazing but she now was beginning to tire of having to undertake constant revisions at the behest of her tutor.

So Faye could not wait for this academic year to come to an end. The dissertation was due for final submission in October only a few months hence now. This day too was a much longed for event when she would be free to look around and to spread her wings. Faye also hoped now to be able to submit her work early and so be free of this particular ball-and-chain.

About an hour later the phone on her desk rang and Faye grinned with mischievous pleasure mingled with a soupçon of apprehension.

"Mr Damien North to see you Miss," announced Peter from the security desk at the main entrance.

"Oh, Peter, could you send him up in the lift and I will meet him up here when the lift arrives? I have not quite finished my report. I will vouch for him myself, of course."

"It is a bit irregular, Miss," said Peter somewhat doubtfully. He was a security man after all.

"Peter, surely you can trust me?" replied Faye in her most persuasive tones.

Peter relented. He was sure no harm could come of it.

"Well, all right, Miss, if you are sure. But can you ring me when he arrives safely on your floor?"

"Certainly. Of course, Peter."

Faye was so obliging and reassuring that Peter allowed her visitor to ascend in the lift but he personally ensured that the third floor button was pressed. Peter received another reassurance in the form of a confirmatory phone call from Faye within a few minutes.

Faye greeted Foxy with a sincere handshake and led him into her office. Foxy Ferguson came in dressed in a very smart but casual suit which looked as if he owned half of London yet did not want to give himself any airs and graces by dressing as if he were going to church before attending the Lord Mayor's banquet.

"I can drop the posh accent now, eh?" said Foxy.

"Yes, but be quick about your business, Foxy," she replied, steering him gently in the direction of Ruth Angell's document safe.

"Trust o' Foxy. You keep watch arrtside, gal and I'll 'ave this open as easy as cracking a walnut at Christmas."

Faye hovered in the corridor. She tied and re-tied her shoelaces more times than she could count while Foxy beavered away at his task with the stamp of the professional patently evident to the observer.

Ten minutes later a cry of delight reached her ears and, after checking that the coast was clear, she re-entered the office and watched while Foxy swiftly took photos with his digital camera of the relevant pages which she indicated. Foxy put the paper's back neatly in Ruth's desk-safe and checked that it looked as if it had never been disturbed.

"Job done, eh? I bet you tied up yer laces more times than most fellas 'ave 'ad 'ot dinners, eh, Faye gal?"

Faye began to feel a little more relieved now that Foxy's work in her office had been completed and their mission was, therefore, virtually accomplished. She locked up her desk and closed the office door as they left.

Foxy suddenly became the gallant gent who escorted her from the lift and bid security Peter a polite "Goodbye and thank you, sir," in his most convincing upper-crust accent.

Peter felt that no harm had been done by his dereliction of duty on this occasion. Poor sod!

Once free of the building, Faye and Foxy hugged each other joyfully and made their way to the appointed restaurant where Barrington was patiently waiting.

Barrington could see by the grins on their faces that success was in the air. A great deal of handshaking and hugging ensued between the three of them.

Barrington, who had collected the Fern Tree's menus on arrival, called the waitress over once they had made their choices. The waitress, Denise, was very taken by Barrington's gentlemen guest who played up to her in a way which she found refreshing. Foxy too decided to ask her for her number on the way out. When Faye and Barrington remarked on Foxy's attraction to Denise, he simply informed them that he was Foxy by name and Foxy by nature.

They ordered the specials of the day together with a carafe of house red for Faye and Barrington to share and a half-pint of lager for Foxy. The men both tucked into a spaghetti Bolognese while Faye consumed a fisherman's pie topped with mature cheddar.

Faye and Foxy related the events of the morning and the way in which they had circumvented security-conscious Peter. Foxy handed over the camera to Barrington who, after flicking through the photos, pocketed it with satisfaction.

Faye said that the relevant information was on page seventy-three of the report in question and that the photos also included some memoranda and emails which were humdingers. She agreed to talk Barrington through the figures once the paperwork had been printed out at his end. They agreed to do this at their next meeting which was scheduled for the next evening.

"You've both done a splendid job," proclaimed a delighted Barrington.

An envelope was passed to Faye and then one to Foxy. All at the table smiled with the utmost gladness.

When the triumvirate left the Fern Tree Bistro later in the afternoon, there was again much in the way of back-slapping, handshaking and hugging between all three of these relentless and unrepentant crooks.

Foxy spoke briefly to Denise as they left and pocketed her number, with a wink at his companions, and with a smile and a kiss blown in the waitress's direction as they walked away.

"Dirty bugger!" said Barrington to Foxy.

"Takes one to know one, yer know."

INTERROGATION

Sandra pitched up at the local Tory party headquarters in a rather defiant mood.

She was scheduled to meet with Helena Dartfield as part of the enquiry being conducted while Sandra was suspended from duty on account of her supposed defection and general disloyalty to the cause. Sandra wondered whether she had joined the Tories or the Communists by the way in which she was being witch-hunted and interrogated.

Sandra had been previously interviewed by a panel consisting of Harrison Smythe, the chief official, and two other senior party-workers at Westbury North HQ. At this meeting, Sandra had felt as if she had been put before the Spanish Inquisition prior to being dragged out to the auto-de-fé, having been proclaimed a heretic, to be consumed by the flames with uproarious cheers and leers from the crowd. The panel had declared that they would need to defer the decision about Sandra's future and pass the buck to Helena Dartfield who would make the final decision.

Sandra, however, had made several decisions of her own about her future with the party, or with any political party for that matter. She believed that working for party HQ, in virtually any capacity, was slave-labour for which they paid her peanuts. And she was not going to be a monkey any longer. Sandra had put in too many underpaid and unpaid hours and had taken too much crap from ministers and from officials who had authority over her. Her work was never appreciated despite the fact that meaningless platitudes had sometimes drifted her way in the form of meagre thanks.

Sandra had recently met one of her colleagues, Phyllis, who had become a fair-weather friend, for a morning coffee in order to discuss the situation. Sandra had thus learned that life was continuing as usual in the office and, in fact, Phyllis had been loaded with even more extra work since her colleague had left – again with very little thanks. Both women also felt that they were actually expected to feel grateful themselves for the privilege of being able to toil long and hard for the institution. Sandra also noted during their conversation that the corruption and the cheating had continued unabated during her period of absence.

Sandra, of course, wished to keep faith with the party in case she might need a reference when she began looking for a new job and so she had agreed to today's meeting with Helena Dartfield with more enthusiasm than she actually felt. She had, in fact, already applied for a number of local jobs but she was either not shortlisted or she was not keen on the position on offer.

Helena was waiting for Sandra in the main office when the suspended recalcitrant arrived.

"Sandra. Very nice to see you," said Helena, devoid of a smile. "Thank you for coming in." Hypocrite! Sandra smiled.

Sandra followed Helena into the office which the MP maintained in the Westbury North HQ.

Helena offered Sandra coffee from the machine outside her office but Sandra refused because she did not want any distractions during her so-called interview. Sandra noted with interest that she would have been expected to get the drink from the machine herself and to pay for it.

Sandra had never really liked Helena and was amazed when she had won her Tory seat at Westbury. But she managed, nevertheless, to tolerate Helena because she did not frequently make her presence felt in the part of the office in which Sandra had resided. Helena, moreover, very rarely appeared at all at the Westbury HQ and she only reacted when trouble was afoot. So Sandra had deemed it a privilege that Helena had felt it mattered enough for her to put in an appearance.

Sandra was prepared for a farce of an ordeal with Helena loaded with smiling condescension and total misrepresentation of the facts.

"Well," began Helena immediately, once they were seated, "you realise that a very serious accusation has been made against you and that this has caused some embarrassing press interest."

Sandra felt as if she had been brought before a high court judge who was stuffy and pedantic. She, however, remained silent for a while in the hope of wrong-footing her senior colleague. A pregnant pause, therefore, ensued.

Helena, of course, expected Sandra to instantly begin to grovel. But her calculation was mistaken. The pause continued for a moment with a smattering of embarrassment on Helena's part. Then the silence was broken.

"I thought that fuss had now been quelled as being unsubstantiated," retorted Sandra, somehow uncharacteristically brave in the presence of the head of the tribe.

"I have been looking into the facts and, it appears, that you have had meetings with members of the Labour party locally. And were seen by a local reporter," continued Helena.

"Yes, I went there to discuss a job they had offered me."

Helena was astounded as such brazen effrontery.

"A job? You went for a job with the Opposition? This is insupportable," she exclaimed.

"But I realised," continued the emboldened Sandra, "that the Opposition party is just as corrupt as the Tories."

"Corrupt!" Helena was in danger of losing it. "There is no corruption in this party, I can assure you!"

"No?"

"No!" Helena retorted emphatically. And then she took a slight backtrack. "I appreciate that it may appear so when we endeavour to put a positive spin on events. But that falls very far short of corruption."

"Like the affair you had with James Fetherington when he was still a married man?" enquired Sandra as cool as a cucumber which had just been slipped into a cocktail ready to be consumed by a fat-cat politician's wife. Sandra noticed the effect which she had engendered in her opponent.

Helena noticeably swallowed hard. She had no idea that her illicit affair with James Fetherington had ever reached as far as party HQ in Westbury North. God, did the entire bloody office know about this? Her affair with James had rotted her socks off at the time but it was relatively short-lived even for James or herself. Stormy and passionate as it was at the time, Helena had soon tired of Fetherington's constant need to appease his wife. The affair was over and done with, therefore, before it hit the press and so, Helena had thought, no harm had been done by her slight dalliance. Since James' separation and divorce from his wife, they had met from time to time but the firework became a damp squib really once it had been doused with the chemicals from a fire-engine's hose.

Helena became suddenly aware of the fact that Sandra had observed her blushes.

Sandra was bolstered by Helena's discomfiture and she was urged to continue on the attack rather than on the defensive. Quite out of character for the normally timid employee.

"I also know that you helped Fetherington to cover up the fact that certain trade-secrets had been sold to a foreign newspaper reporter in order to finance Gregory Tranter's election campaign. And you concealed the fact that Tranter helps himself to the petty cash when it suits him." Sandra, in fact, knew nothing of the sort but was merely testing the water. She drew breath in order to gauge the effect on Helena. Eureka!

Helena felt as if she were going to faint. How the hell did Sandra Mullingar, of all people, get news of that seedy little deal? And if someone like Sandra knew the score, then where did she get this information from? And who else knew? Was there another mole in the camp here or in London who had been feeding Sandra these tasty crumbs? Helena felt that she must acquit herself now without too much disgrace from this unpleasant mêlée.

But Sandra continued riding on the crest of the wave of her success. This was the first time that the simpering and mousy Sandra had ever managed to get a punch in below the belt.

"But, have no fear, I am not about to spill the beans to anyone else," she reassured her superior.

"Do I take it that you do not wish to continue in employment with us then?" demanded Helena, slightly changing tack.

Sandra, for the first time, realised that she could make some capital out of this situation and so she decided to trail her coat.

"I haven't yet decided," said Sandra trying to sound casual.

Helena began to sweat profusely. What could she offer this miscreant in order to keep her mouth permanently zipped without making it look like hush-money? She couldn't keep Sandra on the staff now obviously but there were no grounds really for an ignominious dismissal.

"Obviously, if you wished to leave our employment, we would be prepared to give you a sum in lieu of notice, particularly in view of the fact that you have been a long-serving employee." Helena omitted to say 'faithful employee' in the circumstances and Sandra noted this omission.

Sandra thought this would be a good idea but she wanted to secure a crisp deal.

"Six months' pay would be quite sufficient. Starting from today with immediate effect, of course. Plus a favourable reference. That would give me a chance to find another job now that I am no longer in my prime and I would, therefore, find it difficult to secure congenial employment elsewhere," she announced.

Helena was on the point of offering her the crown jewels.

"I should think that an arrangement of that nature could be accommodated," stated Helena guardedly. "Would you like me to take action accordingly?" She was now anxious to conclude negotiations and the interview forthwith.

"Why not? I think I would be prepared to accept those terms. Will you put that in writing?" asked Sandra now feeling that she was getting the better of the deal. She had only expected one month's payment in lieu of notice.

"Of course. I will get a letter out to you today together with your reference. But I must ask you, in addition, to sign a statement saying that you will not divulge to any outside party any information which you might have in your possession."

Sandra assented but tried to make it appear to be grudgingly. Sandra felt that she would sign the official secrets act with pleasure if it got her out of here with some dosh in the coffers. She had plans after all.

Sandra stood up decisively, thereby taking the initiative. Helena rose swiftly to her feet in sympathy but she felt powerless for once.

Sandra bid Helena a warm farewell, grabbing her hand and shaking it vigorously as if she herself were a politician. She walked out of the offices of the Tory headquarters in Westbury North for the last time with a Cheshire cat grin as if she could eat a banana sideways.

Helena Dartfield meantime ferreted around in her bag for her mobile phone in order to dictate a letter, a glowing reference and a legal statement, which needed to be despatched today, to her secretary. She then returned with all possible speed to the London office in order to sign the documents and to get the legal statement checked by the in-house lawyers. Helena could not wait to get this matter settled and then swept under the carpet for good.

Maurice was waiting for Sandra in the car just up the road. He had provided her with some of the scandalous information which she had hurled at Helena (apparently, he knew someone on the inside who worked in the London parliamentary offices). He was now waiting to take her for a slap-up lunch and another of those river-trips on a just-made-for-two motorboat.

Once on the vessel Sandra gave Rousel a full account of her meeting with Helena – what she had told Helena, what Helena had confirmed and what the outcome had been. Maurice smiled now because he realised that his fact-finding mission was probably complete.

Helena had confirmed apparently that a story had been sold to the press in order to finance Gregory Tranter's electoral campaign-trail. Prior to this moment it had merely been guesswork on Barrington's part but Sandra had managed to call Helena Dartfield's bluff. This was an additional snippet of information which Barry could possibly use. Maurice found that he actually had a growing respect for his latest little concubine.

DISCOMBOBULATION

Gregory Tranter had been called to the office of Ian Jepherson. He knew not whether to be honoured by being summoned into the presence or terrified of what the consequences might turn out to be.

But Tranter decided not to panic. He had received many smiles and tokens of encouragement from the PM recently and, therefore, he had nothing to fear.

Jepherson invited Tranter to take a seat and the PM ordered some coffee from his secretary, Christa Evans-Jenkins. Tranter felt encouraged by this gesture and the fact that Christa had given him a welcoming smile on his arrival on the fifth floor.

The PM was not one to indulge in pleasantries but he did enquire after Tranter's health according to the official code of social etiquette. Again Tranter felt that this was a good portent.

The coffee promptly arrived and Christa poured cups out for both ministers because she knew the preferences of each. Ian took his black while Gregory preferred a dash of cream. Neither, however, availed themselves of the brown crystals of coffee sugar which Christa had placed on Jepherson's desk, because both had reached the age when an excessive amount of simple carbohydrate was not generally a good idea. And, in any case, they both normally got their full quota of sugar from alcohol, making the excuse that socialising was a political necessity for an MP.

"Now about that report which has come to me on the Elisian delegation, Gregory" said Jepherson with a sense of purpose and tone of voice which made Tranter slightly uneasy. Gregory, however, had promised himself that he would keep calm and so he maintained his usual impassive front.

The PM did not wait for a reaction but continued his narrative.

"I have looked at the figures with regard to the Elisian delegation and there seems to be some query which I am sure you can easily iron out."

Tranter swallowed hard but remained silent and composed. How the hell had Jepherson heard about this discrepancy? Tranter was quite sure that he could not have worked it out for himself. Who's been telling tales out of school? Fetherington? He dismissed this idea as James had been covering up for him for years. Simon bloody Risborough, no doubt. That sneaky little crawler. Ruth Angell? Probably not enough in it for her to shop him.

"Query?" queried Tranter, assuming a puzzled frown.

Jepherson now went for the jugular.

"Yes, I have the figures here and this amount looks to me as if it is excessive. Can you actually account for it, Gregory?"

With a twizzle of his wrist, Jepherson swung the documentation on the desk round so that it faced Tranter full on. Tranter pretended to survey the data but he knew precisely the figure at which Ian would have been pointing without even looking. Things could be starting to get tough.

"Err ... This one here, you mean? Err ... Well, yes it does look a bit high." Tranter was stalling for time.

Jepherson had anticipated Tranter's reaction and plunged in now that he had got him on the back foot.

"I gather you and James have maintained that this figure includes a backdated import duty payment from Elisia," said Ian almost defiantly.

Tranter squirmed. *This was going to take some explaining obviously. And I had better come up with a satisfactory answer.*

So Gregory said, "Yes, Ian."

That, of course, was not the answer which the PM had expected to hear.

"Then why was the import duty put in the accounts for the Balance of Payments? Has it been duplicated here? Or has it got into the wrong set of accounts?"

Tranter realised that whatever answer he gave would be the wrong one. The question was of the have-you-stopped-beating-your-wife type. Gregory's cool was melting rapidly. Desperation stakes were beginning to lock in.

If Tranter admitted that the payment was in the wrong set of accounts, on the one hand, then the figures for the Elisian accounts would need to be adjusted. And then the figure would be disputed by the accountants, who had prepared the ledgers for the Balance of Payments, because they would have no record of having received any import duty payment and no evidence that an import duty was actually outstanding in the first place. *Blimey!*

If, on the other hand, Gregory agreed that the figure had been erroneously added to the Elisian delegation accounts by mistake then there would be a sum floating around in the bank account which could not be verified by the auditors.

Oh, hell! How am I going to escape this one? Poor sod! He felt like a timid maiden who had been attacked by a woman-eating tiger. He would have to stall for time while he thought out a solution to the problem. When the sum had been put in the Elisian delegation account, Tranter had believed that it would have gone unnoticed. But he now realised that it had, in fact, been spotted by all and sundry like a swarm of hungry hawks.

He resorted to another round of "Err ..." But the PM remained adamant in grilling him.

"It has reached my ears that the sum in question was a payment which your department had received from the Elisian government as their contribution to your election campaign," said a now-acerbic Ian Jepherson.

Tranter wanted to remind him that it was actually his, Jepherson's, campaign too.

"I shall have to investigate the matter, Prime Minister," said Tranter rather obsequiously, "and report back to you shortly."

"I have been told that it was a backhander from Johann Finkelbaum in exchange for your putting pressure on me to back his election campaign once we were in power," continued the PM undaunted and unconvinced.

"I did not put pressure on you, Prime Minister!" protested Tranter vehemently. "I merely advised that it might be an expedient move. But I had no hidden agenda in making this suggestion, I can assure you."

The gentleman doth protest too much. Jepherson noted Tranter's defensive strategy.

"Well, you had better get your story straightened out and report back to me, as you say, very promptly. I want to hear from you by the end of the week. Needless to say, this is not the kind of faux pas which I expect any of my ministers to make — least of all you. The consequences for the government might be very embarrassing if the news got abroad that we were in any way fiddling the books or taking backhanders from a foreign government without declaring it. I am sure you understand what I am driving at, Tranter. Making the International Development Department's position appear more favourable than it is cannot be condoned."

Tranter agreed that he had heard the PM and his purport loud and clear. Gregory silently noticed that the 'Gregory' had now been replaced by 'Tranter' which indicated his loss of favour with the PM. God please pick me up and transport me instantly from this office and away from Jepherson's gaze.

Strangely enough God granted Gregory Tranter his heartfelt request.

"That will be all for now. But, I repeat, I expect to have heard from you with a satisfactory explanation of that figure by the end of the week. At the latest. Is that clear?"

Gregory nodded and left the room with little of his dignity intact.

Tranter despaired of how he could satisfactorily explain himself or come up with a ruse which would satisfy Jepherson. Basically he was up the Suwannee River. And he knew it. But he would have to think of something bloody quick!

Jepherson knew that he had got Tranter by the short and curlies. But what could be done? That was the key question. Risborough had also told him that a journalist had got wind of the backhander theory and may have passed it on to Ruth Angell. Oh, hell! What a mess this would turn out to be for me personally let alone the Tories.

Jepherson, however, made up his mind, if it came to it, to maintain that the payment was a backdated import duty which had got into the wrong set of accounts. And, if he was then questioned about whether the sum in question should have appeared in the Balance of Payments account, he would simply say that it would not normally be recorded there. There was just a mistake in the accounts. Or something like that. He must have a word with some high-level accountants before he could make a final decision on what angle to take if necessary.

But at the next cabinet reshuffle, however, Tranter would certainly be assigned to another post.

REVELATION

They slept in quite late the next morning and, just as James was about to fire up the engines for another round of shadow-boxing, Calendula noticed the bedside clock.

"Oh, my God," she exclaimed. "I have to meet a client this morning at 10.30 am and I shall be late."

Fetherington was alarmed. He had not expected her to be working this weekend. Why did her bloody, fucking clients always manage to get in the way?

She knelt on the bed to kiss him affectionately before leaving him wanting. She withdrew from his arms and protestations before diving into the shower, dressing at lightning speed, flying out of the door, complete with portfolio, and heading for the lift.

James had to console himself with a miserable room-service breakfast and his memories of an unforgettable night. He believed that he had, at last, found a woman on whom he could shower all his attention and with whom he could gain a degree of sexual satisfaction which not many others had provided him with in the past. James hoped, therefore, that the night's encounter could be repeated on a regular basis for the foreseeable future. He was not really in the marriage market any longer but Verity would be the next best thing. It seemed, quite unusually, as if this particular dose of infatuation was not likely to wear off for James once his initial thirst had been slaked. Worrying but welcomed.

Calendula took a taxi to the Haute Muraille Hotel on the Rue Norvins near the Place du Tertre in the eighteenth arrondissement (administrative district, to you) in Montmartre. The hotel was only a stone's throw away from the famous Basilica of the Sacré Cœur and the Lapin Agile.

"I have missed, my lion cub, ever so much," she announced as she entered the room which she and Barrington had booked into early yesterday afternoon.

"Poooooochie, how wonderful to see you. You managed to escape then? How did you get on?"

Calendula explained that James had talked about his work in vague terms but that the main thrust of her information-gathering expedition had still to occur and that it would probably take her some time to subtly prize this treasure out of him. Barrington, of course, was confident of her infallible success-rate in this field.

They took a stroll into the Place du Tertre to see some of the pavement artists there. For Calendula it was a real trip down memory lane and a chance to meet old acquaintances dating back from the time when she had lived and worked in Paris. She was greeted by some old friends with French hugs and kisses and Barrington was acknowledged similarly as her life-partner now that she had attained an elevated position in the art world. Calendula felt that she would never forget her many Parisian friends from former days and times. With some she discussed their latest work on sale and some the new paint-application techniques which were coming into vogue for artists everywhere.

Because there was a surfeit of tourists and, consequently, punters a-plenty, Calendula and Barrington withdrew to avail themselves of a mid-morning coffee in one of the street cafés in the square.

The couple then returned to their hotel for lunch. They chose the hotel special of the day consisting of a delicious vegetable potage followed by a poulet au citron en papillote which exhibited traditional French cuisine in all its glory.

James Fetherington, meanwhile, took a saunter along the Quai des Grands Augustins and southward down the Rue des Grands Augustins for want of anything better to do while Verity was away from him. He was pining for his new-found lady-love all the while. Poor sod!

James decided to purchase a travel-guide so that he could augment his scanty knowledge of Paris in order to impress the knowledgeable Verity on her return.

He sat and consumed a baguette with tuna, chives and olives and a glass of sparkling rosé in one of the street cafés and read his guidebook. James learned that the Rue des Grands Augustins was in the administrative quarter of Saint-Germain-des-Prés in the sixth arrondissement of Paris. Here Louis XIII, who had reigned as King of France from 1610 to 1645, had received the sacrament one hour after the assassination of his father. A plaque here had commemorated this historic occasion and James, therefore, went in search of this tourist attraction which he duly located at the top end of the street.

The building which held the plague was now a double Michelin-starred restaurant, Le Relais Louis XIII, and on its outside wall James read the famous inscription, although, of course, he would not have been able to translate it without the help of his faithful travel booklet.

Ici, le jeune Louis XIII
fut intronisé, une heure après
la mort de son père Henry IV.

James decided that it would be a great surprise for Verity to be wined and dined in such an august establishment this evening. Accordingly he enquired about booking a table and, because of an unexpected last-minute cancellation, his wish was granted and a table for 7.30 pm was duly secured.

James was also interested to discover from his travel-guide that the philosopher and political economist, Pierre Leroux, who had first coined the term 'socialism' in the eighteenth century, had lived somewhere hereabouts.

Fetherington returned to the hotel mid-afternoon. But Verity was only half an hour late on this occasion and so he was not too enraged.

They took afternoon tea in the hotel lounge while Verity outlined what had occurred at the meeting with her client. She had secured a very lucrative contract for some more work but this would mean that she would have to remain in Paris until midweek in order to tie up the contract and to arrange for payment. Fetherington was marginally disappointed that they would not be travelling back together tomorrow evening. He, of course, had to get back to the chalk-face for an urgent meeting first thing on Monday morning.

Le Relais Louis XIII was an excellent choice, mused James. Not only did it live up to his expectations but it actually far exceeded them. Their fine-dining experience was a perfect celebration for the politician and his new conquest and an excellent precursor to another night of bliss.

Verity chose a sea bass quenelle with a champagne sauce as a starter with roasted duck and candied apricots for the main course. Fetherington decided on potted lobster to begin but joined Verity with the duck to follow. James also ordered a bottle of Puligny Montrachet to drink with their main meal and another of Philipponnat Grand Blanc not only to accompany their dessert but also as a lingering after-dinner drink while their meals were subsiding. He endeavoured to order this wine with the poise of an expert in French wines but, in fact, he knew relatively little about wines of this region and, therefore, just trusted that his choices were apt for the occasion. Verity effected not to noticed his bluff but she was, of course, good at duping the punters.

Calendula smiled. This is going to cost him a tidy little packet. She consumed her meal with much appreciation.

They sauntered back to Les Patineurs full of epicurean comfort and satisfaction. They walked in an interlocked embrace again much to the delight of Fetherington who felt this augured well for the near future.

James was looking forward with eager anticipation to another night to remember. Would she really let her hair down again and satisfy his insatiable lust? Would she really show a bloke a good time?

Calendula was, simultaneously, wondering how she was going to winkle the jackpot out of this particular mark. Was he going to be a hard nut to crack perhaps? Or would he simply roll over and deliver the goods? Would she have to spend a protracted amount of time garnering his trust and becoming his confidante? It was not yet in the bag but, when it was, it would be worth all the time she had invested and the hard work which she had expended.

Back at the hotel Fetherington got the prize he had been longing for all evening. Calendula was on top form and drained him dry of the seeds of procreation repeatedly. He was a smitten creature, a suppliant in her embrace, enfolded by her power and mystique. The secrets of her body he uncovered constantly throughout the remainder of the night which lifted him to a level of ecstasy little known formerly if ever at all. It was as if an angel had wrapped him in a silver shroud and transported him to heaven.

"You exquisitely beautiful creature," he declared. "I wish we could share a bed every night. I have so much stress and turmoil to contend with on a daily basis that interludes such as this are unparalleled."

This was Calendula's cue to engage her brain and pole-vault into action.

"My darling," she said stroking his cheek again, redolent of the previous evening. "What troubles do you have? You do not have a wife? You do not have money worries surely? Are you not happy at work perhaps?"

He took the bait, hook line and sinker.

Fetherington told her of all the hassle he got from his boss, still not mentioning any names, of course, and the fact that there was much in the way of backhanders and double-dealing around the office. James even admitted that some bribes had been given and received. He confessed that he suspected his immediate line manager of misrepresenting the figures in connection with some dealings with Elisia. And that someone else in the office had got wind of this underhandedness and was giving him a hard time. He neglected to mention, of course, that this someone was actually female and that he had fancied the pants off her. This depth of detail could easily be omitted from his narrative.

Fetherington noticed that Verity appeared to have fallen asleep during his discourse and he was relieved that she had not been party to his revelations. James then settled himself down for a nourishing and restorative night's rest after all his hard work.

Calendula smiled to herself as James drifted into slumber and she settled down for the night with a great feeling of satisfaction at the prospect of a job well done. And she looked forward to the financial reward which she and Barrington would deservedly enjoy together in the not too distant future.

By unburdening his soul, however, Fetherington had signed his own death warrant.

PENETRATION

One of Jules' favourite London haunts was the Soho Spa Experience in the heart of the red-light district. Such a seedy side of the capital was familiar territory to Jules who often wished to nurture his taste for the underworld.

The receptionist did not recognise him because he had not visited for some time, now that he resided mostly in Morocco with Hakim, and there was frequently a high turnover of reception staff in the joint. Usually a receptionist would stay for only a couple of months before moving on to a classier establishment which was not raided by the fuzz quite so frequently.

Jules got himself a massage from a suitably dodgy masseur before retiring to the lavender-infused sauna like a wolf on the prowl who is salivating at the prospect of acquiring a partner for the night. This routine was now almost second nature to Jules Axminster who had perfected the art of looking innocent yet utterly inviting in the eyes of his selected quarry.

The sauna was very considerable and considerate in that it had several small sections separated from the larger main body of the room. In one corner of one of the mini-recesses, Jules chose a seat accidentally on purpose next to an older member of society who appeared to be ready for some high-jinks. Jules allowed his leg to brush his target and then indulged in profuse apologies just to keep up the thinly-veiled pretence. He then waited until everyone else in the near vicinity had vacated the sauna either with their chosen partner for the night or to seek tastier goods in the steam-room or in the Jacuzzi where footsie was a regular pick-up routine.

Jules now turned to his intended victim and commenced his onslaught.

"It's great in here, isn't it? I really needed this after such a long and tiring day," he declared as if to no-one in particular.

The lure was heartily accepted.

Jules learned that his compatriot, Colin, was a security man who was currently doing contract work for a number of firms via an agency in London. Surprise! Surprise!

Jules mentioned that he was unemployed at present and that today he had traipsed all over London desperately trying to find work of any description.

Colin told him about the way in which he had become a security guard and how Jules might be able to do the same. It would, of course, mean having to do nightshifts but Jules said that he wouldn't mind doing nights at all.

"I was with the police for a couple of years. But I have been abroad a lot recently," said Jules, "and I am not sure whether that would count against me."

"No," reassured Collin, "They take on anyone these days because they are desperate to get reliable people for unsociable hours. And I could put in a good word for you at the agency."

"Well, my name is Terry Reynolds," said Jules, introducing himself officially to Colin. They shook hands and knowingly looked into each other's eyes.

When back in the changing rooms, Jules smiled when Colin wrote down the number of Safe as Houses, a security recruitment agency in north London. But Jules thought he ought to reward Colin for his services and so he took him back to his somewhat uninteresting but clean hotel room near King's Cross where they didn't ask too many questions as long as you paid the bill in advance.

Thus it was that Jules Axminster marched into Safe as Houses a few days hence for his appointment with senior recruitment consultant Caroline Willborough.

"Good morning, Mr Reynolds, err ... Terry, do take a seat," began Caroline. "Thank you for coming in. We received a copy of your c.v. yesterday. Thank you. Very impressive."

Jules took a seat as he was bidden and waited for his interview to commence. He tried to look unintelligent.

"Did you bring your references, Terry?"

"Yes, I have them here," Jules said as he produced an expertly forged sheaf of papers from an envelope.

"We shall need to check them out, of course," Caroline reminded him. "But Colin Downham speaks very highly of you and that will go a long way towards getting you on to our books."

Jules smiled gratefully at this news but it surprised him not at all considering that Colin had got his money's worth a couple of nights ago.

"Yes, but when can you let me know whether you can employ me? I have been abroad for a while recently tending to a sick relative in Italy and I need to get some sort of job pretty soon."

"I understand. And we shall do our very best for you. But, of course, we do need to follow the correct procedures, you know. We are very security-minded here!" Caroline bantered. Jules smiled courteously, although he was not amused at all by the feeble joke.

"And will it count against me that I have been out of the country for nine months?"

"Not at all, Terry. The fact that you have been in the police for a spell will count in your favour."

Caroline Willborough, of course, was someone who wanted to earn commission for herself and, therefore, turning a blind eye to an absentee employee was not beyond her scope. Indeed she was not as fussy about taking up Terry's references as she made out. He looked a fairly intelligent fellow and so why not collect a hefty agency fee regularly for his services.

"Most companies are desperate for staff these days. You are aware that we are talking about nightshifts, aren't you? And it can be a very lonely occupation," she added.

Jules actually preferred to work during the night rather than the day. It was the time when he was most active and he could probably look at some porn on the net to while away the long midnight hours or he could hack into another bank's computer server when the overnight update of customer accounts was being run.

"Will I be working alone?" enquired Jules. "Not that I mind, of course."

"Sometimes, Terry. It depends on the size of the firm. The banks and government departments, for example, usually require two men at night but the smaller commercial firms only need one man on duty."

"I see."

"Well, all that remains is for me to check out your references and to carry out our usual set of security procedures and then I will let you know what work we can offer you. You should hear from us by the end of the week. Thank you again for coming in to see us."

And there the interview concluded.

Sure enough, on Friday of that week, a phone call from Caroline was received by Jules on his mobile to tell him that the agency could offer to keep him in gainful employment for the foreseeable future. Caroline also wondered if he could start work on Sunday night at a local firm of solicitors in the city and Jules readily agreed.

This assignment proved an interesting place for Jules to work. During his week's stretch at this city firm of solicitors, Jules was again contacted to see if he would be willing to join Colin on a job at the government offices in Whitehall for the following week. Jules acquiesced. He looked forward to spending a night or two with Colin as well as having a sniff round the offices too.

After some distraction in the gents' loo, Jules told his partner that he would do his customary rounds of the Whitehall building and took with him his mobile phone in order to remain in communication with Colin, if necessary, while peripatetically surveying the premises.

Jules made a cursory inspection of the first and second floors and then made his way up to a certain office on the third floor where he managed to download the entire contents of a particular PC hard drive, which just happened to be left behind in the office on that day, on to his high-capacity memory-stick.

After completing his superficial surveillance of the fourth and fifth floors, Jules returned to Colin with the news that all was well in the state of Denmark and that it was proving to be a quiet night.

Once back in his seedy hotel room, Jules inspected the fruits of his night's labours and was decidedly pleased with the results. The entire contents of his memory-stick was swiftly shipped across to a laptop computer with the same specification as the one from which the original had been taken. This computer was then sent via a security company (oh, the irony!) to be delivered early the next morning. He then made a phone call to warn of its arrival and agreed to talk the recipient through the implications of his findings when necessary.

Jules rang the Safe as Houses agency the next day to inform them that he bitterly regretted the fact that he would have to cease employment with them with immediate effect because his aging relative in Italy had unfortunately taken a turn for the worst.

Caroline was sympathetic to his reasons for leaving their employ, reluctantly bid him farewell and reiterated her assurance that a job for Terry would always be available with Safe as Houses should he ever wish to return to the UK in the future. Terry would be a sad loss to the agency, Caroline assured him. And Jules reciprocated Caroline's feelings of sorrow and disappointment and said adieu for the foreseeable future.

Jules would shortly be back with Hakim as a much richer and more contented man.

CONSOLIDATION

When Calendula returned from France, she and Barrington decided that it was high time for a meeting of the board of directors of the Medici Squad.

Calendula had been playing on the swing in the garden which Barrington had erected for her while she was still in Paris. The pond was still a glint in Barrington's eye, however, but he had secretly made arrangements for it to be built in due course when Calendula was next away.

Barrington had had a great time tidying up the garden and gathering some of the produce which he had grown while waiting for Calendula's return. Barrington had made some pickles and apple purée from the garden produce and he had made up some packs of red chard and broccoli which he then froze for later use. Barrington also made several batches of cheese straws which were similarly consigned to the freezer.

Barrington had, moreover, caught up on his piano practice while Calendula was away but the Beethoven sonatina was not really improving much.

Barrington had been forced to leave Paris before Calendula in order to tie things up with their employees, such as Faye, Foxy, Maurice and Maisie, in London before returning to their country estate in Grove Naxton Cross.

Calendula had meanwhile remained in France to see a couple of her clients and to meet up with her daughter Chantal. They had spent a jolly time discussing the latest fashions and inspecting the creations which Chantal had produced for the fashion-design house for which she worked.

Barrington collated the documentation which they had received and then summoned his beloved to the patio for the meeting. They sipped his mulled wine and munched on some chestnuts which Barrington had roasted in their cast-iron fire-pit barbecue.

"Item one. Fetherington has delivered the goods which will be the key to the whole enterprise now I think," said Barrington eager to tie up their current assignment.

Calendula agreed and reiterated her summary of what she had gleaned from the lecher in Paris about the fact that he had been covering up for Gregory Tranter who had engaged in double-dealing with Johann Finkelbaum in Elisia. They both agreed that the backhander in itself was not a crime but the fact that it had been concealed from the electorate prior to the election was. Barrington also speculated as to whether Jepherson, the PM elect, knew of the situation and whether this theory could be verified.

"But," interjected Calendula, "it has been."

"What?"

"That memo emailed from Tranter to Fetherington confirms it. Jepherson knew of the scam."

"My God, you are absolutely right, poochie," replied Barrington riffling through the papers which he had printed out the previous evening from Jules' hoard of goodies. "That can be our exhibit A."

Calendula agreed again.

"And don't we now have confirmation that Tranter's double-dealing with the Elisian government has resulted in the financial cover-up over the latest budget figures and the Balance of Payments account," said Barrington almost to himself as he looked over the financial statements. Barrington's knowledge of corporate accounting was sufficient to detect this proof and to be able to make it stick.

"But what happened to the journalist to whom Tranter sold some trade secrets?" interrupted Calendula.

"We may not need to go into detail about that," suggested Barrington, "but I will include it in our findings and let Turner decide whether we need to follow it up in any way."

"If you say so. It would be nice to get this thing wrapped up so that we can go on holiday," ruminated Calendula.

"And the fact that Fetherington also knows that Tranter has syphoned off some funds from the petty cash before now. That can also be submitted," Barrington continued.

"But is it there in the documentation?" Calendula was playing devil's advocate here in order to make sure that they had covered all the bases.

"Well, no, actually. But can we not forward what we have and let Ronald ask for additional stuff as required?" Barrington asked. "There certainly are some spurious figures in the International Development department's accounts which could be questioned and used as evidence perhaps."

"OK, cos what we have is enough to hang him anyway, I suppose," concluded Calendula.

They remained silent for a minute or two, each letting their thoughts reconcile. Barrington checked through the paperwork again and assembled it into a logical order while Calendula merely let her brain do the deliberation. At last they decided that they had enough documentation to send off to Ronald Turner and, more importantly, to get paid.

Then Barrington came up with a further suggestion as a result of his musings.

"Maisie will leap into action shortly and I will tout this all around the houses later. We can get Jean Paul out of the equation quite conveniently. Maisie can put a pill in his afternoon herbal tea," laughed Barrington. "But we might also mention Fetherington's ding-dong with Helena Dartfield, during his marriage, when we provide some follow-up details. I got this confirmed by Maurice."

Calendula was very pleased with this development. It would mean some ready cash any day now. "And Helena can be taught a lesson for her treatment of Sandra Mullingar. Another bonus," she added.

"Talking of Sandra ... I only have to check with Maurice that we can go ahead and then it will be all systems go," said Barrington. "That will be the final nail in the coffin, of course."

"Can you not get hold of him then?"

"I am waiting for him to come back to me now."

"And then we can plant the bomb?" Calendula ventured.

Barrington considered and then it was his turn to agree with her.

They both murmured with satisfaction at their achievements, the justice which they would exact and, of course, the financial rewards. That was item number two on the agenda sorted.

"But we must keep Ruth out of the equation. She has suffered enough, lion cub," said Calendula.

They both agreed then.

"Not sure how we are going to manage it, however," stated Barrington.

"I do. I know of someone who had a goodly dose of counselling which changed her life and she is looking for someone to rescue as a friend."

"Let's do it."

Calendula picked up the phone.

Barrington changed the subject when she had finished her conversation.

"Do we need to do anything about Ian Jepherson in this campaign?" he asked.

"No, just let him suffer."

"But we have got Faye sewn up, haven't we," Calendula enquired.

"Yes, I have been on to Henry already."

"So we are just about there then."

"Yeah! Do you fancy a shower poochie?"

"No, darling, not again! But I would like another trip to the Peacock's Feather though."

"Anything for my beautiful poochie panda."

PROCLAMATION

Barrington called a morning meeting of the clans in order to ply his wheeler-dealing trade.

He hired a meeting room at the Hotel Russell in Russell Square in London for the occasion and then made a series of phone calls to members of the press. His invitation was gratefully accepted by all contacts.

The invitees comprised the leading luminaries of *The Sun, The Mirror, The Daily Mail* and *The Daily Express*.

The invitations had been issued with an inkling of a story which could be emblazoned across the front pages of the tabloids but the deal clearly stipulated that money would be needed up front before any information could be imparted. The press accepted this stipulation knowing the reputation of Barrington Flint and his associates.

Drinks were ordered by the invited guests despite the early hour but cigarettes were of necessity left unlit. Hotel house rules about non-smoking were very strict and strictly enforced even for sub-mortals.

Barrington had brought a large briefcase to the meeting in anticipation of a full house of journalists. And he was not disappointed. His case was soon filled with plentiful supplies of used notes.

Barrington spoke to the collective assembly of newspaper men and women of the antics of an international corporate lawyer who had repeatedly accepted backhanders and bribes in order to bring acquisition and merger talks to a satisfactory conclusion for the party who had commissioned the deal.

Barrington also issued an information pack to each delegate which consisted of bank statements, email correspondence, recorded telephone conversations and Skype meetings. Some of this information could have been easily disputed by any pedantic barrister in court but the assembled company were not that fussy. They were used to being sued and had an ample budget for such nefarious activity. The press, moreover, knew from experience that certain parties would not even consider litigation in view of the degree of exposure, together with limitless detailed further investigation, that such court proceedings would inevitably entail.

The paparazzi licked their lips when hearing and seeing the foundation for tomorrow's breaking news. They felt the money which had speculatively been invested in Barrington was certainly a bargain which would pay handsome dividends.

After much hand-shaking and back-slapping and, in the case of the female journalists, a discreet peck on the cheek, the press conglomerate left in order to attack their laptops and tablets. Once outside the hotel the fag-packets were brought to the surface once more.

The next day the headlines vibrated with outstanding news and snapshots and blow-ups of Wendell.

The Express stressed the demise of legal practice in the UK with an article headed 'Can You Trust Your Lawyer These Days?' which berated the legal profession and cited examples of other occasions when lawyers had duped their clients. British justice was obviously going downhill fast and had been doing so for some time.

The Sun began with 'Wendell Wonders How He Got Caught' and this article outlined the way in which the lawyer was trapped by getting over-confident and going too far. He had not quit while he was ahead. Poor sod! Another smaller article, entitled 'Shyster Not Work-Shy', in the same daily sketched the way in which Wendell had been tracked down but no sources were, of course, revealed.

The Mail took the angle of 'Backhanders are Backstories' and this news too tracked Wendell's discovery. This editorial also reported on the falling standards in the legal profession and it called on the government to intervene in order to get British justice buoyant again as a force with which to be reckoned.

The Mirror merely responded with 'GMC Housed a Traitor to British Justice' and questioned the way in which a supposedly respectable firm of lawyers could allow one of their senior partners to become a double-dealing agent. This paper also speculated about who else in GMC might have known and this conjecture caused a lot of embarrassment for the firm which they never really managed to live down.

Piers' misdeeds were enumerated by all the gutter-press in meticulous detail and most newspapers quoted from emails and recorded telephone transcriptions with Felix Taynton among others.

The history and growth of Galbraith, Minchin and Claxton worldwide was recounted by many of the tabloids and the initials GMC were likened to the General Medical Council who were similarly maligned as tricksters.

The broadsheets, other provincial newspapers and television crews were also galvanised into action and took up the cudgels by taking residence outside the offices of Galbraith, Minchin and Claxton, Grant Houghton Pharmaceuticals and Wyatt Enterprises.

Comments were sought from Piers himself but he was obviously camera-shy and confined to barracks in Market Drayton.

Mariella, living temporarily in Norfolk, told a few pressmen that she had always suspected that her estranged husband was a fraud and that she had, therefore, left him some while ago as a result of her conclusion. But, she claimed, she knew nothing of the details.

Felix Taynton was also not available for comment but a press release denied any involvement in any sort of deal with the opposition lawyers for the takeover of his organisation by Wyatt's. Felix was, of course, secretly glad that the takeover deal had now gone ahead but he did fear that his position might deteriorate within the new organisation. In time his fears were justified. Sally Plumley, however, remained miraculously unscathed as an ex-employee of GMC.

Wyatt's lawyers, Liarbridge Law Practice, who came in for a lot of stick over the latest news, maintained that the firm too might have been duped by an unscrupulous client in the guise of Felix Taynton. But the wording of this statement was suitably couched in legal jargon that it really admitted nothing. Harvey Grimshaw and Jack Siskins of Liarbridge Law Practice took an impromptu and lengthy vacation once the news broke in order to avoid having to face the music and, fortunately, they were not tracked down for their comments.

Adelina Murphy and Kadienne Patrell of Wyatt Enterprises, similarly, would make no direct comment to the assembled press contingent but a press spokesman stated that the Murphy and Patrell team bitterly regretted that they had been so ignominiously deceived by GMC over the acquisition deal. It was also suggested that Wyatt's were considering taking legal action against Wendell and GMC but nothing further was heard of this intention. Trial by journalism was rife in the US, of course.

Jason Cunningham of Wyatt's in the UK, who had originally recommended Wendell's services to the New York office, claimed that he knew nothing about any misconduct on the part of his former legal advisors, GMC.

Other outfits, such as the advertising agency, Braithwaite and Kelleridge, and the transportation company, On The Road, simply held their breath and hoped that the axe would not fall in their direction.

Wendell managed to escape being sued by Wyatt Enterprises who decided that the adverse publicity which any court case would throw up would undermine its position in the marketplace. But the international Fraud Squad sent Wendell off for a spell in clink.

Mariella's divorce and her financial settlement went through uncontested like a dose of salts once the news of Wendell's financial misconduct broke across the globe and his career as a lawyer was assuredly at an end. Mariella got more money than she had ever hoped to benefit from. Her life changed markedly as a result. Mariella kept the house in Market Drayton, bought a new car and retained her priceless jewellery collection which she later sold at auction. Guy Peregrine, her solicitor, was well satisfied with his remuneration.

Nicholas never resurfaced but then Mariella didn't much care because, by this time, she had met a younger man when she treated herself to a round-the-world cruise. They settled down together in another location, far from Market Drayton, for the rest of their natural and happy days. Willow Cottage was rented out to a wealthy American and this provided her with even more disposable income.

Piers was forced to resign as a partner in GMC, of course, but the good news was that he found that some of the investments which he had secreted away, even from Mariella and that nosey-parker bastard solicitor Guy Peregrine, were enough to live on satisfactorily in a newly acquired apartment near Athens. He mixed successfully with the villagers and even indulged in some petty schemes for helping the locals to evade tax in his chosen domicile. Once a discovered crook always only a slightly reformed man.

EMANCIPATION

"Hello, Andy, you old bugger! How's tricks?"

Andrew Ormerod had answered his mobile phone in a hurry, without looking at the incoming number, but he instantly recognised the familiar voice. The mobile phone which he kept in his briefcase was the one he used exclusively for work. He wanted no-one to be able to record either incoming or outgoing calls as the land line on his desk would do.

"Barry! Barry ... you bloody old sod! Great to hear your voice."

"Got some action for you."

"Have you now?"

Ormerod knew that when the most notorious informant in London said those words it would certainly be worth listening. He gave Barrington his full attention.

"I'm interested."

"I can raise the bar for you on that Elisian matter." Barrington came straight to the point.

Ormerod drew breath and was silent for the count of three.

"Can we have a drink after work?" asked Andrew.

"Might not be a bad idea? Tonight or tomorrow?"

"Either. You choose."

"I'll meet you in the Braided Duck at 7.00 pm tomorrow. Upstairs. OK?"

"Right on. 7.00 pm it is."

Andrew Ormerod, the Editor of the 'News in Parliament Today' page of *The Times*, had been struggling for some while to get a lead on the fact that the Tories had possibly taken a backhander from the Elisian government which was undeclared at the time of the general election. One of his best investigative reporters, John Griffiths, had been working undercover for the Elisian government, when his paper had suspected the scandal. John had heard about this situation virtually straight from the horse's mouth but he had then failed to obtain any documentary evidence to prove it. As Ormerod could not afford to spare Griffiths for any longer, he called him back to London and regretfully allowed the situation to fester.

Andrew had been reluctant to mention anything of Griffiths' findings in the press but he realised that it would be a great scoop if they could substantiate his discoveries. A less scrupulous journalist in the populist press would simply fill in the blanks and risk being sued by the foreign government but Ormerod needed written proof not only in order to avoid court action but also to be able to maintain the reputation of the paper as an ethical broadsheet in the eyes of their intelligentsia readers.

So it was with great curiosity that Andrew went to meet Barrington on the following evening in the Braided Duck in Tooley Street after a twenty-minute walk which the fitness-freak Ormerod took at every opportunity. Although he felt a lot better for his new fitness regime, after keeping it up for almost a year now, he had failed miserably to lose any significant amount of weight which was Andrew's original intention.

Andrew arrived at the Duck slightly out of breath and a slap on the back from Barrington exacerbated this condition somewhat but not as much as it might have done a couple of months ago.

The men exchanged pleasantries about their respective partners, Calendula and Maureen, and then got down to the serious business of putting some drinks down their throats. Barrington downed a scotch on the rocks but Andrew, more abstemious, opted for orange juice which he promptly diluted with water. Barrington ragged his friend about his fitness regime and abstinence from the pleasures of life.

Finally the meeting commenced in the privacy of the upstairs room in the pub which Ormerod was able to obtain for a small fee to the landlord whenever a conference behind closed doors proved to be a necessity.

"I gather you had young John Griffiths out in Elisia?" began Barrington.

"How the hell did you know that?" replied a moderately startled Ormerod who was unable to keep his thoughts to himself. Was there nothing that this crook did not know? And how the hell did he discover this one? But it augured well for what might be revealed this evening of which he could probably make splendid use.

Barrington ignored the question.

"Well, I think you would need to substantiate your suspicions with some hard facts," continued Barrington casually. He observed the change in Andrew Ormerod and liked what he saw.

"Go on," said Andrew smiling at the cunning old fox. "What have you got for me then?"

"The documentary evidence, of course," replied Barrington even more casually and still monitoring the effect of his words.

"Perhaps we should have another meeting very soon then?"

Barrington murmured and nodded.

"Why not come and have supper with us and bring Cal, too, of course? Are you free on Friday evening?"

"Sure!"

The men negotiated terms and times for their supper meeting.

Supper was, as anticipated, a meagre affair because, much to the chagrin of Calendula and Barrington, Maureen was no cook. But sometimes they had to suffer a bit of hardship for the cause. Over the years Calendula and Barrington had become close acquaintances of Maureen and Andrew Ormerod and they had learned to tolerate the suppers at their house. Andrew had never learned to cook either, unfortunately. Barrington silently chuckled. No wondered Andrew was on a fitness regime. Probably that would be the best option in the circumstances for him.

Whenever possible Calendula and Barrington had been the hosts but this ploy only served to increase Maureen's embarrassment at her lack of culinary skills. And so they had dropped the tactic and learned to grin and bear it in silence at the dinner table. At least they knew what to expect.

The first course was some kind of leek soup which obviously came out of one of those supermarket paper-packets with a bit of cream added on top and some bread rolls to make it look authentic. But the Medici Squadron were not fooled. The main course was a mysterious concoction of mince and vegetables with some baked potatoes – Maureen could manage those reasonably successfully – and obviously frozen spinach. The dessert was a homemade chocolate gateau which had certainly not been created in Maureen's kitchen.

Calendula and Barrington made the right noises in the right places but wished that they had taken their hosts out to dinner themselves.

While Calendula and Maureen had a heart-to-heart chinwag after supper about girlie things, Barrington and Andrew retired for a mini-conference. Barrington handed over copies of the documentation which had so skilfully been obtained by Jules Axminster in exchange for a neat little packet of cash in a very large brown padded envelop. Barrington gave Andrew a guided tour of the paperwork in order to highlight its value and the key newsworthy points.

Andrew agreed to hold off publication of the information for a few days until Barrington had given him the OK. Barrington claimed that he might have some additional data and that the time would be more opportune when he gave the word. He assured Ormerod that the scoop could be claimed by *The Times* and that Andrew would get his accolade and, perhaps, his enlarged annual bonus for laudable investigative journalism.

Calendula and Barrington then drove back to their idyllic pad in Grove Naxton Cross in order to enjoy the fruits of some of their labours. But the best was yet to come.

The house had been well prepared for their return by Gladys Taylor who did for them and kept an eye on the place generally in their absence. She liked being paid in cash and, of course, Calendula and Barrington were always more than willing to oblige particularly now that they had a surfeit of liquid funds. When the cash-kitty really built up then they would take a trip to Switzerland but for now some of the cash which they had earned from the night's work could be used to pay their employees.

They were still, however, waiting for Jules' final contribution to the pudding before the trip to Switzerland could be made.

Another shower was anticipated without putting their thoughts into words. The large brown envelope from Ormerod, therefore, sat on the bedroom floor until it was put in the wall-safe the next morning.

FORMULATION

Ronald Turner flicked the butt-end of his fag out of the office window while simultaneously thinking of the office's no-smoking policy with distain. He also attempted to brush the smoke out of the window, albeit unsuccessfully, with a spare copy of *The Observer*.

Turner had decided to call an editorial meeting for his team now that they had the project of the year to work on.

Graham Fifield and Stuart McGill arrived punctually at the appointed hour of **9.00** am although neither knew what to expect. Turner had been deliberately evasive about the contents of the agenda by simply telling Graham late yesterday that he, Dennis, Manfred and Stuart were required to be in the chief's office first thing in the morning.

Dennis Sexton and Manfred Hinds joined the team just before **9.15** am having had to attend another meeting even earlier that morning. Even Dennis and Manfred were able to detect the remains of stale smoke but all had tactfully learned to overlook Turner's unsociable habit. Or habits if you included his propensity for alcoholic beverages.

The assembly of the Political Affairs team, therefore, was a full house for Fifield's department and all were more than curious about what might transpire. Graham knew from experience that a gathering of the clans betokened something big but he had no idea what it was and he had no time to speculate.

Stuart began to wonder whether there would be a cabinet reshuffle because he had not come up with anything interesting recently – and the main reason why he had been employed, he believed, was for his investigative skills. He was consoled, however, by the fact that he was not summoned into the lion's den on his own and so the chop for him was possibly not on the agenda – for the present.

The meeting kicked off abruptly with Ronald announcing that he had obtained, from a reliable source, information and supporting documentation about the goings on in parliament.

"Gregory Tranter and James Fetherington, by gad," Ronald declared enigmatically.

The air could have been cut with a knife. All participants felt a bit stung because they all wanted to get a breakthrough on someone like Tranter or Fetherington but somehow this knowledge about the devious politicians had crept into the office without their cognisance.

"Oh, them. Tranty and old randy pants, Fetherington," said Graham with a sneer.

Stuart blanched. He had an inkling of the subject-matter from his previous stalking exploits but, of course, he had no notion of what would actually emerge about the lascivious politician. Could this be something to do with Fetherington's Paris trip perhaps?

Turner savoured the moment.

"We have discovered that Fetherington has been covering up for Tranter's misdeeds," he proclaimed.

Stuart wondered who 'we' referred to. The Royal 'we'? Or to Turner alone? What did it matter anyway?

Ronald continued now that he had captured the responsiveness of his audience. They were like a bunch of dirty old men eager for the stripper to totally disrobe in order to achieve the desired effect on their physiology.

"Tranter took a huge sweetener before the election from Finkelbaum in Elisia. This payment was not declared when it should have been and, therefore, they have tried to disguise the payment in the accounts for the Elisian delegation trip," the political chief editor announced.

"So the electoral success was based on this false accounting, then?" interrupted Graham. He had seen this sort of thing before many times.

"And it would also affect the Balance of Payments," Ronald reminded the assembled company.

"Does Jepherson know the score, I wonder?" pondered Dennis.

"Feast your eyes on the supporting documentation, chaps," proclaimed Turner with a giant-size grin as he handed over a pack of information to each delegate. A lot of reading and exclamation then ensued.

"Juicy. Yes?" said Manfred with his eyes popping out like thirty-two-foot-reed bombarde organ stops.

The news-hungry participants at the meeting were first asked by Turner to study the Elisian accounts. And then the various email exchanges to and from Fetherington, Tranter, Jepherson and Finkelbaum but he kept back the report summary which he had received from Barrington the previous day. He had spent most of the night dissecting it with relish. Turner, however, saved for last the stuff which Jules had got out of Elisia which he almost surreptitiously revealed finally as the icing on the gingerbread.

There was virtual silence as the team digested the contents of this paperwork and mulled over the implications of the discovery. And all were internally writing up the story.

"Now for the various angles we need to take. We will get this stuff out in tomorrow's edition. Front page!" concluded Ronald.

All present, felt that such a remark went without saying.

"Now for the plan of action. Graham, you can cover the main story both from this end and from the Elisian angle. Dennis, consider the implications on the Balance of Payments," announced Turner. "Manfred, can you do an angle on Fetherington's career? And can you also remind readers about Fetherington's sexual inclinations? Let's savour the moment."

McGill sat on the edge of his seat desperately hoping that he would be given a commission. He held his breath but cyanosis did not set in.

"Sonny, you can write a subtle bit about how *The Guardian* is in possession of documentary evidence. Give nothing away but just indicate that they had better not even think of trying to sue us. And hint at the fact that Tranter could have dipped his paws in the cashbox too." Stuart was much relieved. He even overlooked the fact that he had been addressed as 'sonny' once again.

"And I want to see it by lunchtime today everyone. So get going. Now!" bellowed Ronald. It never occurred to him, of course, that any of his team would question this edict.

All members of the conference, in fact, couldn't get out of the office quick enough in order to make their mark on the world and to gain a few brownie points into the bargain. Soon the personal computers started buzzing, coffee was brewed and the phones were switched to silent.

Fifield wrote up his copy under the headline of 'Tranter and Finkelbaum in financial misconduct cahoots.' He summarised when the deal with Tranter and Finkelbaum had been struck and how the money had been transferred from the Elisian government to the UK account. He also spoke in detail about the fact that the protagonists in the drama had attempted to conceal their misdeeds in the Elisian delegation accounts.

Dennis, in his article, discussed the implications on the Balance of Payments and the way in which the voters had been duped, referring to a number of occasions in the past when such practices had been attempted in order to pull the wool over the eyes of the electorate.

Manfred outlined Fetherington's involvement and documented the career of both Tranter and Fetherington to date and the way in which they had amalgamated as a twosome. He also speculated about occasions when the two might have, in the past, been up to their usual tricks.

Turner was secretly working on his own unique coup d'état which he had concealed from the rest of his pack. If he was going to create waves, he would do it in style.

The meeting reconvened with the copy for checking at 12.35 pm. Ronald read each reporter's copy through with his usual pedantic scrutiny and made changes when he saw fit. The journalists had already read and checked the contributions of others in the cohort. That way there was no undue duplication of information or conflicting accounts.

Graham was asked by Turner to add some additional material while Dennis was advised to be more specific about his analysis of the Balance of Payments account in order to stress the fact that the electorate had been conned but without actually saying it.

Manfred luckily got his copy approved without amendment.

Stuart trembled slightly as he handed his copy over even though Graham had given it the once-over. Ronald grunted and then made some cosmetic changes more to keep Stuart in his rightful place than to gild the lily. Even though Stuart's copy was considerably shorter than that of the rest of his crew, he still had taken the most time to complete it. But that was about on par for a junior reporter. He would mature with age.

Ronald then distributed his contribution for the rest of the team to gloat over and gloat they certainly did.

"How the fuck did you get hold of this stuff, Ronald?" asked Fifield.

"A good newspaper man never reveals his sources," replied the other blandly.

Graham knew better than to probe further but he had for many years suspected that Turner had a bloody brilliant lapdog working for him. If only I could discover who it is, I would be made for life. Perhaps I can discover who it is if I really keep my nose to the ground? Graham had found a new mission in life.

FASCINATION

A letter was waiting for Faye one evening when she had returned home late to her small flat in Pimlico after a spell in the LSE library in order to do some of the last bits of research and fact-checking for her dissertation.

She opened the letter expecting it to be a bill or an invitation to part with some of her income for some superfluous reason. It was, however, from a company called Dunbar Appointments plc, a name with which she was not immediately familiar.

Faye read without much enthusiasm initially until it occurred to her that the content of the letter might be of great interest to her. Faye then read the letter with mounting curiosity and excitement. She reread the letter several times in order to absorb the glad tidings which it conveyed.

Dear Miss Windsor-Harris

Post of Head of Economic Research

We act on behalf of one of our valued multi-national corporate clients who is currently seeking a senior researcher to head up a team of junior employees in the Economic Research Department at their head office in London.

Your name has come to our attention in view of the fact that you are currently completing your MSc degree from the London School of Economics in Statistical and Corporate Research. We understand that you are at present employed by the government in a capacity which would render you highly suitable for consideration in applying for this post and we are, therefore, writing to you to ask whether we could put your name forward as a worthy applicant.

> *If this post would be of interest to you, then I would kindly ask you to ring me on my direct line in order to make an appointment for us to meet and discuss the position further.*
>
> *Yours sincerely*
>
> Henry Montgomery
> *Managing Director*

Faye took a long, hot, musk-rose bath and contemplated her next move. The musk-rose scent was a bath oil which she had picked up just after Christmas. She had been looking for an excuse to try it out and this would be an ideal opportunity.

Should she ring Mr Montgomery first thing in the morning or would that look a bit too keen and desperate? But if she waited a couple of days would that then seem as if she were not interested? Had a similar letter also been sent to any other prospective candidates? How the hell did Montgomery find out about me? Did it matter? Perhaps head-hunters just made it their business to find out such things? Could this be the break that I have been waiting for? Will it matter that I have not yet completed my master's degree? It does not appear so from the letter. Hell, I had better get on with that degree pretty smartish. I wonder when they would want me to start? I'd die if I didn't get it. But would I want it? Would I be disappointed when I attended the interview? Oh, Christ!

Faye headed for the staff restaurant the following afternoon in order to replenish the supply of cheese biscuits which she always kept in the top drawer of her desk in the office and, on the way, she made a discreet phone call to Henry Montgomery. She explained that she was unable to talk at length but that she would be willing to meet him to discuss his proposal, as outlined in his recent letter, at a mutually convenient time. Accordingly an appointment was made for Thursday next at 6.30 pm at Montgomery's office in Baker Street. Faye wanted to tick off the hours prior to this meeting as her anticipation mounted.

At the appointed hour Faye walked up to the first floor of a large building in Baker Street and into the offices of Dunbar Appointments plc. The offices were slick, spacious and plush. This gave Faye confidence that she would be dealing with a reputable organisation. She was asked to take a seat by a secretary who was just about to leave for the day and to wait for Henry who would be with her shortly.

Henry arrived almost instantly and he showed her into a comfortable meeting room off the reception area where still and sparkling mineral water was already provided. Henry asked Faye whether she would prefer tea or coffee but she stated that she would be more than content with sparkling mineral water so as not to cause him any undue trouble and in order to get down to the business for which she had agreed to meet him.

It transpired that a job in which Faye would be very interested was on offer. She would be working for a multi-national manufacturing company which produced prestigious video and stereo equipment and then sold their products worldwide. Faye had certainly heard of this company and she knew their reputation for high-priced high-quality, high-tech goods which sold like hot cakes.

Fuck! Faye was certainly interested in having her name put forward for this job. She could not wait to hand over her curriculum vitae which she had updated the previous evening in order to make herself sound more stunning than she actually was.

Henry read through her career résumé and declared that it would not need any tweaking for his client and he obtained Faye's agreement to make contact with the Head of Human Resources as soon as he could get hold of her. Faye noted, with interest, that the head of HR was a woman and she saw this as a good sign of future success from the cosmos.

Faye squandered some of the money which she had recently earned from Calendula on a new summer dress in pale blue chiffon lined with silk and some navy leather sandals in readiness for her interview with Fiona Myers, the Head of Human Resources, and Sir Donald Norland, the Chief Executive of Verclam Briars.

Faye thoroughly approved of the meeting room into which she was shown for her lengthy discussion of the job at Verclam Briars for which she had been put forward by Henry Montgomery. She was asked about her current job and what she had undertaken by way of research projects. Sir Donald seemed particularly interested in her predictive analysis on voting trends and some other projects which she had undertaken in connection with overseas markets.

Sir Donald gave her an explanation of the work which Faye would be expected to undertake and the need to recruit a high-level head of department to supervise the team already in place.

Faye was later, at a second interview, invited to meet the rest of the team which she would be supervising and a few days later she was offered the job for which she was longing. Faye was, in fact, over the moon that she had been offered this post and welcomed this change in her fortunes so heartily. She felt that the move which she had intended to make next year was remarkably coming to fruition long before it was due and, moreover, at a salary which would mean that she would have more disposable income in order to improve her lifestyle and her living environment.

Faye wrote a letter of resignation, addressed to Ruth Angell, and she was then required to work out her notice in her current employment.

Faye managed to hand in her dissertation on time, having burned some midnight oil in the process, and began her new job with relish and certainty that she would gain her MSc in due course. The job, in fact, turned out to exceed Faye's expectations and she enjoyed every moment of it. She travelled abroad, which she found greatly stimulating, and she had her own office. Her junior staff were competent and willing and her department produced the majority of their research reports on time and to a high standard which pleased her immediate superior Sir Donald.

Faye was frequently invited to lunch with Sir Donald and, more importantly, to dinner with Henry Montgomery with whom she had struck up the kind of friendship which led to more invigorating things.

The political scandals and intrigues at Whitehall, of course, continued to rage unabated with a degree of ferocity which Faye was relieved to have left behind when she finally walked out.

Ruth was desolate when Faye elected to leave the Research Central team and, after her colleague had left, she sunk into a deeply depressive phase of her life which threatened to become a permanent state of mind and being.

Henry eventually left his nagging wife and set up home with Faye. They became a happy and contented couple, almost as blissfully happy as Faye's friends Calendula and Barrington.

Faye ceased to work for Calendula when she was earning enough money to enjoy a lifestyle to which she soon became utterly accustomed. But she kept in touch with her old school-chum for the occasional social lunch and catch-up.

Liberation

Ruth sat in Hatty's Wine Bar in total despair. Her colleague Faye Windsor-Harris had found herself an impressive job elsewhere and she missed her company greatly.

Ruth remembered that time when she had poured her heart out to her ex-colleague here in Hatty's and how relieved and comforted she had felt as a result of the experience. When Faye left, she had promised to keep in touch but somehow this parting sentiment never actually materialised. Faye had not left her new office number or her private number and so she, Ruth, could not keep in touch. And, in any case, she did not want to keep pestering her ex-colleague for a get-together if an approach from Faye was not naturally forthcoming.

Her relationship with Fetherington had virtually disintegrated. Ruth had noticed the way in which James invariably took evasive action whenever they threatened to bump into each other. They hardly acknowledged each other even if they did meet these days. At ESIDR meetings, they simply sat and glared at each other frostily across the boardroom table and he still always managed to nick the prawn sandwiches. Ruth maintained that he would choke himself on the prawns rather than allow her to have her choice.

Ruth felt, furthermore, as if she were continually living in a pressure-cooker at work. She was constantly hassled by Guy Chaffinch who criticised her statistical work and complained about her findings for every report which was submitted to him.

Faye had been replaced by another senior researcher, Brian Rossiter, but his skills did not in any way match up to his predecessor's attributes in Ruth's view. While waiting for Faye's replacement to arrive, the work had piled up and the backlog was not yet cleared even now. The whole situation, moreover, seemed to be blamed on Ruth. She had started to work longer hours, coming into the office earlier and leaving later. And then simply decanting to Hatty's at the end of a tiring day.

Even more upsetting than anything else was the fact that she had never ever heard from Keith Viner again after their trip to the London Eye. This had ripped her to shreds. How could such an enchanting evening not be something which Keith wanted to repeat as he had promised? Ruth would have given him anything he might have requested. Not only her body but also her home, her money, her car and her eye-teeth. But no word, no contact and no further lovey-dovey meetings. For this reason alone, Ruth had promised herself that sooner or later she would actually hurl herself into the lake in St James' Park or off Westminster Bridge one dark night.

Ruth felt that she had not a friend in all the world and no-one wished to become her lover. Ruth would give to a lover all her undying affection, gratitude and passion. Why did it happen to others and not to me? Why has life treated me so cruelly and there is simply no way out of the morass? She hated herself and her life. She hated her work and the people in it – especially that bloody randy James Fetherington. She would have thrown herself at him at one time but now she simply hated his guts. The bastard! The arsehole! She wanted to buy a gun and kill him and then shoot herself.

She began planning the way in which she could end it all but all the possibilities and suggestions which she came up with all seemed to be impractical. And, in any case, Ruth was actually too scared to go ahead with any plan which she thought might work. She hated her emotive pain but dreaded physical pain still more.

On her third bottle of wine Ruth wondered whether this evening would be a good time to approach Westminster Bridge. The night was beginning to draw in and perhaps there would not be too many people there at this late hour of the evening.

"Do you mind if I sit here?" came a voice from out of the ether.

Ruth looked up in surprise but was greeted by an open and friendly face. Ruth merely nodded her assent.

The stranger sat down and proceeded to start a conversation about the food at Hatty's. She asked Ruth whether she could recommend anything on the menu. Ruth hesitated and then suggested that the fish was usually a good choice and this also reminded her that she had not had a bite to eat herself that evening.

The stranger ordered a battered cod with chips and peas and this decision stimulated Ruth to ask Joe for the menu. Ruth then asked for some smoked salmon and prawns with minted mayonnaise, green salad and new potatoes. At least that lousy Fetherington could not take the prawns away from me here.

The meals arrived together for Ruth and Zoe. Ruth was pleased about this because she found that Zoe was someone with whom she felt at ease. They talked continually about their lives and Ruth learned that Zoe had been in a high-pressured job herself once which had nearly driven her to suicide. Ruth listened intently to this piece of information about her new companion as she was anxious to find out how the situation had resolved itself.

Zoe explained that she had sought solace from a counsellor-psychotherapist woman who had helped her to make realisations about why she was continuing to punish herself in a thankless job. Zoe told Ruth that she had found the counselling experience to be one of great enlightenment and that this inner knowledge had resulted in her resigning her job, telling her boss what she thought of him, walking out of the place and slamming the door hard behind her.

"And did you then manage to secure another job or were you up the creek without the proverbial paddle?" enquired the enraptured Ruth.

"Well, I did struggle for a short while but I spent about a week or two trawling all the agencies in London and eventually I found a job quite easily. It took less time than expected. And I had the confidence and the energy to do it after the counselling."

Zoe was apparently a legal executive and, although jobs were scarce, if a number of agencies were searching diligently then it was inevitable that the right job would soon come up out of the paving stones especially in London.

Ruth was intrigued. This woman before her seemed to have emerged from the dungeons like Phoenix from the flames. This observation set her thinking and hoping.

Eventually Zoe pulled from her handbag a card which she handed to Ruth. This gave the name of one Leander Deane, psychodynamic psychotherapist and counsellor. Ruth placed this card in her wallet and contemplated her future.

Zoe and Ruth exchanged numbers and agreed to meet in a couple of weeks for another meal and a chat. When they did so in Hatty's Bar two weeks later, Ruth reported that she had gone to her first appointment with Leander a couple of days ago and that she was due to see her again next week. Ruth said that she had been inspired by Zoe, that she was very pleased with the way her first counselling session had gone and that she was looking forward very much to her second appointment. Ruth mentioned that she had cried a lot over Keith who had let her down and that she had ranted even more about James who was a total fucker! Zoe seemed to think that Ruth was making tremendous progress when she heard this news.

The two friends arranged to meet in a fortnight's time in order to review Ruth's further progress in cracking open the locked box in her mind and taking the dead-weight off her shoulders.

Ruth and Zoe then met regularly and Zoe noted the great strides which Ruth was making with the help of Leander over the coming weeks and months.

Ruth felt noticeably better in herself after only a couple of sessions. She did not put up with such crap from Chaffinch anymore and she openly told Fetherington at one of their ESIDR meetings that he was a cheat and a liar. Fetherington and the rest of the committee were stunned by this forthright accusation from Ruth. But she stood her ground. She argued her case with an analysis of the figures which Fetherington had attempted to falsify and pass off as a clerical error in recording the backdated payment from Elisia in the wrong set of accounts.

Fetherington for the first time appeared not to have the upper hand with Ruth and the fact was duly noted by all present. Fetherington was actually so stunned that he failed to reach the prawn sandwiches before Ruth. Of course Ruth and Fetherington continued to glare daggers at each other whenever they met but Ruth, at least, did not seem to suffer from the encounter or to react to any of his cutting and derogatory remarks.

She had also decided that she did not want to go on punishing herself in an atmosphere which she loathed. Eventually one of the agencies which Ruth had contacted came up with a more interesting position for her. The money was more or less the same but the work was infinitely more enjoyable, less pressured and she was very much appreciated by colleagues and superiors alike. Ruth's future prospects for promotion also seemed to be more hopeful in her new position.

Ruth and Zoe continued to meet and became lifelong friends. Because both were single, they took their holidays together and often compared notes about that first auspicious meeting when Ruth had been seriously considering the suicide route from which her faithful friend Zoe had rescued her.

Hatty's Wine Bar suffered a loss of income now because Ruth had ceased to become a regular patron and their profits for the year took a serious nosedive as a result. Joe, however, felt relieved that he did not have to regularly witness Ruth's distress and he was gratified that her meeting with Zoe had turned out to be such a fruitful liaison. And he believed that Hatty's had been instrumental in bringing about this transformation in Ruth.

TEMPTATION

James had spent yet another exhausting week of bickering, exasperation and apprehension. But, at least, it was Friday again.

He had sat through yet another lunchtime meeting today with Gregory Tranter in order to discuss the voting trends report and Fetherington's comments on the matter. How much time can two individuals waste over one stupid fucking report? Fetherington was on the point of telling Tranter to read the bloody thing himself rather than rely on his précis of its contents and then take issue with him over every tiny detail of his summary. But Fetherington had to tolerate his superior in the interests of securing his promotion in the future.

When the lunch in the staff restaurant felt as if it were coming to an end, Fetherington began looking forward to making his escape back to his office, where, no doubt, that martinet Beryl would ambush him from her perch outside his office with her usual zeal. Sign this, check that, phone this person, email the other. Christ, she was worse than that bloody Tranter! And Beryl always managed to curtailed his propensity to leer at Claire and Zena. So there was no respite for James at all. Poor sod!

James was also worried because things had gone quiet since he had returned from Paris after those unforgettable nights with Verity Baxter. He had returned on the Sunday evening because the exigencies of his work dictated his homecoming while she had remained in Paris for her own professional reasons. She had to see her agent or a client or something.

James had tried her mobile number several times with a view to repeating the weekend but he had always got her voice mail, left a sexy message but then got no response. James was not unduly worried by this but he still would have liked to have seen her this weekend at least. Or made a future date to which he could look forward.

But now he was winding things up at his desk and anticipating with relief the massage which he had booked at Harmony Holistics with

Jean Paul. This experience never failed to relieve him of much of his stress provided that he could switch off from his job sufficiently in order to relax and forget himself. Fetherington, however, had also booked a sauna session which would precede the massage as this tactic often ensured that he could relax sufficiently in order to gain maximum benefit from Jean Paul's soothing hands.

When he arrived at the South Kensington establishment, however, he was slightly peeved to learn that Jean Paul had suddenly been taken ill and was, therefore, unavailable for his massage. And Eleanor, the receptionist, protested that there had been insufficient time to contact him. While James was taking in this news, Eleanor told him that Selina Mason was free to step in at the eleventh hour so as not to disappoint him. Eleanor spoke highly of Selina's skills and qualifications and, when James saw a photograph of her in the clinic's brochure, he instantly decided that she would, indeed, make a very good substitute for Jean Paul on this occasion.

Accordingly James took his sauna and was then led by Selina upstairs to Tuscany on the first floor. James, of course, made full use of the opportunity to observe Selina's curvaceous and oscillating buttocks as she escorted him up the stairs.

Selina invited James to lie down on the massage-couch while she hung up his towelling robe. James willingly obeyed and submitted to her tender touch. She did not render such a firm and vigorous massage as Jean Paul but she had other attributes which James appreciated very sincerely. Out of the corner of his eye, James was aware of her full breasts, her slender waist, her delicate perfume and her thick auburn hair.

But James wanted to relax and so he sunk into the couch and zoned out in order to enjoy the experience. It was difficult for him to relax, however, being so aware of the woman in close proximity to him who was applying such a tender and sensuous touch. He felt himself transported into a realm which he had hitherto not experienced. James imagined caressing her body, running his fingers through her hair and then urgently seizing her with almost violent passion. All the while his thoughts vortexed and leapt about, Selina continued with her magic touch.

James began to relax still further while being lost in his thoughts and bodily sensations. He felt himself getting aroused yet he felt powerless to return to conscious awareness in order to curtail it. And then it seemed as if her hands were getting close to the focus of his passion and he was unable to resist the inevitable consequence.

"James," she whispered in a seductive voice, "I am just going to get closer."

He was speechless as her hands began to approach the target of his arousal. James had reached the point of no return. Poor sod!

The relief for James was overdue and magnificent.

But the phone rang to announce Selina's next client. Why is it that telephones are continually the bane of my life?

When he asked to see Selina again, she urged him to make another appointment. Well, OK, but that wasn't exactly what he had in mind. But still.

At the end of his massage session, James gave her a long and lingering kiss of gratitude as he fondled her breasts and pressed himself against her. James left Harmony Holistics in a bubble of bliss. That was the kind of relaxation which he had craved and an angel from heaven had donated it to him free of charge. Well, he had to pay a high price for the massage, of course.

As James drove home, he even felt as if he hardly cared whether Verity returned his calls or not that weekend.

James spent a peaceful weekend pottering around the flat, doing some essential shopping and moping about his inability to contact Verity. He had, however, booked another session with Selina so, at least, he had that to look forward to. Maybe I could book a regular weekly appointment with her?

Fetherington spent Monday at home reading reports and writing some of his own in draft ready for typing. He told Beryl that he did not wish to be disturbed all day.

On Tuesday morning the phone rang at 7.00 am and, unexpectedly, it was Tranter who was in a foul mood.

"What the hell have you been up to now, matey?" demanded an irate Tranter.

Fetherington stammered, wondering what on earth old Tranty might have found out about his précis writing or his constituency activities.

"Have you read today's papers?"

James confessed that he hadn't yet. He was about to consume a couple of croissants for breakfast and intended to digest the papers while munching them.

"Well I suggest you do. And ring me back in order to provide a suitable explanation." Tranter slammed the phone down.

Fetherington was completely nonplussed. He dived for the papers which were still lying on the mat in his Mayfair apartment. He sat down on the sofa in the lounge and prepared himself to be astonished. He was.

The headlines unnerved James in no uncertain terms.

The Sun headline read 'Randy Fetherington Likes the Common Touch'. *The Mirror* stated that 'Massage Turns into Sex Orgy for Fethers'. 'Birds with Fethers', said *The Mail*. And so it went on.

The Times was only slightly more reasonable and sober with 'James Fetherington Exploits Masseuse' and *The Telegraph* restricted itself to 'Politician Indulges in Scandalous Liaison'.

James was close to tears and quite unable to decipher how the news of his Friday-evening escapade had reached so many tabloids and broadsheets in such record time. That bloody Selina must have done a kiss-and-tell stunt! And, what was even worse, he had managed so far to keep his sexual inclinations away from the press and the public. Could he ride this storm? Probably not. The entire globe would come to hear of this one.

James switched on the television. A bank of journalists had camped outside Harmony Holistics and it appeared that Selina Mason had done a bunk. Grace Norris, the proprietor, gave a television interview stating firmly that her clinic would not in any way condone such behaviour and she would never knowingly have employed any disreputable staff.

The police and the press had attempted to trace Selina Mason but, it seemed, that such a person did not, in fact, even exist.

Fetherington was astounded. He had been set up by someone. He had obviously made an enemy somewhere along the line but now, of course, it might be a complete waste of time to even attempt to discover who.

James glanced out of the window and was greeted by waves and jeers from a host of media correspondents. Oh, Christ! Now he would be house-bound for weeks.

The phone rang again. But Fetherington had no plausible explanation to provide for his superior. Tranter ranted at Fetherington for what seemed to James like hours and told him that he was suspended from duty pending an enquiry into his unseemly conduct.

That poor sod Fetherington knew now that his career as a politician was over. Well, it was, at the very least, imperilled. Perhaps it could be retrieved when the storm had died down? What's a bit of sex-play these days, eh? No, he was finished. Probably? Maybe? Certainly! Perhaps? Definitely! Oh, hell.

James had assumed that his meeting with Tristanica Rezze, the creative design agency, and PR consultant Pippa Gresham about next year's Russian trip, scheduled for tomorrow, would have automatically been cancelled by Beryl by now. And he was right. James also thought that Beryl was no doubt gloating. It was more than likely, in fact, that his trip to Russia had been cancelled too because he might not even have a job next year.

James reviewed his future prospects but decided that he didn't actually have any worth speaking about. He hunted around the flat for some alcohol to take his mind of things.

He could have been consoled by Verity but, when he tried her number again, he discovered that she had blocked his calls. This was the end of the world for James. Poor sod!

He was pilloried at every staging-post.

And things could not possibly get worse, surely? Could they? Hmmm!

DETERMINATION

Sandra awoke bright and early with the dawning day.

She had made a decision in the night watches during her slumber. The Angel of Enlightenment had visited her during the night and she was truly renewed and recreated by this visitation. Sandra had now decided to change her life radically and to emerge triumphantly from the fray.

Sandra rose up from the bed like a *Gyps Rueppellii* (Rüppell's griffon vulture, to you) soaring above the African Sahel. But she was not now an endangered species, although she certainly had been in the past. And she was not about to expire from lack of oxygen at the altitude which she had attained.

For Sandra the wakeup call had been heard loud and clear and she had grabbed the message with open arms. And Sandra would not now allow anything or anyone to stand in her way. Her engines had been revved up and she was all set for take-off. Beware a woman on a mission!

She kissed Rousel lightly, showered, dressed and walked back into the bedroom which they had booked at the Drooping Palm Hotel, which overlooked the Irish Sea in the far distance, on the Isle of Anglesey off the north-west coast of Wales.

"I need to return home now," she announced to the gob-smacked Maurice who was expecting to wake up for some more shag and sugar. "Immediately."

"Pardon? Ma petite? Qu'est que c'est? Qui se passe?" was Maurice's bewildered response to the uncharacteristic and prevailing circumstances. He had still not really come to his senses but the rude awakening was beginning to dawn on his consciousness.

"No, I need to straighten things out at home. If you will not drive me home, Rousel, then I shall go by public transport."

"All right, all right, all right. But, but, but ... my precious, beautiful Sandra, are you sure?" Maurice protested lamely. But he was certain that this woman actually meant business. And she would brook no argument. Beware a woman on a mission!

Maurice was in a quandary as to how he could retrieve the situation effectively. Maurice wondered whether this job was just about to go sour. Had Sandra seen though him? Had she realised that he was an imposter? Had she discovered that he was a fake or a plant? Was she about to read him the riot act? Was she about to sock him one on the jaw or worse? Was he destined to lose his income?

Sandra then explained what she intended to do and Maurice was slightly mollified.

Maurice dressed at breakneck speed, having decided not to attempt to lure her back under the sheets but simply to go with the flow.

Maurice settled the hotel bill while Sandra paced up and down outside the entrance. Maurice consoled himself with the fact that he had probably extracted all the information and favours which he could make use of from Sandra and the fact that she did not appear to be overtly cross with him particularly.

They journeyed home in virtual silence.

Sandra Mullingar crashed open her front door and strutted into her humble semi-detached in Lymingworth.

Ted came into the hall in order to remonstrate with her.

"Where the 'ell have you been, woman?" demanded the cantankerous and discomforted Ted.

"Shut up. Just shut your bloody gob!"

Ted was rooted to the spot. His property had never had the audacity to speak to him like that before. Sandra had, in fact, never answered him back in her life. He simply spluttered and blustered but was lost for words.

"I'm leaving you!" she proclaimed. "And now!" Sandra strutted up the stairs.

"What? What? You're what?" he screamed, following her ineffectually.

Sandra pulled a case out of the wardrobe and began throwing things into it but with a relaxed attitude and a purposeful design.

"What the hell are you thinking of woman? Have you gone crazy?" Ted was beginning to lose his grip and approached Sandra in a threatening manner.

"And don't you dare even think of striking me. You bastard! I have put up with you for too long. I have pandered to your every demand and not received an iota of thanks or gratitude since the day we were married. You have treated me like a skivvy and barked your bloody orders at me like the selfish bastard that you are! You have treated me like dirt and I am not putting up with it for one second more. Not one second more, understand!" Beware a woman on a mission!

"You fucking bitch! You fucking cunt! Where will you go and what will you live on? You won't get any money out of me."

Sandra remained bizarrely calm and smiling. She was like the axis of the storm, the minutely calm eye-of-a-needle in the centre of the typhoon. She was supremely the dynamic epicentre of the hurricane.

She continued her packing and serenely left the house while Ted resumed his fuming tirade of calling her all the names under the sun and threatening her with fire and brimstone. How he didn't hit her, he was at a loss to understand. But perhaps he was actually a coward? Judge for yourself.

When the door had slammed hard shut, Ted collapsed in tears of rage on the kitchen floor. Poor sod! She had meant every word she had said.

Why did she not tell me that she was unhappy before? Perhaps I was a bit inconsiderate? Maybe I should have shown her a bit more affection or taken her out once or twice? But why? She has never behaved like this in the past? Oh, my Sandra. What shall I do without you? My Sandra. How will I cope? How will I manage? I can't cook. I can't do all the washing and cleaning. I don't know how that washing machine works. Oh, my God! I can't live without you. You're a fucking bitch to have left me. I hate you! Will she come back? Will I have her back? No, she has gone for good.

This internal harangue continued within the hapless Ted for days, weeks, months. He switched from plotting his revenge on Sandra, to self-recrimination and back to hatred for his wife as frequently as a whirlwind changes direction. He tried drowning his sorrows in drink but that was hopeless. In the coming weeks he had the mother-and-father of all hangovers every morning and he virtually killed himself with ready-meals. Ted had fortuitously learned how to use the microwave. He had actually used it once or twice since their marriage many years ago. So that was not an insurmountable difficulty for Ted.

The washing machine, however, broke down the first time he tried to use it. But Ted soon learned how to go down to the launderette and get someone to show him how to use the machinery there. But Ted's helper was not at all interested to hear of his morbid troubles.

Ted's friends down the pub were also unsympathetic and his own mother actually sided with that bitch and said that he deserved it! Fucking hell! What a bloody cheek! She left me. She's the one who should be punished not me.

No-one had ever got closer to suicide yet failed to admit that it was his own fault when his wife had left him than Ted Mullingar. Poor sod! But don't feel sorry for him.

Very soon after the earthquake had occurred, Sandra found herself a little flat far, far away from Lymingworth. She returned, in fact, to north Wales, a place where she really felt at home and which had been the catalyst for her road-to-Damascus experience.

North Wales provided Sandra with work. She worked in a café for a stretch before finding a lucrative position as an office administrator for a large firm of lawyers in Bangor. This firm of solicitors efficiently engineered Sandra's divorce proceedings and obtained a very handsome financial settlement for her. Sandra had long ago banked her so-called redundancy settlement from Tory party HQ in Westbury North. Beware a woman on a mission!

With some money in her purse, Sandra bought herself a little bachelor pad just outside Bangor, mortgage free, from the proceeds of her various financial settlements. This was an ideal location not only for work but also for visiting her beloved Anglesey and Holy Island as well as taking mini-excursions into the mountains and coastal areas around Bangor.

Sandra was not at all interested in finding a replacement for Rousel who seemed to have disappeared completely from her life after their last momentous stay at the Drooping Palm. But, instead, she found herself silently thanking him for the pivotal role which he had played in her gaining her freedom from a dead-end, corruption-ridden job and, more importantly, liberation from a selfish, grossly uncouth and dictatorial spouse.

Sandra made many friends among the Welsh locals who welcomed her as a new and interesting member of the community. She joined a nearby book club. She became an active member of the local history society. She organised village fetes and became a keen ornithologist. She studiously avoided joining any political party and never ever voted at any election again for the rest of her days.

Sandra Mullingar was now happy. Bless her!

CULMINATION

The news broke one sunny morning in mid-August like an anemophilous Tsunami tidal wave. It killed no-one physically but its effects were just as devastating. It killed many metaphorically.

The timing was perfect because the summer recess of parliament had just taken place and all members of the government were beginning to relax until the autumn.

The front page of *The Guardian* broke the news proudly parading its flagship position of erudite authority to the world.

Tranter and Finkelbaum in Financial Misconduct Cahoots

We have today received disturbing news that should be brought to the attention of the voting public.

It is reported that cabinet minister, Gregory Tranter, the Secretary of State for International Development, is known to have received monies from the Elisian Federal Government which he did not declare to the electorate.

A sum of £12 million was passed from the Elisian Federal Government's account into the Conservative Party Election Fund in order to boost the trade figures which were published at the time of the election campaign in March of this year.

This princely sum was paid to the Tories so that prime minister, Ian Jepherson, would reciprocate by backing the subsequent Elisian election campaign. The deal was struck, we believe, with the full knowledge of both Ian Jepherson and premier Johann Finkelbaum in Elisia.

Mr Tranter, it seems, put pressure on the prime minister publicly to back the Elisian election campaign when Johann Finkelbaum was endeavouring to secure his re-election in May.

This was the way in which the payment was justified by the Elisian Federal Government and, in their case, the gratuity reaped significant rewards when they were returned to power with a substantial majority.

Graham Fifield
Chief Correspondent for Political Affairs

James Fetherington also came in for some more stick in a follow-up article in *The Guardian* from Graham Fifield.

Tranter Used James Fetherington as Cover-Up Man

Apparently, James Fetherington, Under Secretary of State for International Development and Gregory Tranter's right-hand man, was blatantly asked to cover up Gregory Tranter's misdeeds.

Fetherington, it seems, knew of the Elisian deal and the fact that pressure had been brought to bear on the prime minister, Ian Jepherson. Fetherington had apparently maintained at a recent meeting of the Executive Sub-Committee for International Diplomatic Relations, chaired by Simon Risborough, member of parliament for East Bressex, that the sum from Elisia was a backdated import duty – even though he knew this was not so.

Graham Fifield
Chief Correspondent for Political Affairs

This article continued in some depth, in a somewhat speculative vein, by considering who else might have known the truth of the matter, who in the house might also have been duped and who might be accountable as the news all came out in the wash.

A further discussion ensued on subsequent pages which essentially repeated, embellished, speculated and elaborated the main purport of this appetite-wetting article from Fifield.

The same articles were repeated, more or less word for word, in a late-morning edition of *The Observer*.

Another article in *The Guardian* outlined the effects and implications on the UK Balance of Payments and the way in which the Elisian payment would have deceived the electorate into thinking that the Conservative government were handling the UK economy better than it actually was.

Yet another article thus appeared as front-page news in *The Guardian* and *The Observer*.

UK People Duped by Tories Over Elisian Deal

The UK Balance of International Payments would have been affected by an influx of cash to the tune of some £12 million which would have duped the British public in two ways at the time of the March election.

Firstly the Conservative Party would have appeared, according to the much-publicised Balance of Payments, to have been handling the economy more efficiently than was, in fact, the case. And secondly, and perhaps more importantly, the sum from the Elisian Federal Government was disguised in the accounts in order to ensure that it was not officially declared. This cash-injection, of course, may have also been used for the election campaign but, as always, spurious funds do arrive in conservative party accounts from various sources.

We also understand, in fact, that additional funding could have come from a newspaper source to whom Gregory Tranter sold some insider information but the details are, as yet, unclear.

The Guardian Media Group have evidence that false accounting was practised in order to disguise the incoming payment from Elisia. An attempt was made, for instance, to pass off the sum in the accounts for the expenses for the recent Elisian delegation cited erroneously as a backdated import duty payment. No record in the Elisia accounts has been identified, however, as evidence of such an outstanding import disbursement.

Dennis Sexton
Senior Correspondent for Political Affairs

Sexton's article too was elongated on subsequent pages, the normal allocation of three pages for Political Affairs in *The Guardian* and *The Observer* having been extended to six pages of comment.

The careers of Ian Jepherson, Gregory Tranter and James Fetherington were paraded before the public by Manfred Hinds who was certainly not backward in referring his readers back to the news about Fetherington's recent encounter at Harmony Holistics.

A much smaller article, which was almost lost because of its minuscule size and insignificant position, also appeared in the two newspapers within the Guardian Media Group plc conglomerate. A little-known correspondent penned the article but with little hope of any further limelight. His words, however, had been heavily censored and doctored by his superiors.

Documentary Evidence of Political Affairs Announcements

Both newspapers in the Guardian Media Group have made their claims about the pecuniary kickback from the Elisian Federal Government supported by documentary evidence.

Both The Guardian and The Observer newspapers have received reports, printed copies of accounts and duplicate copies of emails in order to substantiate the shocking evidence which has been published today concerning the underhand dealings of prime minister Ian Jepherson and premier Johann Finkelbaum.

Stuart McGill
Junior Correspondent for Political Affairs

This article was designed to stem the tide of criticism from other newspapers and especially the tabloids who would have been bitterly sore to discover that they had not scooped the scandal first. The other motive for trailing this article was to keep the Tories from attempting to sue and, even if they did, to make the public aware of the fact that *The Guardian* and *The Observer* could both fight back with powerful and plentiful ammunition.

A second article, published both in *The Guardian* and *The Observer*, contained some even more appalling news on the following day.

Tranter Helped Himself to a Couple of Million

It has now come to our attention that some money was siphoned off by Gregory Tranter personally from the payment which the Tories received from the Elisian Federal Government. The original payment from Elisia would have totalled £14 million at today's exchange rates but £2 million, at least, found its way into Tranter's personal account.

Mr Tranter, Secretary of State for International Development, was not available for comment.

Ronald Turner
Chief Editor for Political Affairs

Readership figures for *The Guardian* and *The Observer* newspapers virtually trebled which was far beyond the expectations of most of the management and staff while this news was still hot.

Andrew Ormerod, of *The Times* newspaper also substantiated the involvement of the Elisian government in the scandal by stating categorically that his newspaper was in possession of documentation, in the guise of email correspondence and bank transfer slips, which confirmed that monies had been paid directly into the Conservative Party's election expenses bank account. Some of this documentation he actually printed in *The Times* but neither the British government nor the Elisian government elected to provide any comment or dispute.

The tabloid hacks smarted with envy when reading the scoops in *The Guardian*, *The Observer* and *The Times*. Newshounds from *The Sun*, *The Mirror*, *The Mail*, among many of their opposite numbers elsewhere up and down the country, arrived in London in their droves and beetled off down to Downing Street and Whitehall. Helicopters flew in from Scotland and from across the globe. The worldwide media teams also assembled for some fun and games and all were prepared for playing a lengthy waiting game.

Shops, hotels, public houses, guest-houses and restaurants flourished in London and the Home Counties.

The parliamentary summer recess had to be delayed for a while and, some thought, indefinitely.

The UK residences of Jepherson, Tranter and Fetherington, and even Simon Risborough and Chancellor David Dulchester, were put under 24-hour surveillance. Every member of parliament quaked in their boots or their high-heeled shoes in case they were implicated.

Jepherson had to cancel his Caribbean vacation much to the annoyance and disappointment of his family who castigated him like crazy for abusing his hard-won position. Jepherson and his wife Hazel, together with their disappointed children, Malcolm and Jessica, were left to unpack their luggage and forced to relinquish the cost of their vacation because of their enforced sequestration. Jepherson's faithful secretary, Christa Evans-Jenkins, however, was paid overtime to bring them food and provisions, including newspapers, in order to sit out the media siege. And Christa managed to evade the press cordon very skilfully by arriving disguised as a delivery operative.

Fetherington was under self-imposed house-arrest in his London flat with the phone permanently off the hook. He could only monitor calls from his mobile and not the land line. He raided the freezer and hoped that this would suffice because Mrs Maskell seemed reluctant to attend to his needs these days. She had told him that his conduct was most improper and that her husband would not allow her to work for him any longer.

James' ex-wife Glenda did not ring but she merely gloated at his demise – although she did worry about whether he would be able to keep up the maintenance payments and whether he might seek to re-open legal proceedings by pleading impoverishment. She knew, however, that he had private means and, therefore, she gave a short and discreet press interview to a single journalist from *The Times* in order to make this known to the general public as a means of deflecting any redress from her ex-husband. It did the trick.

Tranter and his wife, Stephanie, became the main target of attack. And, as they were house-bound, starvation threatened the entire family. Deliveries from Waitrose and Fortnum and Mason, however, allowed them to survive once the delivery vans had managed to get through the barricade of paparazzi. Janice Tranter, their daughter, who was hitchhiking across Europe and Asia, before returning to university in York in the autumn, managed to keep a low profile. Her calls to her parents were fortunately not intercepted and so she avoided any unwanted and unwarranted publicity.

Ronald Turner envisaged his bank manager patting him on the back and thanking him for clearing his overdraft. He also looked forward to an extended holiday with Dotty in The Seychelles at the end of the year.

Graham Fifield, Dennis Sexton and Manfred Hinds all had similar aspirations for the future. Fifield treated himself to a last-minute quick getaway. Dennis settled down to finishing his latest novel which was due at the publishers in the autumn. And Manfred and his girlfriend went away for a dirty weekend in Paris of all places.

Stuart (Sonny) McGill, who could not afford to spend any money on a holiday, merely manned the phones in the office but he was under strict instructions not to disturb any of his colleagues while they were away enjoying themselves.

Ronald Turner remained in the office also in the hope that he might be able to dredge up some more political dirt while the majority of his team were on leave. His hopes were in vain, however. And so he spent a sweaty summer puffing smoke out of his office window and getting drunk at lunchtime as usual without too many glaring looks from his colleagues.

CELEBRATION

The Dom Perignon Rosé was on ice in several transparent ice-buckets.

A marquee had been hired for the occasion together with two extra-large rectangular trestle tables, with white damask tablecloths and napkins, and a dozen or so white-wood chairs with royal blue velveteen seat-covers. One table held the drinks and the other was to house the diners. The large marquee covered the tables in case it rained and also served as a vehicle for holding decorations. Silver cutlery and crystal glasses were also on sparkling exhibition.

Several floral displays had been delivered that morning of freshly scented carnations, red roses, pink and yellow tulips and calla lilies which adorned the tables. Festoons of helium-filled balloons also graced the set. The hand-painted bunting was hanging out in startling profusion in order to complete the party picture.

Each guest had his or her name written in ornate calligraphy on a table-tent by each place-setting for the occasion. The male table-tents read Mr Jules Axminster, Mr Harold Ferguson, Mr Henry Montgomery, Mr Thomas Dryden, Mr Ivan Phelps, Mr Maurice Moreau and Mr William Frampton. The female guests comprised Miss

Faye Windsor-Harris, Miss Maisie Clifton, Miss Vera Clough and Miss Gemma Gallagher.

Barrington performed the role of head chef and Calendula had designed the bunting and produced all the beautifully crafted table-tents. Barrington was also ably assisted by a team of local waitresses who came to serve the guests with drinks and food and, of course, would help with the clearing up chores tomorrow.

Their villa in the countryside of southern France was groaning with the splendour of the occasion. The weather was considerate and so the garden became the ideal place for the celebration.

The guests arrived in dribs and drabs and were greeted with champagne cocktails and nibbles consisting of things on sticks and caviar bites.

When all had assembled, the gong was sounded for the lingering six-course supper.

Course number one was a lobster bisque followed by a platter of locally cured ham with olives and rocket accompanied by baguettes made by the baker in the village. The main course consisted of sea bass stuffed with cranberries, almonds and red onion with new potatoes and artichokes.

Then appeared a salad consisting of wilted spinach, shredded carrot, pine nuts and finely grated orange peel in order to cleanse the palate French-style. Next to arrive was the cheeseboard which consisted of handmade brie, camembert de Normandie, Époisses de Bourgogne and the rich and creamy ewe's Ossau-Iraty.

Finally the guests were offered a choice of either fresh fruit salad laced with brandy and cream or a chocolate gateau made to a recipe which Barrington had been perfecting for most of his life.

The wines which accompanied the feast were a selection of French delicacies. These wines consisted of a rich red Chateauneuf du Pape from the Côtes du Rhône region, a Côteaux d'Aix rosé from Provence and Languedoc's own sparkling Blanquette de Limoux produced near Carcassonne.

The guests chatted with merriment about their various coups and chuckled at the successful outcome. Those persons who had been saved from the fray were also remembered affectionately and their health and prosperity was lavishly toasted. Congratulations were the order of the day all round.

No-one except the co-ordinators and purse-string holders, Calendula and Barrington, held the whole picture and knew all the secrets but the cast could appreciate the ingenuity of the entire enterprise for that year's harvest.

The party went on for most of the night until the guests were almost too tired to return to their respective and respectable hotels.

Once the guests had finally retired with grateful thanks and many hugs and kisses and promises to do it all again soon, Calendula and Barrington sat in the garden taking stock of their hard work and success with pride.

Calendula mused about the gaiety of the atmosphere and the success of the party all round. Barrington recollected the deposits they had made in Switzerland on the way down to their abode in France and felt more than satisfied with this year's operation.

Calendula and Barrington reviewed their enterprise as if dissecting a play after the first night but it was not found wanting.

"Shall we retire, poochie? Shall we quit while we're ahead? We now have enough money to live on for the rest of our lives, you know. Many times over," asked Barrington.

Calendula met Barrington's question with another. "Good God! What a ridiculous suggestion, lion cub. What would we do all day and where would we get our kicks from?"

Barrington could see the logic of this argument and so let the matter drop. He realised that they both needed the excitement and that they wanted to have the opportunity of entertaining their guests and beloved friends many more times in the future on occasions such as this evening.

Tired as they were it seemed like the right time for a shower.

I felt my life come back, and glow; I felt my trust in God revive; I felt my joy of living and of loving dearer things than life. It is not a moment to describe; who feels can never tell of it. But the compassion of my sweetheart's tears, and the caressing of my bride's lips, and the throbbing of my wife's heart (now at last at home on mine) made me feel that the world was good, and not a thing to be weary of.

Richard Doddridge Blackmore
Lorna Doone

VENDETTA VICE

Vendetta Vice is the second novel in the Medici Squadron series which traces the antics of Calendula Fortescue-Bligh and Barrington Flint of the Medici Squadron.

The talented pop-music band, Vendetta Ice, have effortlessly achieved worldwide fame largely due to their sensational lead singer, Rouchuka, but also as a result of the determination of guitarist, Rocker Blaize, and business manager, Gerry Paxton. Certain members of the company, however, undertake some nefarious behind-the-scenes activity which excites the interest of Calendula Fortescue-Bligh and Barrington Flint of the Medici Squadron.

SPARRING PARTNERS

Sparring Partners is the third novel in the Medici Squadron series which traces the antics of Calendula Fortescue-Bligh and Barrington Flint of the Medici Squadron.

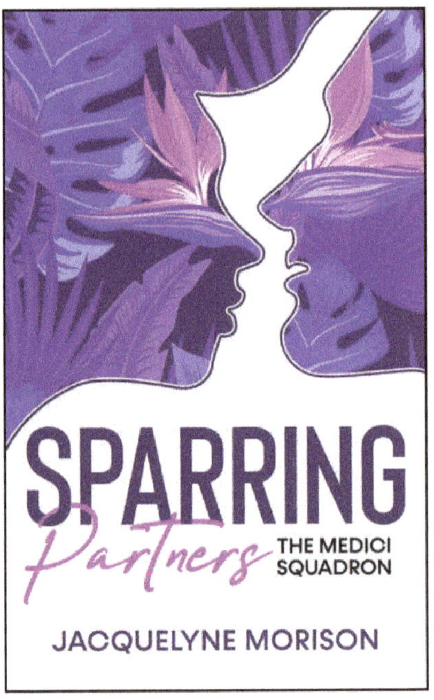

Lucinda Ketterworth is a self-made entrepreneur who runs the hugely successful Squirrels Bank Hall, a health retreat, which attracts shoals of the idle rich. Lucy also offers an additional service for her guests in order to accommodate their needs fully. Members of the Medici Squadron, headed by Calendula Fortescue-Bligh and Barrington Flint, however, decide to unearth Lucy's salacious extramural activity with a view to exposing her duplicity.

9 780099 299736